MW01061446

DON'T MIX THE BITTER WITH THE SWEET®
All Rights reserved © 2006 **Street Knowledge Publishing**

Published by: **Street Knowledge Publishing** Written by: Gregory Garrett Edited by: Dolly Lopez Cover design by: Marion Designs/ www.mariondesigns.com Photos by: Marion Designs

For information contact:
Street Knowledge Publishing
P.O. Box Box 345
Wilmington, DE 19801
Email: jj@streetknowledgepublishing.com
Website: www.streetknowledgepublishing.com
Myspace: www.myspace.com/streetknowledgepublishing

ISBN: 0-9746199-6-5

Don't Mix The Bitter With The Sweet

Written By
Gregory Garrett

Street Knowledge Publishing LLC
Website: www.streetknowledgepublication.com
Myspace: www.myspace.com/streetknowledgepublishing

Dedication

To my grandfather, Willie Garrett Sr., thanks for always having my back and instilling in me the essentials of being a responsible man.

To my children, Ashley and Ki'Rel, you are the world to me. I love you

Acknowledgments

I give thanks to GOD for blessing me with the talents of creative writing. To my father, Willie Garret Jr., stepmom Phyllis, my big sisters Tuwonda and Mona, Aunt Beverly and everyone in my family, thanks for the love and support throughout all the rough time.

Big ups to the homies in FCI Seagoville that kept it real and motivated me to keep writing: Orpheus "O" Hill, Bruce Banks (good lookin' out on all the copies), Botley, Tyrone, Key-Baby, Fred, D-Town, Donel Clark, Slim, Red, Shorty, Ant Lee, D-Wade, Big Tank, Elton, Junior, Buggy, C. Coats, Nudy, T. Johnson, E.P., D-Mo, KJ, Red Jiles, Ray J, Nick, Lil'Rich, Self, Day-Day, Wayne, Re-Re, PeeWee. If I forgot anybody, I still got love for you!

To all the haters and fakers, you know who you are…How you like me now! To my baby momma, Jackie, thanks for turning a negative situation into a positive.

To my girl Rhonda, thanks for being my "Down Chic" when I needed you the most. I will forever be grateful for the time and patience you put into me. I love you! Big shout out to Tyler Tx, the Wild Bunch and them boyz reppin' that Northside; Keep holding it down. I.D., Money D, Hops, Mitch, Carlos, Reg, Pone, Petey. RIP Jacqueline "Black Jackie" Jones.

Most importantly, to Linda Williams, thanks for everything. I am truly grateful. Without you this wouldn't be possible. I owe you big time! To JoeJoe and the Street Knowledge Team, thanks for all the help. You, JoeJoe, turned nothing into something. Good Lookin' Out! We fam now.

To The Reader:

A lot of us sometime choose the wrong   paths in life which allows us to lose focus on what's important.

We become blinded by the material outlook of certain things that creates an image that's right when we know it's wrong.

 In the process those bad decisions become detrimental to life's progression.

At times it seems as if we've gotten away or beaten the odds but usually what's done in the dark eventually comes to the light.

The moral of the story evolves around making the right decisions and choices in life.

Sometimes we may have to go through certain adversities, a degree of hardships, grief or set-backs to obtain the basic necessities we seek to live a prosperous, spiritual and happy life.

So to my readers, take advantage of what life has to offer and appreciate what life has given. "Don't mix the bitter with the sweet!"

Prologue

"Girl, I told you it was gon' be crunk. Look at all these niggaz waitin' to go in," Jasmine said cheerfully admiring the increasing number of available niggaz.

Stepping out the car, Naija, herself, was not enthused. She still didn't know why she let Jasmine talk her into coming to the club anyway. It wasn't so much of an issue about the club itself, but she knew Dontae would be calling her tonight from federal prison, something that became a constant ritual, basically, to keep tabs on her whereabouts. *I know he gon' trip!* She thought. She could hear him now. "You, been with some nigga? You fuckin' over me now? You don't love me anymore?" Constantly, it was the same ol' tune.

Naija tried her best to give him the support he needed; frequent letters, money, flicks with panty shots and waited on him to call. At times, it seem like her best wasn't good enough. Now, a year into his bid, her life has been completely on hold. Everyday was routine; to work and back home. Definitely, no enjoyment for herself. Her idea of fun was sitting at home with her mother and baby sister watching sitcom reruns and the Lifetime Channel. Occasionally, her and Jasmine would hangout. However, her whereabouts had to meet Dontae's approval with him always saying, "Make sure you be back at home at sucha and sucha time and you bet not be out fuckin' with no nigga!" She felt like she was the one locked up. On top of it all, no sex! Naija considered herself a virgin all over again.

After ten long minutes of waiting in the line, Naija and Jasmine finally made it in the club. The bass from the speakers rumbled the whole room. "Hey, that's my jam!" Jasmine said, dancing to the song "Juicy" by Notorious B.I.G.

Their rare appearance, and being Naija's first, drew a lot of attention from different niggaz and a few females who were hatin' because of their good looks.

Dressed in tight mini dresses, Jasmine in black and Naija in red, both girls were dimes. A nigga couldn't go wrong. Naija was built like an Amazon; exceptionally tall, full breasts, small waist and thick thighs. All featured with a pecan brown complexion, hazel eyes and long sandy brown hair that hung at shoulder's length. And it was all hers! Jasmine on the other hand was a bit shorter. She had an athletic body sculpture on a petite frame. Her mocha complexion and beautiful brown eyes accentuated her girlish good looks along with a short feathered hairstyle.

From a distance, Tony watched them as they sashayed through the crowd. "Who is that?" he murmured to himself with his eyes focused directly on Naija. He watched them closely, observing to see if they were with some niggaz. After a moment of evaluating, he saw they were alone, which meant fair game. Quickly, he stopped the waitress.

"See those girls over there by the bar?" Tony gestured with a slight nod of his head in the direction of the bar.

The waitress looked, trying to locate the specific girls he was talking about.

"It's a thousand girls over there," the waitress said sarcastically.

"Right there!" Tony pointed. "Those two wearing the red and black mini-dresses."

"Ooohhh! Okay," she said, finally locating Naija and Jasmine.

Dumb bitch! He thought. "Go see what's up with them. Tell'em to order whatever, it's on me." He gave her a $50 dollar bill. "Keep the change."

The waitress maneuvered through the crowd, making her way to Naija and Jasmine. They stood scanning the crowd. Naija was feeling cold turkey. Her guilty conscience was eating her alive thinking about Dontae. This was her first time back in a club in months. The last time she went out, Dontae made such a big fuss about it, she lost the desire to go out anymore. Since then, Jasmine had tried to get her to go out on numerous occasions, but Naija always found an excuse, saying she didn't feel like it, or any lie she could come up with to justify the fact she was waiting on Dontae to call, mainly respecting his wishes. Convincing herself, she thought, *What harm can one night at the club hurt? It ain't like I'm fuckin'. I'm just giving myself a break.*

"Excuse me ladies," the waitress said, getting Naija's and Jasmine's attention. "That gentlemen over there," she pointed, then continued, "says order what y'all want to he'll take care of it."

Naija and Jasmine looked in Tony's direction, straining their eyes to see the mystery man behind the friendly gesture.

Noticing that Naija and Jasmine were looking his way, Tony casually raised his hand, indicating that he was the one paying the bill.

"Can you see him?" Jasmine asked Naija.

"Barely. Its too dark in here," Naija responded, squinting her eyes. "He probably ugly anyway."

"Who gives a flyin' fuck what he look like! You might miss a golden opportunity worrying about what a nigga look like. The nigga can look like Sam Cassel. It's all about the free drinks and what he might have to offer, to put a bitch ahead of the game," Jasmine schooled Naija. "Besides, it ain't like you ask him. He volunteered."

"But you know how niggaz is. Once they buy you a drink they expecting some pussy wit it," Naija said, truthfully. "By the way, who in the hell is Sam Cassel?"

Clearing her throat, the waitress asked with a slight attitude, "Are y'all gon' order, 'cause I got other things I could be doin'."

Naija and Jasmine looked at each other, smiling. Being friends as long as they've been, they damn near could read each other's mind just off expression. They were both thinking about getting dead on the waitress' ass for trying to get an attitude like she was some important bitch. Their intentions weren't to come to the club to fight, mainly to have a good time. But, if a bitch got out of line, it was on!

"Girl...tell Ms. Thang what you want to drink before I go off in this mothafucka!" Jasmine said to Naija while giving the waitress a hateful look. Jasmine was hoping the waitress got 'fly' at the mouth so she could slap the taste out of it.

"Get me an Alize' Blue," Naija told the waitress.

"Make that two Alize' Blues," Jasmine chimed in.

The waitress walked off, mumbling obscenities under her breath as she rolled her eyes. In more ways than one, she realized she had let her mouth over talk her ass like so many times before.

"I don't know who that bitch thinks she is. That's what the two-dollar ass bitch get paid to do is wait on a mothafucka!" Jasmine said still upset.

"I don't know either, homegirl. But she can get her ass tore up in here," Naija said.

The girls slapped hi-fives. Within minutes, their drinks were being served, but by another waitress. Naija and Jasmine looked at one another and smiled.

After a few sips, Naija became relaxed. Her mind was no longer on Dontae. She was lost in the moment as the club atmosphere begin to take control of her mind. Soon Jasmine was dragged away to the dance floor by a brotha with cornrows she knew.

Work it girl, Naija said to herself as she continued to watch Jasmine do a series of booty shaking dances. The more she watched the more she started to feel the music. Slowly, she began to move to the beat.

Any nigga in their right mind could see Naija was thick as hell. Slowly, Tony crept up behind her and whispered in her ear, "Want to dance?"

Naija was startled by his presence behind her. She quickly turned around, almost dropping her drink. She was captured by Tony's height advantage over her, considering she was tall herself, standing at 5'10. More so, his dimples, a physical attraction that seemed to always catch a female's eye.

"You scared the shit out of me!" she said, holding her chest.

"My bad," he apologized, "I see you got that drink."

"Yeah. Thank you," she said, smiling, showing a set of perfect white teeth.

Naija was grateful that Tony was the kindhearted gentleman who bought her and Jasmine drinks and not someone ugly. This helped ease her doubts. Unlike Jasmine, Naija did have certain standards she went by.

"So do you want to dance or what?" Tony asked again.

Persistant, she thought. *But cute!* "C'mon!" Naija said, setting her drink down and leading the way to the dance floor.

Jasmine noticed Naija and Tony coming. She felt somewhat jealous, wishing she would have waited around a little longer. Maybe she could have gotten her hands on Tony first. Judging by his appearance, she figured he had to be a baller. *Damn he fine!* Jasmine thought.

Reading Jasmine's expression, Naija licked her tongue out at her when she made it to the dance floor.

While getting her groove on, Naija couldn't help but notice the mixture of platinum and gold jewelry Tony had on. Each piece sparkled from the flickering of the dance floor lights, creating a light show. Not only was she fascinated by that, his appearance was neatly groomed; tapered fade haircut, trimmed beard and mustache. Also the Versace outfit and Kenneth Cole loafer' set it off, glamorizing his image.

The DJ was mixing it up with old and new school hits. Finally, Naija was having some fun. Something she was lacking for months. The short mini-dress she was wearing limited her from getting down and dirty.

Soon the tempo was broken down to a slow jam. The song "Read Your Mind" by the R&B, singer Avant flowed gracefully through the speakers. Naija was leaving off the dance floor when Tony slightly grabbed her arm, motioning with a tilted nod for another dance. How could she not resist those dimples. She was hesitant at first. *What the hell!* she thought as she walked into his arms.

As they danced together, Naija comforted herself in his embrace. Their hips moved in a synchronized motion, rocking from side to side. She was mesmerized as she clutched onto his broad back, enjoying the sensation. It's been a year and a half since she been able to relax in the arms of a man without a C.O. (Correctional Officer) telling her she was doing too much touching. Even if it was only a dance rather than sex, it felt good. The warmth. The protection. Helplessly, a burning desire ran through her body wanting to be released.

Tony began to slow grind her pelvic area, arousing himself to an erection. Naija wanted to tell him to stop, but in a way, it kinda felt good. She closed her eyes and let the sound of the music meditate her mind. After the song, they walked off the dance floor. Naija was heated. Not in a mad way but in a sexual way.

Jasmine was waiting on Naija, expecting some erotic details.

Again, Naija read Jasmine's expression. Jealousy.

"Damn bitch! You all over that nigga for someone who always praises her faithfulness," Jasmine said a bit aggravated. "Its like that?"

"Don't hate...congradulate!" Naija smirked. "You the one who brought me here to have a good time, huh?"

Jasmine rolled her eyes, finally managing a smile. She was glad to be able to get Naija's mind off Dontae for a change.

Throughout the night, Tony and Naija kicked it. He was the perfect gentleman, hoping it all paid off later tonight when he tried to get the pussy. His homeboy, J-Rock and Jasmine were introduced to each other and that triggered an instant attraction. For Jasmine it didn't take much, especially if the nigga was getting money. The four of them hung out, dancing, drinking, talking and getting high. Tony sensed the doors of opportunity opening to get in Naija panties. Although Naija was high, she was fully aware of her actions.

Unlike Naija, Jasmine was lit. Her hormones were raging. She was all over J-Rock, ready to get her freak on.

After the club, Tony and J-Rock invited the girls to breakfast. Naija and Jasmine definitely accepted the offer because their stomachs were howling.

Following Tony's Escalade to the Waffle House, Naija and Jasmine discussed their interests in the two men, both agreeing they were rather cute.

"You lucky bitch! I invite yo' ass to the club and I end up with the scrub and you get the dubs!" Jasmine said, jokingly. Her infatuation for niggaz rested solely on material possessions: big cars, big wheels, big house, big jewelry, big money. And, to top it off, a big dick to go with it!

Naija figured it out that Tony was a major do' boy. But how major? In the past she was exposed to drug activity through

Dontae, meaning she knew first hand about the game and what it took to be major. Tony's whole demeanor told her his status was large.

After eating and talking, the night became restless for Naija and Jasmine. It was 3:00 a.m. in the morning. Combined with the need of sleep, weed and alcohol, the mixture of the three was disallowing them the desire to drive home. Establishing the fact that Naija and Jasmine didn't need to drive home all fucked up, Tony convinced the girls to stay at his crib. Naija was leery, not fully comfortable with the idea. Some persuasion from Jasmine gave her a change of heart, simply because she knew Jasmine wanted to get with J-Rock. Naija didn't want to carry the label as a cock blocker.

Arriving at Tony's house, Naija was impressed with it both inside and out. Whatever doubts she had about his status in the dope game, the house told the story. Looking around she thought, *Is this really this nigga house or is he just frontin' to make himself look like he livin' large?*

Noticing her admiration, Tony gave her a tour of the house while J-Rock and Jasmine made their way down the hall to a nearby bedroom.

After a walk throughout the entire house, Tony and Naija finally ended up upstairs in his bedroom. Intrigued with the vaulted ceiling, marble floors, black art, leather and brass furnishings, she pictured the house on a scene of "MTV Cribs" because of its décor. She never would've expected Tony to have an eye for the elegance the house presented. *Looks can be deceiving*, she thought.

"You stay here by yourself?" Naija asked, as she sat down in the chair, attentively making sure she didn't miss the answer.

"Yeah, all by my lonesome," Tony said with a sad face, playing on her soft side as he settled himself on his bed.

"So what do you do for a living?"

Tony looked lost. *What?* he thought. *This bitch must be the police.*

Naija read his expression, knowing the question would catch him off guard.

"You don't have to answer that. Its not like I was born yesterday," she assured him.

Tony chuckled.

As time passed, Tony tried to have sex with Naija but, she kept refusing, when at times her no's seem like yes's. Their constant kissing led to the fondling of her breasts down to the fingering of her most private possession. Although she was tempted to go all the way, she held strong just enough for Tony to further his interest in her.

For the first time, Tony's name behind the baller lifestyle kept him from getting some pussy on the first night. Sitting down, holding a intelligent conversation was never a issue before. Always sex! Usually, he never knew the past sex partner's last name and barely remembered the first. With Naija things were different. He saw something long term rather then temporary. Hopefully, she was worth the wait.

The next morning when Naija made it home, her mother and sister stared at her strangely after she walked in the house. It was not like Naija to stay out all night. Here it was 10:23 a.m. in the morning.

Her mother's expression clearly showed her mind was in the gutter.

"What?" Naija shouted, noticing the stunned looks on her mother and sister faces.

"We ain't said nuttin! You must be guilty," her mother said sarcastically.

Naija smirked, unable to comment.

"Dontae done called you a thousand times," her mother added exaggerating, while sensing Naija was somewhere she wasn't suppose to be, solely relying on mother's instincts.

"Momma, what you tell 'em?" Naija asked blankly, hoping her mother told Dontae something he would believe.

"Hell, I told him you was with Jasmine. Ain't that who you was with?" her mother asked curiously, pausing as if waiting for the answer. "He been calling since 6:00 a.m. this morning. He better be glad I like him or I'da cussed his ass out for callin' my damn house that early in the morning. It was bad enough last night, calling all them damn times."

Immediately, Naija's thoughts went into a whirlwind. She stormed into her bedroom, trying to conjure up a good lie to tell Dontae. "Could I say I spent the night with Jasmine?" Suddenly, she remembered he had the number to Jasmine's house. "Damn!"

As she started to undress, the phone rang. Her instincts told her it was Dontae. She checked the caller I.D.--anonymous caller. *I know that's him*, she thought. She knew it was no way around talking to him, even though she didn't have to answer the phone. She had the option of having her mother or sister tell him she hadn't made it home yet. Unfortunately, that would only make matters worse. At some point in her life, she was going to have to deal with the drama, so it might as well be now. She let out a long sigh, then picked up the phone receiver.

After listening through the recorded message from the Federal prison, she pressed five.

"Hello!"

In seconds, the harsh words burned her ear like fire.

"Bitch where the fuck you been? You been laying up with some nigga? You ain't shit! I've been callin' yo' ass since last night and early this morning. And don't lie and say you spent the night with Jasmine 'cause I done already called her house too, and her momma said she hadn't made it home since last night."

Naija couldn't get a word in if her life depended on it. She constantly stayed on the receiver for a verbal beat down. The more Dontae assaulted her with his mouth, the more her faithfulness was becoming less appreciated. For the first time since his incarceration, she questioned herself about moving on with her life.

After fifteen minutes of insults and accusations, finally it was over and she hung up. "I love you too!" she said sarcastically. In a matter of speaking, she felt bad about not being at home when Dontae called, however she wasn't sorry this time around.

Three Years Later

Chapter One

Thursday, the first week of June, Dontae walked out of the prison gates of FCI-Big Springs and inhaled. "Damn! The air does smell different on the outside than on the inside," he said, remembering the old myth amongst inmates.

Seeing his mother, Dorothy, and his uncle, Man-Man, standing waiting on him in the prison parking lot, Dontae took one last look at the place he once called home for the amount of time spent on his bid and said a silent prayer; thanking God for finally allowing him to be on the outside looking in. Afterwards, he hurried and greeted his family with a hug.

Today, Dontae Johnson was a free man after serving a 60 months sentence for a minor possession of crack cocaine. To many, this is a mere slap on the wrists. Most niggaz go to prison and become rehabilitated, laying aside their ghetto past and steering clear of the glamorous life.

Not Dontae! Getting out of prison marked a new day to a new beginning.

Kicked out in the streets with virtually nothing, he didn't have a pot to piss in or a window to throw it out of. But all that was about to change in a matter of time. He was determined to stack some major paper.

Before going to Federal prison, he was nowhere the baller status like niggaz that had a name in the dope game. Truthfully, he was one of those brothas who just got caught up in the system, classified as another nigga in the way, basically, getting the next nigga rich, while he struggled with petty hustling--slinging nickel and dimes rocks on the corner, or in some dope trap. Back then, he didn't have a purpose defining his criminal activities. Only experimenting with the game 'cause all his homeboys were doing it. Dontae didn't know firsthand about dealing with large quantities of drugs. Scoring a few ounces of dope, he figured was big time to him.

While in prison, Dontae developed a for sure connection with his celly and friend, Sergio Rodriguez, who Dontae did the majority of his bid with.

Sergio was serving a 20-year sentence for conspiracy for 60 kilos of cocaine. He was a Mexican kingpin in his early sixties, originally from Chihuahua, Mexico, but resided in Phoenix, Arizona, where he caught his case.

Sergio took a liking to Dontae about three years ago, after being placed in a four man room with Dontae. Sergio liked the way Dontae carried himself, mostly his quietness and knowledge of respect, slow to speak, quick to listen. These were among the many traits to set well with Sergio which came as a big surprise, compared to the average youngster in prison--wild and dumb. After analyzing Dontae for a few weeks, Sergio was drawn to his style. From that point on, they became good friends. Sergio practically cooked spreads every weekend; tamales, burritos, nachos--all the Mexican favorites. Money was no problem. Whatever Sergio had, Dontae had it. Every night, they would sit up talking about past life experiences and the cocaine business. Don't be greedy, make your money and don't let the money make you; don't mix business with pleasure and keep your enemies close! These were Sergio's favorite quotes. Over the course of time. Dontae grew more interested in returning to the dope game but at a higher level. And Sergio was just the person that had the control to put Dontae at the top of the game. Seeing the potential in him, Sergio set up a meeting with his son, Hector, through visitation.

They all discussed prices, drop off's and pick up's. Dontae had all the information he needed to get his hands on some major weight if he decided to re-enter the dope game. Dontae wrote down all the names and phone numbers to each family member that had a hand in the business. Officially, everything was set up. Next, it was putting everything else into play once he got home.

Traveling back home to Dallas was a long ride from the boonies of West Texas, where Dontae served his prison term at FCI-Big Springs. After leaving the prison, his mother stopped in the next town and bought a twelve pack of Budweiser. Four hours later, he was slightly buzzed after drinking four beers himself. That shit went straight to his head and out his dick. His mother must've stopped a hundred times for Dontae to take a piss on the side of the road. For the rest of the ride, he slept.

Arriving at home, of course, family was waiting on him. Motherfuckers he hadn't seen or heard from in ages, popped out the woodwork in his face with open arms. *Its funny how family, friends and loved ones act like they so glad to see a nigga when you get home but while on lock its out of sight, out of mind,* Dontae thought. To be cordial, he greeted everyone with hugs and smiles, keeping his animosity bottled up inside. Next, everyone wanted to sit around and kick it, mainly his cousins that were near his age. His relationship with his cousins was nothing like it use to be when they were growing up as kids. As they got older, each one went their separate ways.

Dontae wasn't high sprung on kickin' it with the family. At least not right then. He felt there was plenty enough time for that. First things first. He figured it should have been self-explanatory; that any nigga getting out of prison--his first priority is some pussy. Everything else is irrelevant until after the first 'nut'. Therefore, his primary focus was just that preferably from his ex-girl Naija, but since there was a failure to communicate over the past few years, his friend, Keena would have to fill the void.

Keena was just a sidekick broad Dontae was messing around with before he went to prison. It was nothing real serious. Unlike the rest of his so-called friends, she managed to 'keep it real' during his prison bid, which eventually gained his respect for her. Her frequent letters and occasional fiend shots helped his time run a bit smoother. Although their relationship was with no strings attached, he still had sort of a soft spot for her. Yet and still, Keena couldn't replace the feelings he had for Naija.

During his bid, Naija fell off on him. Word on the streets-- she was fucking this nigga name Tony. Of course, she denied it so, Dontae gave her the benefit of the doubt, because there was no proof. As time passed, the rumors spoke for themselves. Naija became less responsive to his needs. Later, she turned her back on him completely without saying a word, the same way all trifling hoes do that say they gon' ride with a nigga in prison. From Dontae's standpoint, he didn't feel like the Lone Ranger. It happens to the best of 'em!

Finally, reality set in and he decided to give her the space she needed and focused primarily on the remainder of his time. Despite it all, he still loved Naija. True love has no boundaries. Perhaps, there was still a chance of them getting back together.

Starting out in his bid, everything was cool. Naija was a soldier. She was faithful and very supportive. She was at Dontae's every beckon call. The visits weren't really a big deal, considering he was trapped away in West Texas, just as long as she 'kept it real'.

Their relationship began in their sophomore year in high school. At that particular time, Naija had just moved to Dallas from Tyler, a small town in East Texas, and started her new school year at Skyline High School.

Dontae and a few of his homeboys were hanging in front of the school building that morning, waiting on the 8:30 a.m. bell to ring for class. As usual, Dontae was entertaining the fellas, being the typical class clown. A reputation that spoke for itself.

"Why did yo' momma cross the road?" Dontae asked the crowd of boys, then waited patiently for the answer. After seeing that no one was going to respond, Dontae finished the joke. "To get her crusty ass on the other side to pay her pimp before he go upside her head."

All the boys laughed along with Dontae. Suddenly, the other boys stopped laughing and focused their attention behind Dontae. He noticed the expression on their faces that read something unimaginable. Quickly, he turned around to see what the amazement was all about. There she was walking in his direction. Naija Taylor! Instantly, he was attracted to her smooth brown skin and a body that would make Janet Jackson jealous. She was the pure definition of 'country fed'. It seemed as if all the ham hocks, red beans, chitlins, and hot water cornbread she ate definitely agreed with her, because it showed in her hips, her thighs, her curvaceous butt and everywhere else that was visible. Fine wasn't the word. More like 'brick house'.

As she passed by them, wearing tight Guess jeans and a matching pink T-shirt, she flashed a pretty smile then entered the building.

Dontae shook his head about the possibilities. *Thick bitch! I can do somethin' wit that*, he mumbled to himself.

Throughout the early part of the day, he was on a mission to win her. After introducing himself to her, he met her after each class, offering to walk her to the next class or carry her books. Each time she turned down his offer.

During lunch period, he noticed her sitting by herself and he walked over to her table.

"Is this seat taken?" he asked.

Again she flashed a pretty smile and politely said, "No"

Dontae hurried to sit down before she changed her mind.

"Are you a stalker?" Naija asked, teasingly.

Dontae laughed at the accusation. "Naw, I'm not a stalker. What makes you think that?" he said, looking at her to see if she was serious.

Smiling, she looked over at him while she ate. Judging on his appearance, she figured he was rather cute, far beyond the likes of a stalker. *However, looks can be deceiving,* she thought.

"I'm just playin'. No need to get offended," she said, finally becoming comfortable with his company.

Coincidentally, they took English together, fifth period class. During the days to pass, he kept her amused with silly antics. Naija learned quick why he was called the class clown. Finally, she gave in to giving him her phone number. Between school and late night phone conversations they started drawing closer.

Naija made friends quickly because of her good looks and her athleticism in all sports. She was the jock among the girls. All the girls wanted to hang with her based on all the attention she got, hoping they could get recognized by some of the cute boys that paid them no mind before. And then, there were the girls that were hatin' for the boys that were all up in Naija's grill' fascinated by her supernatural beauty.

Later in the school year, Dontae was able to talk Naija into being his date to the sweetheart ball. Afterwards, they hooked up becoming inseparable, then advancing on to something serious. After graduation, their plans were to get married and start a family. Influenced by a hustler's lifestyle, he entered the dope game full speed. Being a novice in the game, quickly he got caught up in the hype. Everything seemed to be heading in the right direction. Soon all the plans of a fairy tale life came to an end when he was arrested and sent to Federal prison.

After making a few phone calls, Dontae was able to track down Keena on her cell phone to let her know he had touchdown. She screamed into the phone, totally excited when she first heard his voice. She assured him that she would be there to pick him up at 6:30 p.m. At first he was a little frustrated that she was making him wait longer to get the pussy, but soon figured…what the hell, two additional hours was nothing. If he could go almost four and a half years without some pussy, a couple of more hours wasn't shit.

He changed clothes into something more suitable than those gray commissary sweatpants, then went and sat out in his mother's front yard and kicked with his dope fiend uncle, Man-Man, while the rest of his family were saying their goody-bye's. Again, Dontae played the role.

Finally, Dontae has some alone time. Although Man-Man was talking his ear off the same way he was doing on the ride back home, Dontae was listening but, at the same time he wasn't listening. He was still zoned out on Naija.   Dontae had mad love for his uncle, disregarding his drug addiction. Growing up, Man-Man was one of those relatives you could say or do anything around without getting in trouble. Their relationship was more like brothers, and that's how Dontae saw Man-Man, as a big brother.

Back in the day when Jeri curls was the shit, Man-Man was the only person Dontae looked up too. Having a deadbeat father, Dontae turned to his uncle for advice and guidance on being a man. When Dontae realized his dick was made for other reasons besides pissin', he went to Man-Man for a talk about the birds and the bees.

Man-Man informed him on everything there was to know about fuckin', and even schooled him on the art of eating pussy.

"See young nigga, it ain't all about getting' in the pussy, Wham Bam! Thank you ma'am! and you through. Hell naw! You gotta take your time getting her in the mood, kissin' all over her body. You have to get it in yo' head, its not about you when it comes to the bedroom. It's all about pleasin' her. Its alright if you can slang much pipe, but sometimes you have to take things to another level. The main thing is you gotta lick it before you stick it!" Man-Man explained.

Dontae couldn't believe his ears. The desire to eat pussy was something he never imagined.

"What?" Dontae shouted, wincing at just the thought. "You mean to tell me, I got to put my tongue down there where she pee at?"

"It ain't as bad as it sounds. First you got to make sure she clean down there. Don't get it twisted. This doesn't mean you have to eat every girl you do somethin' wit'," Man-Man paused, making sure Dontae was gathering every valuable piece of information.

After a satisfied check, he continued. "You gotta make sure she special. Once you establish that, then you put yo' thang down on her and she will be beggin' fo' mo', especially if it's her first time. I guarantee you!"

Given the information, Dontae felt he had everything down pat. Over the first few years, he mastered sex with flying colors. However, his first experience with oral sex was sickening. It was Naija's seventeenth birthday. Dontae wanted to do something special, and giving her his oral pleasure was considered the ultimate gift. They were already six months into their relationship, far beyond sex. Trying something new would definitely spice things up some more.

Everyday, Man-Man would pick Dontae up from school. This particular day, Naija rode home with Dontae instead of riding the bus like she normally did. Arriving at Man-Man's apartment, he left Dontae and Naija there alone. In the bedroom, they undressed and engaged in a level of intimacy, kissing and touching. Remembering his uncle's advice he laid her down and began kissing all over her body. Finding his way between her legs, he sniffed, making sure she didn't have an odor in her pussy. *It don't stink,* he thought as he played in her pussy. To him, the sight was gross. He never actually took the time to analyze it up close and personal before. He was beginning to have second thoughts. Finally, he decided its too late to chicken out now. Slowly, he licked her putty-cat, tasting the bitter taste on his tongue. "Eeewwww!" he shouted, spitting the awful taste out of his mouth as he jumped up off the bed to go rinse his mouth out. Unfortunately, the thought of the taste lingering in his mouth was enough to cause him to throw up.

When Man-Man made it home, he was expecting some good news. Undoubtedly, the information wasn't no way what Man-Man imagined.

Dontae explained his grotesque encounter, leaving Naija shameful.

Man-Man laughed hysterically. "Next time put some Kool-Aide power on the tip of yo' tongue. That way you can create yo' own flava until you get use to it," Man-Man teased.

"It ain't gonna be no next time!" Dontae emphasized.

Dontae stayed sick for the next two days, throwing up all kinds of shit.

In those years, Man-Man was Dontae's idol. Man-Man could do no wrong in Dontae's eyes. He was a smooth dresser and a slick talker. With him being a light-skinned brotha with long Jeri curls, women of all flavas were attracted to him. As the years passed, crack cocaine hit the scene heavily, destroying everything that got in its way. For Man-Man, he fell victim of circumstances. The drug started out as a casual high then gradually advanced to becoming an addiction. Slowly, the Man-Man Dontae once knew and respected as a player and mentor became a totally different person.

While sitting and waiting on Keena to come, Dontae and Man-Man rapped about the status of the dope game around town. Again, Man-Man was doing all the talking, more so lying.

"Yeah nephew, its rollin' out here. All you got to do is get the work and I'll move that shit for you. You just kick back and get paid. I'm good for a least $10,000 a day," Man-Man said, blowing himself up.

The last part of Man-Man's narration really caught Dontae's attention. *$10,000 a day! Nigga, you probably smoking that much up in a day,* Dontae thought to himself.   "Nigga, if you movin' that much dope, then why is you broke as a mothafucka?" Dontae said, staring at Man-Man, hoping to get a logical answer.

Man-Man was at a loss for words trying to come up with a good lie to tell in an attempt to gain his nephew's trust.

"'Cause I was waitin' on you, baby! We might as well get this money together," Man-Man said, trying to sound convincing.

During the course of conversation, Keena finally pulled up in her Nissan Maxima, promptly at 6:30 p.m. It seemed as if Dontae hopped in the car before it even stop rolling.

"Damn! You must be really glad to see me," Keena said smiling.

Dontae sat in silence, horny as a dog in heat. *I'll be glad to see any bitch...blind, crippled or crazy. It don't matter. Bad as I need some pussy!* he thought.

Turned on by her appearance, he leaned in and kissed her passionately. Lust aroused him instantly, forming an erection. Breaking their tender kiss, Dontae looked at her, eyes roaming her entire body as he noticed the short skirt she was wearing.

"What?" Keena said softly, following his eyes.

"You lookin' good as a mothafucka!" Dontae said in a smooth tone of voice.

Keena smiled.

"Thank you," she said, blushing. "You lookin' good your damn self!"

Dontae was right. Keena was looking good. Her butterscotch skin was glowing, radiant as ever, thanks to her fragrant Victoria's Secret body oil. She was a foreign mix--half Black and half Asian. She had long silky, jet black hair that she normally wore in a ponytail but today she let it cascade down the sides of her face. Her main attraction were her chinky eyes and long slender legs that were revealing beneath the short tennis skirt she wore.

Reaching over, Dontae slid his hand underneath her skirt, finding the edge of her panties. Gently, he slipped his fingers inside, reaching the center of her pussy. She was already wet and inviting. As he fingered her, she closed her eyes, hypnotized by the feeling. Her breathing became heavier. The desire was taking control. Quickly, she stopped him, pushing his hand away.

"Save all that for the motel room," she said, panting, trying to catch her breath.

Dontae knew she was just as horny as he was. "Let's go," he announced.

Driving down Forney Road, turning right on Jim Miller Road, they soon pulled in at the La Quinta Inn Motel. Dontae practically played in Keena's pussy the whole ride to the motel, fully returning his own lust. He hopped out the car and quickly paid for the room.

Walking in room 101, he turned on the lights and the air conditioner while Keena turned on the television.

"I don't know why you turned on the TV 'cause what we came to do doesn't require no TV," Dontae said playfully.

Keena laughed. "You sho' right!" she agreed.

The room was extra clean and spacious. The Jacuzzi tub in the bathroom was something that caught their attention. They both had plans to add that to their sexscapade.

Keena laid down on the bed, kicking her shoes off.

Dontae sat down beside her and started massaging her shoulders.

"Ooohhh! That feels good," she moaned softly, closing her eyes.

Dontae wanted to enhance the mood instead of rushing into things. He felt the more he turned her on would arouse her more to an orgasm, because he knew once he stuck his dick in her it was a 'wrap. Once he got the first 'nut' out of the way, it was on and poppin'.

He kissed the back of her neck. Her response was just what he expected. *It seems like all that shit I read in those Black Men magazines does work,* he thought.

Keena let out a lingering moan. She turned around to face him and kissed him wildly. The freak in her was gradually making its appearance.

Sliding his hand underneath her shirt, he groped her breasts, feeling the hardness of her nipples. Carefully, he pulled her shirt over her head exposing the fullness of her breasts. Her nipples stood at attention. Licking his lips, the appetite to devour the swollen flesh overwhelmed him as he gently cupped her breasts, positioning himself to suck her nipples. He took his time tantalizing and teasing, marking his spots with bright red hickies.

Keena tossed her head back and forth, giving in to the pleasure that he was giving her. He laid her back down on the bed and unzipped her skirt, pulling it and her panties down together in the same motion.

Standing over her flawless body for a brief moment, he undressed quickly. She watched him closely as her eyes widened when he exposed his manly features in front of her.

As he got ready to handle his business, she stopped him. "Did you bring some rubbers?" she asked.

That instant the whole mood changed. Dontae was too busy worrying about getting the pussy, that he totally forgot about picking up some condoms. For a minute he thought about going bareback. *Hell naw! This bitch might be burnin' or somethin'. I don't know where this ho pussy been,* he thought as he snatched up his clothes to get dressed.

"Where you goin'?" she asked, thinking he was mad because she wanted him to use a rubber.

"You said I need some rubbers. So that's where I'm goin'…to get some."

"Hold up! Look in my purse."

Dontae walked over to the table and grabbed the box of condoms out of her purse.

"You came prepared, huh?"

"Always! I ain't tryna get pregnant. At least not right now. And I definitely ain't tryna catch nuttin'!"

"I feel you. It's better to be safe than sorry."

"Already!"

The mood had died out temporarily, causing a problem for Dontae to put the rubber on. His shit had went soft.

"Help a nigga out," he said, gesturing for her to give him some head.

Gently, she grabbed his dick, stroking it lightly, then placed it in her mouth. After feeling the warm suction of her mouth, he was back hard instantly. Desperately, he slid the condom on and started on his journey of Keena's body, placing kisses everywhere. He took her feet in his mouth, slowly sucking her toes. She squirmed from the feeling.

Shit! This nigga done learned a lil' sumptin' in prison, she thought.

Dontae slowly maneuvered his way up her legs, still applying soft, delicate kisses. Stopping between her legs, he nibbled on the inside of her thighs. She gasped, anticipating his next move. He saw he was in total control. *Yeah bitch, I know you want me to eat your pussy. NOT! It don't get that good just yet,* he thought as he bypassed the appetizer and worked his way on up.

The sexual intensity begin to overtake Keena. She grabbed him into her arms, holding him tightly. She whispered in his ear. "Fuck me!" That only turned Dontae on even more. He mounted her missionary style, penetrating her fully. Her wetness accepted him inside with a demand for pleasure. He let out a mild grunt as the tightness of her flesh surrounded his dick.

"Damn, you feel good," he said softly as she wrapped her legs around his waist. He cupped her well rounded butt to position himself to give her every inch of him. Minutes later, he turned her over, positioning her in doggy-style. She accepted him in her again, with much gratitude. She repeatedly moved back and forth, grinding away at God's creation to women. He thrust himself further and further, hitting his mark as she arched her back then buried her head in the pillow. *Take this dick bitch,* he mouthed silently to himself. She braced herself, clutching a fist full of covers beneath her. The squishing sounds of her pussy expressed her appreciation, arousing him even more. Dontae entered in and out powerfully, while admiring his work. He was at his boiling point. Finally, they both reach the peak of satisfaction.

"I'm cummin'! I'm cummin'! Goddamn this pussy good as a mothafucka! Aaah shit!" Dontae squealed.

Keena pumped her body faster as she felt him swell inside her, reaching her G-spot. In minutes, they were releasing the beast within them. Dontae collapsed on top of her, sweaty and exhausted.

She rolled from beneath him to look at him face to face. As she cradled his face, she wondered if it was all a dream.

"Welcome home baby," she said, gladly pleased.

● ● ● ● ● ●

A slight breeze was blowing, barely cooling off the humid evening. It was 8:00 p.m., gradually getting dark when Tony and Naija pulled into his mother's driveway in Cedar Hill, in his candy colored brandy wine Hummer, sittin on 26 inch Dalvin wheels, still spinning and the stereo knockin' the rap song "Can't Knock the Hustle" by Jay-Z.

Tony and Naija were buzzing from the two blunts they smoked on the way to his mother's crib. He grabbed a bottle of Cool Water cologne out of the console, spraying some on to kill the weed smell in his clothes before going in his mother's house. Naija did the same with her Burberry perfume, figuring it wasn't a bad idea. She knew his mother 'tripped out' at times. Also she put on her Channel sunglasses to hide her glassy eyes. Since she had been involved with Tony, smoking weed became something she depended on daily.

As they walked to the door, Gloria, Tony's mother, met them coming in.

"How many times have I got to tell you to quit coming over here with all that loud racket in them cars," Gloria said harshly. "You know I got all these nosey ass white neighbors and they itchin' for any reason to call the police just to find out how a single black woman is stayin' in this big ol' pretty house. Then you ain't makin' it no better coming over here in all them fancy cars. Sometimes I wish you wouldn't have bought me a house out here. I was satisfied right there in Oakcliff. As you youngster's say…In the hood where I don't have to worry about the neighbors being curious, "Cause they already know what time it is."

"Momma, quit sweatin' the small stuff!" Tony said, kissing her on the cheek as he passed by her, walking to the kitchen to get something to eat.

Naija politely spoke and followed behind Tony.

"Small stuff my ass!" Gloria griped.

Tony ignored his mother's nervous accusations. He knew she was just running off at the mouth, like usual. Although he did get a big kick out of blasting his music whenever he stopped by purposely to agitate the neighbors. He remembered how she cried when he first showed her the elegant five bedroom, red brick contemporary style home and told her it belong to her. The house was a Mother's Day gift he purchased after reaching his first million dollars, five years ago. His mother was in total suspense when Tony came by to pick her and Q'Tee, his baby sister, up to go out to eat. At least that's what his mother thought. There was a change of plans. The drive was longer than when she expected. Her suspicion came after she noticed the upscale neighborhoods they rode through in the suburbs of Cedar Hill. Throughout the years, Gloria had always dreamed of living in the same elegant homes one day. *If only my husband was still alive*, Gloria thought while staring out the window.

"Tony, where is we going? And why is you got me out here with all these white folks? It's bad enough I work around them all day," Gloria asked, growing suspicious as to her whereabouts.

Tony held a straight face and kept on driving, ignoring the question. He was laughing like crazy on the inside.

Angry that Tony hadn't answered her, his mother turned to him in her seat and looked at him sternly.

"Tony KeJuan Williams! I know good and damn well you hear me talkin' to you," Gloria announced bluntly. "Don't make me knock you through that window."

Q'Tee couldn't help but laugh in the backseat.

Before having to feel his mother's vicious backhand, Tony pulled in the driveway of his mother's new house.

His mother looked at him, trying to figure out why they were at a strange house. Suddenly, Tony flashed his dimpled smile as he presented her the house keys. Right then, she was ecstatic, shedding tears of joy.

"Is this for me?" Tony nodded. "Thank you, baby!" his mother expressed with much gratitude as she reached over to hug her son.

It was definitely a Kodak moment. That was just the start of Tony's overly expressed love for his mother. Over the years the gifts continued to come. It's funny how dreams come true. The abundance of Tony's wealth relieved her of all pressures of financial disadvantages. Even though she made good money due to the skilled profession of a registered nurse, Tony still catered to her every need, knowing that his father would more than willingly do the same if he was still alive. Tony felt it was his obligation to step up and be the provider for his family.

As Tony and Naija entered the kitchen, Q'Tee was finishing up the last of the dishes. Tony playfully, kissed his sister on the cheek.

"Stop boy!" Q'Tee squealed, disapproving of his brotherly love. "No tellin' where yo' lips been."

Naija was amused by the remark while she dropped her head to smile as she thought about the fact he had just got through eating her pussy an hour ago.

Q'Tee wiped her face where her brother had kissed her with the back of her hand then attempted to hit him with the towel she was using to dry the dishes. After the brief tantrum, she acknowledged Naija by speaking, despite her dislike of her.

"Hey Naija," Q'Tee said dryly.

"Hey Q'Tee," Naija responded the same.

"Whatever y'all mess up be sure to clean up after yourselves. Ain't no maids around here," Q'Tee exclaimed, purposely for Naija.

"I gotcha!" Naija assured.

Naija knew Q'Tee didn't care for her being with her brother. Fuck it! Jjoin the club! This is something she grew accustomed to. Not only by Q'Tee, but the triflin' hoes that wished they were in her shoes. As for as Q'Tee, her and Naija managed to get along. They barely talked unless put in a situation that they had to. Nevertheless, it didn't bother Naija how Q'Tee felt, or anyone else for that matter, because she was going to continue to play her position. She felt like bitches have their right to their own opinions, just as long as opinions didn't become physical!

Naija and Q'Tee conversed briefly about college and various other things that women discuss, trying to be social. True enough, Q'Tee did have her certain dislikes about Naija, mainly because she knew Naija was playin' her brother for his money. However, Q'Tee stayed out of his business because she didn't want to give him the freedom to get in hers. But at the same time, she didn't want to see him hurt.

Q'Tee left Naija and Tony in the kitchen and went to her bedroom. She lay across her bed, drowning herself in thoughts.

She had graduated from college a few weeks ago and now it was time to put her degree to good use by finding a job suitable to her qualifications. The part-time job at the mall was just something temporary, until something better comes along. However, the job did have its advantages with the employee discounts.

Currently, there were so many things she wanted to get situated in her life. First, secure a good job. Secondly, get her pre-owned Hyundai out the shop so she could trade it for a new car. Getting a new car was a must have; not just any car. She wanted something that would turn heads wherever she went. Thirdly, her own place to stay. "I love you momma but a sistah gots to have her own space." In the back of her mind, she knew all she had to do was ask her brother to get her a car and an apartment. Out of all likelihood he wouldn't hesitate to make things happen. But for once in her life, she wanted to do things on her own.

Lastly, she wanted a stable relationship. Someone she could love and grow old with together. Just the thought reminded her, she hadn't had sex in almost a year. Immediately, she thought of Jaleel. She knew she needed to put their issues behind them and move on. Their ways of thinking definitely didn't see eye to eye. He still wanted to be a gangster which was something that wasn't a part of her criteria anymore. When they first start kickin' it, the gangster image was cool. But now it was played out, especially considering the direction she was trying to go in life. She wanted something more stable. She didn't mind him hustling, instead, he was "hustling backwards." This meant all the extra money he made taking penitentiary chances selling crack, he spent it on getting his homeboys high on "water," sipping syrup, shooting dice, smoking blunts or just having fun and then end up having to start all back over again--never saving for a rainy day. She wasn't against him treating himself to the benefits of his money, but the consistant nickel and dime status wasn't playa at all. The point given, she had to move on.

After eating, Tony went in the family room with his mother while Naija cleaned up the kitchen. He told her he wanted to get rid of Q'Tee's old car and buy her a new one but he wanted it to be a surprise. Tony was very proud of his sister, though at times he didn't show it. Now that she had graduated from college, he wanted to show his gratitude.

"Boy, you not gonna keep buying all them damn cars and puttin'em in my name," Gloria frowned. Practically every car that Tony purchased was in his mother's name because of her legitimate job status.

"Mamma, I told you to quit sweatin' the small stuff," Tony said nonchalantly.

Suddenly, Tony's pager beeped. Checking the number, he recognized it instantly. Looking at his diamond encrusted Rolex watch, it was 9:37 p.m.

"Naija! Are you finished in there?" he asked, walking in the kitchen to get a trash bag.

"Give me five more minutes," she told him.

"Hurry up so we can go. I got other things to do," he demanded as he turned to walk to the spare room in the house.

Naija was distraught by his tone of voice but didn't bother to respond back out of respect for his mother. Quickly, she finished wrapping the remainder of the food and placed it in the refrigerator. Afterwards, she grabbed her purse and waited on Tony.

Inside the spare room, Tony opened a hidden safe in the wall located inside the closet. He counted out $280,000 and threw the money in the trash bag.

As soon as Tony and Naija left his mother's house in the Hummer, he called the number in his pager on his cell phone to receive the instructions on where to purchase the drugs he needed. After hanging up, he called J-Rock.

"Wuz up wit' it?" J-Rock yelled into the phone.

"Where you at?" Tony asked.

"At the Executive Club watching the strippers," J-Rock hollered over the loud music in the club.

"Say my nigga. I'm 'bout to swing by there and pick you up in ten minutes," Tony said, and hung up.

"Hey" J-Rock heard the click before he could respond back. He looked at his cell phone as if he was staring at Tony. "Stupid mothafucka!" he said while placing the phone back on the side of his hip. He quickly gulped down the Crown Royal and Coke he was drinking. With a few minutes to spare, he stopped one of the strippers named Diamond for a quick lap dance.

Tony thought about taking Naija home first because he didn't like her being around when he was taking care of business. He sure as hell didn't feel like driving all the way on the other side of town to drop her off at home in Los Collinas, and then have to drive back to Oakcliff to pick up the dope. It didn't make sense, especially when he was already minutes away from picking up J-Rock and the meeting spot to buy the kilos of cocaine. His mind was made up to let Naija tag along.

A little over ten minutes, Tony pulled up in the parking lot of the Executive Club.

J-Rock was standing outside waiting. He saw Naija in the front seat and gave her a curious look. *Why she tagging along?*

Tony must be really sprung or tripin'! J-Rock wondered as he hopped in the backseat.

"What it do?" J-Rock said loudly.

"Damn nigga! Why you all loud and shit?" Tony said harshly.

The anger built up in J-Rock once again, pertaining to Tony. He stayed cool.

"My bad dog," J-Rock said in a way of apologizing. Noticing the trash bag in the backseat, J-Rock took a peek being nosy. Seeing the money, he knew what time it was.

Tony filled him in on everything that was about to go down. Tony reached in his console and handed J-Rock a 9mm handgun. J-Rock took the gun, and the thought of blowing Tony's brains out crossed his mind, but that would take away from his plans.

Moments later, they pulled in at the Deluxe Inn on Camp Wisdom Road. Tony and J-Rock both got out, leaving Naija to wait in the Hummer with the motor running. J-Rock tucked the 9mm in the waistband behind his back, while Tony grabbed the trash bag out the back with the money inside, and they both walked upstairs to room 212 and entered inside.

Nervously, Naija waited. She definitely didn't want to be with Tony while he was buying drugs. Since she was already there, there was nothing she could do.

As she listened to the radio, jamming FM K104, she noticed the irregular activity of a white man that kept pacing back and forth, making sudden stops as if he was waiting for someone.

She watched him as he approached the Hummer and dropped his keys. As he bent down to pick them up, he was startled at the sight of Naija. To play it off, he just smiled. Immediately, she became more nervous than before, as well as suspicious. She watched him closely as he got in a Chevy Malibu. She checked her lady Rolex; it was 10:05 p.m. She wondered what was taking Tony and J-Rock so damned long. Finally, they arrived back to the Hummer, carrying suitcases. Focusing her attention back to the white man in the Malibu, she saw him exiting the parking lot, then speed down Camp Wisdom.

After Tony and J-Rock loaded the suitcases and got in the Hummer, she tried to explain to the best of her ability about the white man. Only Tony brushed her off, telling her that her mind was playing tricks on her.

Silence was among the three of them during the ride. The music was the only thing that could be heard in the vehicle as Tony drove carefully, trying not to commit any traffic violations. The 20 kilos in the backseat, along with the 9mm was enough to send them all to prison for a long time. Tony thought about what Naija tried to explain to him about the peculiar activity of the white man. *Could he have been an undercover?* he thought, as he checked his rearview mirror making sure no one was following him. Nervousness was beginning to set in. *I knew I shouldn't brought this dumb broad along.* Finally, Tony turned in the parking lot to let J-Rock out.

"Holla at me in the morning," Tony said, reaching back to pound fists with J-Rock.

"Bet!" J-Rock said, returning Tony's fist pound. Giving him back the 9mm, he said "You straight with all this work?"

"Yeah, I'm cool. I'm gon' take it to the crib and just drop it off at the stash house in the morning," Tony assured J-Rock, yet and still he was a bit nervous.

Thirty minutes later, that seemed like forever, Tony and Naija arrived at home. Tony let out a sigh of relief. Now he could relax after the scare Naija gave him.

Naija hopped out the Hummer, slamming the door. She was still upset that Tony didn't take her seriously, like she was just plain stupid.

Tony watched as she walked away quickly to the front door.

Jinxy bitch! he said to himself as he grabbed the suitcases from the backseat. As he walked to the front door, he didn't notice the Chevy Malibu that followed him home, pass by slowly, snapping pictures.

Chapter Two

Knock! Knock! Knock! The heavy tapping on the other side of the door awoke Dontae suddenly. He covered his head with a pillow to absorb the constant noise.

"Dontae, get your ass up so you can go report!" his mother yelled from the other side of the door.

Hearing his mother, he realized he had to get up and take his mother to work so he could use her car to go report to his parole officer.

"A'ight momma!" he shouted after sticking his head from underneath the pillow.

He looked at the clock on the nightstand. It was 6:30 a.m. *It's like prison wake-up call over again,* he thought as he massaged his early morning hard on. Sluggishly, he got out of bed and walked to the bathroom to take a piss, still tired from last night. He only received about three hours of sleep after practically being up all night with Keena. After five rounds of pure rugged sex, they went out for breakfast at Denny's, then later, back to the motel room for more sex, including a must be told dick sucking. At three in the morning, she dropped him off at home so she could go home herself and rest up and be at work by 7:30 a.m. in the morning.

After cleaning himself up and getting dressed, Dontae was still feeling a little groggy as he walked into the living room. Dorothy, his mother looked at him, shaking her head, suspecting he had a well enjoyed night. She smiled.

"Looks like you had too much to handle," Dorothy said teasing. She reached in her purse, afterwards, handing him some money.

Dontae looked dumbfounded as he accepted the money from her.

"What's this for?" he asked blankly, thinking she wanted him to stop and pay a bill.

"That's for you," she said. "I know you want to buy you some new clothes and have a few dollars in your pockets."

Without counting it, Dontae stuffed the money in his pockets then hugged his mother.

"Thank you momma!" he said happily.

The $700 she gave him, for Dontae the money was appreciative, but far from what he was planning to get his hands on. Besides, the $700 highly replaced the $50 gate money he received from prison that he spent last night on a motel room and food.

Dorothy had been saving the money six months prior to Dontae's release date, adding $25 or $30 every week. She loved her son dearly and wanted to do everything she could to help him out. At times she thought, maybe if his father would have stayed around in his life, its possible Dontae would have made better decisions.

Dorothy was a full-figured woman that still showed signs of having a voluptuous figure in her younger years. Street smart she was; mastered at a young age, by the illegal activities of the different people in her life. In her late forties, she showed no signs of aging. She possessed a smooth coffee brown complexion. Beautiful in her own way, both inside and out.

Growing up with five other siblings, Dorothy being the third to the oldest, deprived her of a normal childhood. Her biological mother wasn't responsible enough to raise six children so every time she got pregnant she would dump each child on "Big Mama," their paternal grandmother. Big Mama accepted each child with open arms. She created a loving environment, though the struggle to feed six mouths, not including herself, was difficult at times.

Dorothy developed quick. By thirteen she had full breasts, thick thighs and a perfectly round butt. And by sixteen, she was the talk of the school campus because of the way her body was fully proportioned. Boys were all over her. Her attention, however, was caught by a senior name James Wright. He had everything--Good looks, a car and the star quarterback on the varsity football team. College scouts definitely were interested in his talent. And so were the girls, only sexually. One day at school, James approached Dorothy after third period class in the hallway. She was in complete awe when she saw him.

"Hey cutie," he said, flashing a debonair smile.

That moment a chill went through her body. She blushed, unable to speak.

"I was wondering if I can call you sometime," he continued.

Dorothy had to look around to make sure he was talking to her. "Who me?" she said, pointing to herself.

James grinned. "Yeah, you."

From that point on, they eventually became girlfriend and boyfriend. As the months rolled on, he pressured her into having sex with him. Unfortunately for Dorothy, she was still a virgin. However, she was madly in love with him so to speak, and didn't want to lose him to another girl who was willing to give him what he wanted. Soon, she decided to give in. Picking her up one night in his car, they rode to a nearby park and parked. There, she was introduced to sex for the first time in the backseat of his car. Months later, she ended up pregnant. But when she told him, he denied it being his. The news got to his parents, quickly assuming Dorothy was trying to stick a baby on their son to mess up his chances to go to college or maybe on to the NFL. Defining their better judgment, his parents transferred him to another high school and changed their phone number. Dorothy never saw James again.

Bringing another mouth into Big Mama's house only added to the turmoil. To help take care of her baby, she exposed herself to the street, selling drugs and sleeping with older men who were obsessed with her body. They paid dearly. Later, she involved herself with various hustlers who were willing to take care of her and her baby.

● ● ● ● ● ●

Dontae sat in the lobby of the parole office, waiting on his parole officer. His appointment was at 9:00 a.m. He checked his watch to what seem like the umpteenth time. To be exact it was the third time in ten minutes. The time read 9:16 a.m. *What's taking this cracker so long,* he thought. As he waited impatiently, his thoughts drifted to Naija, who had been a closed chapter in his life for quite some time now. It was no doubt that he wanted to see her. More so, get back with her. Just to feel the warm flesh of her body all over again. Instantly, images of her appeared in his head. The thought of them making love, slowly started his dick to rise.

For the past few months, prior to his release date, he just couldn't shake free of the thoughts that he tried so hard to erase from his memory.

Finally, the parole officer came, breaking Dontae's trance. He introduced himself as Mr. Clay Edwards. He and Dontae shook hands, and afterwards he handed Dontae a cup to go piss in.

"When you're finished, drop your urine sample in the lab down the hallway, third door to your left, and they'll direct you to my office," Mr. Edwards said.

After Dontae finished his business, he delivered the cup to the lab as instructed. He signed the paperwork and was led by the technician to Mr. Edwards' office.

Mr. Edwards was a balding white man with a gray beard who appeared to be in his late fifties. Dontae was hoping he wasn't one of those white supremacists that stereotyped all Blacks as a drug dealer, gangster, or rapper.

During their meeting, Mr. Edwards explained to Dontae his conditions of parole and what was expected of him to meet those requirements. Undoubtedly, their meeting went fairly well. Despite Dontae's better judgment of character, Mr. Edwards was the total opposite of what Dontae expected. The longer they talked, Dontae found out Mr. Edwards was involved in an inter-racial marriage; his wife being Black, along with three bi-racial children, one son and two daughters.

Spending over thirty minutes of lecturing, more so shooting the shit, Dontae was relieved to be finally leaving the parole office. Hearing his stomach growl, he remembered he hadn't eaten anything that morning because of rushing to get up and take his mother to work by 7:15 a.m. He stopped at the nearby convenient store to grab a bag of chips and soda until later on.

Getting out the car, he noticed a female in some tight Daisy Dukes pumping gas in her car. "Damn that bitch fine!" he said, admiring her from a distance. Slightly focusing his attention on her, he recognized the familiar face of Lisa. Back in the day, he tried so hard to get in her panties but she played hard to get.

"Lisa!" he yelled.

Quickly, Lisa looked up to see who was calling her name. *Who in the hell is calling me,* she said to herself while scanning the lot in the direction she heard the voice. Soon, her eyes were locked in on a nice looking brotha making his way towards her, waving his hand. *Who is that?* Admiring the stranger, she was glad she had just come from the beauty shop just in case someone tried to 'holla'. She knew she was looking 'fly' even though she just threw on the shorts and T-shirt.

The closer Dontae got, the more she recognized his face.

"Dontae?" she said, walking to him to get a better view.

They greeted with an embracing hug.

Lisa was stunned by the firmness of the way his body felt.

While in prison, Dontae stayed on the weight pile, pumping iron and working out, especially after Naija turned her back on him. That was the only way to relieve his frustration and stress. After months and months of consistency, his hard work and dedication paid off.

He was handsomely built--tall and dark complexioned, an added attraction to most women. Standing at 6'2, he possessed the strong features of his father, something he will never know. His chiseled face helped define his boyish grin.

Stepping back from each other, they expressed their pleasantries.

"You sho' lookin' good," Lisa said, overwhelmed as she looked him up and down. "How long has it been since I saw you last?"

"Probably the last time I tried to get in your pu..." Dontae cut the sentence short.

Lisa hit him playfully. "Boy you ain't changed one bit."

"On the cool, it's been over four years," Dontae answered, truthfully.

"It's been that damn long?" she said, trying to calculate the time in her head. "I remember hearing you went to jail. But it don't seem like it's been that long ago."

"Believe it or not. It's definitely been that long," Dontae said. "So what's been up with you?"

"Nuttin'! Just tryna survive, now that I have a son."

"Oh yeah!" he said, surprised. "By who?"

"This nigga name Chris Jackson. You probably don't know him. He's from Fort Worth."

Dontae figured she was right. He didn't have a clue who her baby daddy was. He quickly erased the thought from his brain.

Dontae and Lisa stood and talked for what seem like hours, until the store clerk came outside demanding Lisa to come in and pay for her gas so that she could move her car. Afterwards, they continued catching up on old times.

"What's up for tonight?" Dontae asked.

"I'm probably goin' to the Ice club with some home girls. You remember Marquita and Briana, don't you?"

Thinking for a few seconds, Dontae remembered them clearly.

"Yeah, yeah. I remember them," he said, chuckling as he thought back to his sexual experience with Marquita that was interrupted when her boyfriend showed up at her house unexpected. "How could I not remember Marquita. Y'all still tight?"

"I just know you can't," she said, matter-of-factly while rolling her eyes at him. "Yeah! We cool to a certain extent."

Little did Dontae know, his sexual experimentation with Marquita was the reason Lisa was hesitant to get with him in the first place. Honestly, she was always tempted after hearing he had a big dick. Unfortunately, Dontae went to prison before she could find out personally.

Dontae noticed her somewhat funky attitude, but didn't know what to take from it. In a matter of speaking, he figured she may have been a little heated about the sarcastic remark about Marquita. *Who gives a fuck! Neither one of them hoes is my girl.*

To me, they just a piece of pussy, he thought. Truthfully, he was hoping he could get a second opportunity with Marquita. There was definitely some unfinished business to tend too.

Checking his watch, he realized time wasn't in his favor. He had spent way over an hour taking to Lisa. He didn't trip, she was for a worthy cause. He wanted to go to the mall and then holla at a few homeboys before he had to pick up his mother from work.

"Say Lisa. I'ma holla at you tonight at the club. Maybe we can hook up later or somethin' if you don't have nuttin' else planned after the club.

"See what I'm talkin' about! You ain't changed one bit. Here it's been over four years since we saw each other, and you still tryna get in my stuff," Lisa said smiling as she placed her hand on her hip.

"There you go playin' hard to get again. You need to quit trippin' and let me show you what you been missin' all these years," Dontae said, nonchalantly.

"No you didn't!" Lisa said surprised by his straight forwardness. "Boy you somethin' else! We'll see." She couldn't help but laugh, arousing her curiosity to see what he had in them jeans.

Agreeing to see each other at the club and finish their small talk, they parted ways.

As Lisa walked to her car, Dontae stared at her butt cheeks hanging beneath her shorts. *Yes Lord! I definitely gots to get in them guts tonight,* he said to himself as he turned to walk into the store.

Twenty minutes later, Dontae arrived at the Red Bird mall. Once he went inside the building, he was completely mesmerized. My, my, had it changed. There were several new and remodeled stores. The main corridor presented exquisite new styles and designs and a dancing water fountain gracefully displayed its geysers in the center of the floor. Small kids got thrills out of watching the streams of water jump back and forth, while couples and senior citizens sat nearby enjoying the wondrous scenery.

Walking through the mall, he felt like a new man. Freedom is the ultimate feeling. He was getting stares from all types of women as if he was the only man alive. *Am I looking this good to draw this much attention?* he thought. The question answered itself as a sexy white girl with an ass like a sistah, waved at him when she passed by, eyeing him up and down. Admiring her big booty, he said to himself. *These white girls are comin' up!*

Slowly, he added an extra bounce in his step.

Dontae browsed in several stores. There wasn't too much he could buy with $700, considering the high ass prices on all the name brand gear. A couple of outfits and maybe a pair of tight sneaker was about all he could afford. Basically, he kept it simple, trying hard not to get broke which was a difficult task because of being enticed by so much 'fly' shit. Only God knows where his next dollar was coming from, hopefully soon. He settled for a few Polo shirts, jeans and Nikes.

Browsing in Dillards, he saw a baby blue Sean John warm-up that he just had to have. Checking the price tag, it was $150. Dontae shook his head, looking at the warm up once again. "I gotta rock that tonight, especially with my new Air Force Ones."

Reaching in his pocket, he pulled out his money and recounted it. He had $220, which meant buying the outfit would leave him with only $70 to his name. *Not including the tax*, he thought. He sighed, figuring after he tried the warm up on, he would decide if he still wanted it.

As he modeled in the mirror in the Sean John, the young sales assistant was impressed with Dontae while catching a sneak peek at his butt when he turned around.

"Does this look okay on me?" he asked while posing.

"Looks perfectly fine to me," she said with a gracious smile. She was hoping he payed close attention to what she said.

With her approval made his decision was more justifiable to spend the $150. However, he knew it was her job to say "yes" anyway just to make her commission, even if the outfit didn't look good on him.

As the sales assistant totaled up his clothes, she entertained Dontae with casual conversation.

"Who you dressing to impress?" she asked curiously.

"No one in particular." He paused. "Just treating myself. Q'Tee!" he continued after noticing her name on her name tag while reaching in his pocket to grab his money to pay for his clothes.

She looked down at her name tag as if she didn't know it was there, quickly realizing that's how he knew her name.

"That will be $155.46. You mean to tell me there's no one in your life?" she said, accepting his money.

"As we speak, no! But who knows what tomorrow may bring," he teased with a warm smile while receiving his change.

Warmth embraced her body as she became captivated in the moment, alerting her curiosity. She wondered how a nigga that fine and good looking not have that special woman in his life unless he was runnin' game or was a faggot.

"I'm pretty sure you're going to make some woman's lucky day," she replied smiling, wishing it were her.

Dontae smiled back, attracted to her flirtatious hints as he gathered his bags to leave. He couldn't help but notice the print of her erect nipples poking through her blouse.

Admiringly, she became aware of what he was staring at. She blushed, pushing her chest out more to give him a better view.

Feeling slightly embarrassed after being caught staring at her breasts, he said, "I hope to see you around."

That was Q'Tee's cue to get in where she fit in.

"As a matter of fact, that can be arranged. I mean, if it's some truth in what you just said," she said softly.

Dontae was intrigued by her assertiveness. He was definitely willing to take her up on her offer. He never was the one to turn down any pussy, especially if she was attractive and literally throwing it at him.

Q'Tee's dark complexion made her extremely attractive. Her full lips sparkled from the lip gloss she was wearing as if they were asking to be kissed. Her brown eyes made her look innocent but the way she stared showed a wild and freaky side waiting to be exposed. She stood about 5'5, with small breasts and she wore her hair in a stylish French roll with a strip of hair hanging down the left side of her face. Whatever else she was lacking in other areas, her butt took up the slack. She had a curvaceous "ghetto booty".

Years ago, dark women were never an interest to Dontae, considering he was dark himself, until he went to prison. After looking through so many pornographic magazines, he begin to have a fetish for the dark meat. He wanted to see if they really lived up to the reputation "the blacker the berry the sweeter the juice".

"So what do you have in mind?" Dontae said, sitting his bags down to give her his undivided attention.

"I'm about to get off in the next ten minutes. So if you're not in a hurry maybe we can take a few minutes and talk some more, comfortably."

Checking his watch, it was 12:35 p.m. He figured he had some time to burn. Besides, the time spent just might be beneficial. After last night's experience, his hormones were still at its peak.

"Yeah. I'm down with that," Dontae began. "First of all, before I get all attached to you, do you have a man? 'Cause I don't need no drama!"

"No, I ain't got no man. But I need one. Do you know anybody that's available?" she said, hoping he caught the hint.

Q'Tee wondered if Dontae could be the chosen one to fill the empty space in her life, and be able to fill her other emptiness, more so.

After she got off work, her and Dontae stopped at an empty bench in the middle of the mall and sat down.

Catching a whiff of her perfume, he was drawn to her presence.

"What's that you're wearing?" he asked.

She smirked, pausing to respond. She was confused as to what he was referring too. "Excuse me!" she said, slightly frowning.

"The perfume you're wearing," he said after noticing the dumbfounded look on her face. "What's the name of it?"

"Ooohhh! It's DKNY," she answered, fully understanding the question now.

She had sprayed on some more just on g.p. (General Purpose) to make herself more alluring.

"It smells good."

"Thank you."

Silence fell among them for a brief moment.

Dontae contemplated on what else to say to her. His making skills were pretty rusty. Fortunately for him, Q'Tee broke the ice with a conservative approach.

"So, what's you name?"

"Its Dontae," he announced, extending his hand to her.

"Nice to meet you Dontae," she replied, accepting his handshake.

"Excuse me for asking, but is Q'Tee a nickname or your birth name?"

"It's my nickname. My real name is Quatesha. Q'Tee was a name my father gave me when I was a little girl which is pronounced like 'cutie'. He said everywhere he took me everyone that saw me would say I was a cute child. So it was something that stuck with me all these years and, of course, it became a household name with family and friends. To my advantage, the letters in my original name brought the nickname into existence," she explained proudly.

Now officially introduced, they briefly discussed life's occurrences and so forth. Both of them were cautious not to reveal too much about their personal relationships because of being skeptical on which direction their friendship was heading.

Q'Tee highly praised her brother for always being there for her through thick and then. However, his overprotective attitude was something she couldn't tolerate. Usually the case was him thinking he had her best interest at heart.

As their conversations grew deeper into childhoods and family, Q'Tee found herself very relaxed with Dontac just by the way he kept his eye on her the whole time, never looking away one bit, even though he was tempted to because of the variety of sexy and attractive women that kept passing by.

She expressed herself wholeheartedly.

Dontae, himself was feeling Q'Tee as well. He felt a certain vibe with her because of her determination to beat the odds. Something they both had in common.

At the age of ten, her father was gunned down in a drug deal gone bad. That left the burden on her mother to raise two children on her own. During this time, her brother became protective of her and her mother. Sometimes too protective! Her mother's struggles pushed Tony, her brother into the street life. As Q'Tee got older, the negativity surrounding her is why she chose to further her education to avoid the uncertainties of becoming a victim of the streets. With that right decision, she is now a twenty-two year old college graduate of the University of Houston, majoring in business and accounting.

"Oh, my God! Look at the time," she said after glancing at her watch. Quickly, Q'Tee stood up.

Dontae looked at her awkwardly, rather confused.

"You got somewhere to be? he asked.

"Something like that. My brother is going to kill me!"

"What's wrong?"

"See, my car is in the shop and my brother has been picking me up from work. Usually he's been 15 minutes late. So I figured I'd kill some time talking to you," she explained as they walked to the exit.

'My bad. I didn't mean to hold you up," he said, apologetic.

'It's not your fault. As the saying goes, time flies when you're having fun," she said, sincerely, hating the moment was coming to an end.

Q'Tee had spent well over thirty minutes talking with Dontae. Disregarding his good looks, she was expecting him to be a busta like all the other niggaz she allowed herself to spend time with. Miraculously, he was different. Thank God! It has been a long time since she was able to sit down and have a sensible conversation with a man. Unexpectantly, she savored the moment.

Q'Tee and Dontae walked out of the mall together. She looked around the parking lot and quickly spotted her brother walking back to his Lexus. It was obvious he had been looking for her. More than likely, he was pissed, considering the fact she knew her brother better than anyone. He was someone that always stressed his time was precious.

"There go my brother," she said, heading in his direction, hollering his name.

Q'Tee approached her brother with a hug to smooth his attitude. Reading his facial expression, told her he was mad for having to wait so long. *Fuck'em! He'll get over it*, she thought.

Shaking away from his sister's hug, Tony checked the time on his Rolex.

"Damn! You took long enough. You been off over thirty minutes ago," Tony said, highly pissed.

Q'Tee ignored her brother's remarks and introduced him to Dontae.

"Tony, this Dontae. Dontae, this is Tony, my overprotective brother."

The two men greeted one another with a traditional soulful handshake.

From the moment Dontae saw Tony, he knew Tony was a heavyweight in the dope game; the flashy car, the chrome wheels, the jewelry, the whole persona of being the man. He had all the characteristics of a baller.

"Nice car," Dontae said, making small talk but at the same time, hoping he didn't sound like a lame.

Instead of responding right away, Tony shot Dontae a blatant stare, sizing him up. After a brief pause, he uttered, "Appreciate it." then walked to his car.

Realizing Tony wasn't much of the friendly type, Dontae decided not to waste anymore time making conversation with him. He focused his attention back on Q'Tee, something that was worth his time. The two of them talked some and exchanged numbers, while Tony stared from his seat inside his car. His facial expression proved he wasn't impressed.

Tony honked his horn a couple of times, signaling he was ready to go. Dontae and Q'Tee, both paid it no mind. Dontae remembered Q'Tee mentioning how protective he was of her. But in a sense, Dontae couldn't blame Tony because if he had a sister, he probably would act the same way. But at the same time, Dontae didn't want Tony to get the impression he was a punk, because he definitely would get down for his if the situation called for it. Then again, the last thing he needed was some drama on his second day home from prison.

"I guess I'll let you go before your brother, have a fit,"

Q'Tee laughed. "You are never lyin'!"

"I'll call you," he said, reaching to give Q'Tee a comforting hug.

Dontae walked to his mother's car, thinking about the possibilities of hookin' up with Q'Tee. She was smart, sexy and cute. Most of all no kids! So far, so good. Was she wifey material? Could she cook and clean? Was she responsible? Was she a ho? Is she a messy broad? "Wait a minute!" he said, snapping back to reality. "It ain't like I'm about to propose to her. The question should be, Is the pussy good and can she suck a dick?"

Dontae figured in due time, he will find out the true story defining Q'Tee.

●●●●●●

"Uuugghh! Tony will you quit asking me all them damn questions!" Q'Tee screamed. "I told you for the fourth time, we met in the mall...end of story! Now please. Stay out of my goddamn business."

Their ride home wasn't pleasant at all. It was a verbal showdown. Tony kept asking questions about Dontae and Q'Tee was becoming more and more annoyed by his constant pestering.

"All I want to know is what's up on the nigga," Tony pleaded. " I'm just tryna look out for you."

"What you want me to do, Tony? Write an autobiography on the nigga? For the fifth time, I just met him. So there's nothing to tell you about him. Just the fact that he fine as a mothafucka and cute enough to make a bitch want to drop her panties. Is that enough information for ya', brother dearest?"

"I ain't tryna hear all that kinda shit!" Tony said, getting upset at Q'Tee for talking like she was a ho.

"That's what you get for tryna be so damn nosey. I don't see how them hoes put up with you."

"If you only knew," Tony said with a slight grin.

"Believe me, I know. It got to be the money 'cause it ain't yo' face. And it definitely ain't yo' dick 'cause I done heard you ain't workin with nuttin'!" Q'Tee said, laughing uncontrollably.

"Fuck all that! It's something about that nigga Dontae that rubs me the wrong way."

"You say that about every nigga that try to talk to me."

Tony didn't stop there. The questions kept coming. Where he from? Is he hustling? Are you going to hook up with him? How old is he? Blah...blah...blah! 21 questions was in full effect. The bickering continued.

Q'Tee turned up the music in his car in hopes of drowning him out. That didn't work. It only helped a few seconds before Tony quickly turned the music down.

"Girl, don't do that shit!" he snapped.

Q'Tee rolled her eyes and stared out the passenger side window. She figured if she ignored him and didn't say anything back, he would finally get the message that she didn't want to be bothered. Not quite. The silent treatment didn't work either.

Tony babbled on. "Q'Tee, I know you hear me," Tony shouted, realizing she wasn't responsive.

At this point, she was highly pissed off. She tried so hard to ignore him but he would always say something to strike a nerve.

They hollered, screamed and yelled at each other the entire ride to their mother's house.

Tony's and Q'Tee's differences in character were like night and day. Tony, the oldest of the two was self-centered and cocky. Some would say a bully that liked to throw his weight around, mainly because he had money. He was passionate towards family and friends, but became a raging pit bull if someone crossed the line.

Q'Tee, however was the sweetheart of the family--spoiled since birth, getting her way with her charming good looks and heartbreaking smile. Caring and considerate, she gave herself wholeheartedly to all things beneficial in her life. But still ghetto in her own way.

Pulling into their mother's driveway, Q'Tee breathed a sigh of relief. Now she could finally distance herself from Tony. Actually, she loved her brother dearly, but at times he could be a pain in the ass. And today was a prime example.

She hopped out the car, with Tony seconds behind her, running his mouth.

"Tony, you need to worry about that gold digging bitch you got at home instead of focusing your time and energy on me. Cause I'ma do my thang whether you like who I'm doing it with or not. Believe that!" Q'Tee said, walking briskly.

Hearing all the commotion, their mother met them coming in the door, noticing the tension between them.

"Can the two of y'all ever get together without fussing?" Gloria asked.

"Momma. He need to stay out my motha..." Q'Tee caught herself, realizing she was talking to her mother. She definitely didn't want to have a slip of the tongue in front of her. Gloria didn't play that. "Excuse me, momma. But he need to stay out of my business," she corrected herself, hoping her mother would be on her side and persuade Tony to leave her alone.

"Hey, momma," Tony spoke coming in behind Q'Tee.

"Tony, what have you done this time?" his mother asked.

"Momma! Q'Tee ain't talkin' 'bout nuttin'." Tony affirmed.

Mrs. Williams gave him an unconvincing look.

Mrs. Gloria Williams, the mother of Q'Tee and Tony, was short and plump, giving her a stout look to herself. She wore her salt and pepper hair cut short in the back and curled on top, similar to the legendary old school songstress Anita Baker. It was nothing too fancy. Despite her size, she presented herself in a classy way. Her dark caramel skin gave her an enriched type of beauty that was genetically passed on down to her daughter.

Having enough of Tony's mouth, Q'Tee walked in the family room and flopped down on the couch. She grabbed the remote and flicked on the TV.

Tony raided the refrigerator for any leftovers the way he usually does every time he stops by. Instead of taking time to warm up any food, he settled for a cold boloney sandwich. Afterwards, he walked in the family room to say good-bye. He kissed his mother, then headed to leave. Slowly, he turned around, catching Q'Tee looking right at him with the same frown she had on her face for the last fifteen minutes. Tony made sure his mother wasn't looking at him and then pointed a middle finger at Q'Tee. Quickly, he hurried to the front door without waiting for her to respond back.

Q'Tee lunged forward off the couch, stumbling to catch herself while startling her mother.

"Girl, what's wrong with you?", Gloria asked blankly, soon realizing Q'Tee and Tony were still at each other's throats.

Finally making it to the front door, and out of breath, Q'Tee stopped herself. "See, I'm not gon' even trip," she said as she watched Tony run to his car.

She figured she had enough arguing for one day. All she wanted to do was kick back and relax, preferably, after a good old fashioned fuckin'. Sad to say, a warm bubble bath will have to do regarding the fact she didn't have a man to help her in her time of desperate need.

●●●●●●

The mid-day temperature was already at its peak, topping out at 98 degrees. It was 1:47 p.m. and hot as hell. When Dontae made it back to the Pleasant Grove area, the hood to him, few people were outside, unless, they had to be. Neighborhood children were ripping and running wild, full of energy. The majority of people were inside, staying cool, waiting to come out later once the heat died down some.

As Dontae rode through several hang out spots, he noticed parts were still the same and some parts showed signs of improvement.

After cruising several blocks, unable to find anyone hanging out, he rode by the projects. If he wanted to find something to get into, the projects, was definitely the spot to be.

Driving through the projects, he quickly spotted Reg and Isaac in the courtyard talking to two red bones, named Kayla and Ne-Ne. They appeared to be young, no more than nineteen or twenty. Other than that, they were all that. Their bodies were bangin', completely filling out the T-shirt dresses. Any nigga passing through would definitely stop and stare. More than likely, that probably was the case with Reg and Isaac, because they were notorious cock-hounds.

Parking his mother's car, Dontae hopped out yelling. Quickly, Reg and Isaac turned around, recognizing Dontae instantly. As they got ready to walk off, Kayla and Ne-Ne stopped them.

"How y'all just gon' up and leave us over here by ourselves after y'all stopped us to talk?" Ne-Ne asked with an attitude.

Neither Reg nor Isaac bothered to respond back. They just looked at each other and turned back around and kept walking.

Ne-Ne and Kayla were in complete awe with their mouths hung wide open. It was a rare occasion that they got dissed because of their good looking and bangin' bodies. Damn near every nigga they came across was sweatin' them. Being rejected was something they weren't use to. It usually was the other way around.

"No they didn't!" Kayla said to her home girl, totally not understanding this picture.

Despite Reg and Isaac's unconcern, Kayla and Ne-Ne still stood and waited. If it wasn't for Reg and Isaac's baller status, the girls wouldn't have given them the time of day.

Meeting up, Reg and Isaac gave Dontae warm welcome hugs and pounding fists. Reg was a dark-skinned brotha whose eyes stayed naturally red from all the weed he smoked. Some people would think he was high all the time. Isaac was a couple of inches taller, with braids and brown skin. They were both friends of Dontae's from back in the day, who he hung around with committing petty crimes, such as breaking in cars and purse snatching, later advancing to drug dealing. Fortunately, they missed the long arms of the law.

"What up my nigga!" Reg said cheerfully. "When you make it to the crib?"

"Yesterday!" Dontae said visualizing his release for a short second. "Man, I'm just glad to be home."

"That's what that is. I feel you on that shit." Isaac said, shielding his face from the direct sun. "Say y'all, lets go over here and stand in some shade. It's hotter than a bitch standing here."

As they all got ready to relocate to a cooler spot, Dontae took a quick glance, noticing the two fly bitches Reg and Isaac were talking to when he pulled up were still standing in the courtyard as if they were waiting on Reg and Isaac.

Stopping Reg and Isaac, Dontae asked, "What about them hoes back there?"

Reg and Isaac turned and looked in Kayla and Ne-Ne's direction.

"Fuck them bitches! A nigga can catch up with them later. They ain't nuttin' but some sack chaser's," Isaac said, confident the girls were easy fucks.

In Dontae's mind, he knew his homies didn't know how valuable a piece of pussy is until a nigga go to prison. He was hoping they would never have to experience the feeling.

The three of them walked a few feet to a nearby breezeway of the apartments. Dontae couldn't help but notice the reflection of Reg and Isaac's iced out platinum jewelry. Their Rolex watches with diamond bezels, two carat diamond studded earrings, pinky rings, link chains with diamond encrusted crosses and medallions and customized bracelets, made them look like they were paid in full. The boys were definitely getting money.

While in prison, Dontae had heard Reg and Isaac were getting money. Instead of the low level drug dealer's they used to be, they were now major niggaz.

"You niggaz been makin' plenty noise out here in these streets," Dontae said, looking closely at the diamond in Reg's medallion. "Y'all names ringin' all in prison and shit. I don't know if that's a good sign or what. Is it that sweet out here?"

"Already! Its gravy out here, my nigga," Isaac said, boasting. "On the real we just tryna get it while the getting' is good, playboy."

"I feel ya'! I can't blame a man for tryna keep his head above water. Right now I'm just kickin' back chillin'. Checking out the scene, so I can put my pieces together. I don't want to jump into shit to quick and fuck around and be hit like good weed."

"Yeah, dawg. Do yo' homework first. It's a buncha bustas out here that be hatin' on a real nigga tryna get his paper," Reg said, giving the real scoop on what's happening in the streets. "It's a trip how niggaz hate to see a playa come up in the hood when they have the same opportunities as the next nigga. All they have to do is apply themselves, get they grind on and quit waitin' on the next nigga to do somethin' for 'em. It's wild out here, homie."

"It's always gon' be like that though. Haters is what makes the world go round." Dontae spoke like a true vet in the game.

They all agreed, nodding.

"Whenever you get ready, just holla at us. We can put you down with some work to help you get on yo' feet," Reg said, being a real homeboy.

"I'm straight. I gotta a little sumptin' sumptin' already set up. Once I feel things out, the work is just one call away," Dontae said justifiably.

"Do yo' thang, hustla. The invitation is always welcome if thangs don't work out with that," Reg said with no hard feelings. "What yo' pocket lookin' like?"

"Hurtin'!" Dontae emphasized, rubbing the outside of his pants pockets. "My momma gave me some bread this morning. Hell, I went and blowed that shit at the mall. I got close to $70 to my mothafuckin' name."

Reg and Isaac both reached in their pockets, pulling out large knots of money.

Dontae stood wide-eyed, amazed at the amount of cash these niggaz were holding. *Man! I gotta hurry up and get me some paper*, he thought.

After shuffling through the large bills, Reg and Isaac together gave Dontae $2000.

"Damn! Christmas came early for a nigga," Dontae said accepting the money graciously. "Man, that's good lookin' out."

"Yeah, we don't want you runnin' 'round like a bum with yo' hands all stuck out. Plus, you ought to be able to buy plenty pussy with that," Isaac said laughing.

"Oh you got jokes now," Dontae chuckled. "You know I ain't never been pressed for a bitch!"

That remark alone made him think for a few seconds. *Except for when it came to Naija turning her back on me*, he thought, as he stuffed the wad of cash in his pocket.

Now he was eager to go back shopping to get some of the stuff he had to put back on the rack because of the lack of funds. Then again, he had plenty enough time for that. He figured he would splurge at the club.

Looking at the time, he realized he had to go pick up his mother from work. He rapped a little longer and then decided to leave.

Reg and Isaac walked him to the car.

Again, Dontae noticed Kayla and Ne-Ne. This time they were leaning in a maroon Chrysler 300 sitting on chrome 22 inch wheels out in the parking lot of the projects.

"What's up for tonight, Dontae asked, getting in the car.

"Probably hit the club," Reg said, knowing the club was first option on a Friday night, unless he had some pussy already set up. "What's up, you need me to swing by and pick you up?"

"I'm cool. I'ma roll my momma shit." Dontae said, knowing he might have a possible hook-up with Lisa and didn't want to be stuck out without his own transportation. "Which club y'all goin' to?"

"The Ice Club. That's where everybody goes on Friday night," Reg answered.

"I'll see y'all out there," Dontae said pounding fists with them as he got in the car to leave.

As Dontae drove out of the projects, the game re-entered his head. His intentions were taking him faster than expected.

●●●●●●

After talking to her mother and watching B.E.T. music videos in the process, Q'Tee went in her bedroom, closing the door behind her. While moping around and getting her things ready to take a bath, she thought of the memories she had in her room involving the sleepovers with some of her friends, especially her home girl, Tiffany, who she shared all secrets with.

An incident she will always remember was the time she lost her virginity to her ex-boyfriend, Jaleel. How could she ever forget that horrible day. Replaying that particular day in her mind, she laughed at having to save Jaleel from a serious beat down from Tony after bursting in her bedroom, while he was getting dressed. Dick swingin' and ere 'thang!

During her freshman year in high school, Q'Tee was at the tender age of fifteen. Among the girls she hung out with, she was the only one who hadn't had her cherry popped. Everyday, the girls bragged to Q'Tee regularly about how they were getting 'theirs', revealing the most graphic details. Out of the bunch, Tiffany was the main one rubbing Q'Tee's virginity in her face. One day after volleyball practice, Q'Tee, Tiffany, and some more girls were talking while getting dressed. As usual, Tiffany had to be the one to crack on Q'Tee first.

"Q'Tee, if you don't hurry up and get some dick soon your pussy hole gon' close up permanently," Tiffany said meddling.

All the girls laughed uncontrollably.

"Yeah! If not that, all those cobwebs are gon' take over," another girl, named Renee, joined in.

Being the center of their entertainment, Q'Tee finally convinced herself she was determined to have sex with Jaleel.

When she made it home, she knew her mother was at work until midnight, and her brother usually stayed out hustling until late night. This gave her the house all to herself. Quickly, she called Jaleel and invited him over. Since his older cousin stayed two houses down at the time, made it convenient for Jaleel to come across town from the Southside to Oakcliff.

After hanging up with him, she figured it would take him a while to get to her house, because his cousin had to go pick him up and bring him back to her house. All the time she waited, she begin to get butterflies in her stomach. She was unsure if this was what she really wanted to do. But the constant reminder of her homegirls criticizing remarks pushed her to go on through with it. Plus, the much talk about the feeling sex brought only aroused her curiosity.

Forty-five minutes later, Jaleel arrived at her house. Once inside her bedroom Q'Tee dropped her robe, standing only in her bra and panties. Seeing her half exposed gave Jaleel all the more reason to hurry up and undress.

Jaleel was a young thug. This was nowhere near his first sexual experience. Coming up in the projects, sex at a early age came with the environment.

Q'Tee hopped in the bed and crawled under the covers. She pulled off her panties and bra, tossing them to the floor. As she watched Jaleel get undressed, she said, "I hope you brought a rubber."

Jaleel whipped the condom out of his pocket, easing her nervousness just a bit. Placing the condom on, he climbed in the bed with her, yanking the covers off her, fully exposing her nudeness.

"Jaleel!" she creamed, trying to cover herself.

His eyes lit up at the sight of her pert nipples and hairy poonanny. Quickly, he laid himself on top of her, kissing her fully on the lips. She could feel the hardness pressing against her sensitive flesh. Just that alone felt good as she closed her eyes and wrapped her arms around his neck. As he released his kiss, he slithered his tongue down to suck her nipples. The feeling sent a spark between her legs, increasing her wetness. *I see what Tiffany 'em was talkin' about now. This shit is feelin' good,* she thought.

Caught up in the moment, she was unaware of Jaleel positioning himself to penetrate her. Suddenly, without warning, he thrust his dick inside her, literally ripping her hymen apart. Q'Tee gasped, trying to catch her breath. Effortlessly, she let out a faint scream as the tears begin to fall. She tried her best to push him off of her but he was too heavy.

"Jaleel st...stop! It hu...hurts!" she managed to say between his strokes.

It seems as if her pain turned him on more. His gangster mentality told him he was puttin' his 'thang' down. Instead of taking consideration to this being Q'Tee's first time, he simply pounded away at her. Realizing he wasn't going to stop, she gritted her teeth and took the agonizing pain until he finished. As he rolled off of her, she jumped up off the bed, looking down at herself to examine the damage and saw all the blood running down her legs.

'Boy! Look what you done to me!" she screamed, frantically swinging her fists at him.

"Girl, that ain't nuttin' but some cherry juice," he said, laughing as he fought her off.

Feeling weak in the knees, she stormed out of the bedroom to clean herself up. Just her luck, she had to run into Tony coming down the hallway.

"Q'Tee! Whatg the fuck is you doing walking through this mothafuckin' house butt ass naked?" Tony yelled harshly. "I know you better not have no nigga up in here!"

Q'Tee was absolutely terrified, unable to speak. *I done fucked up now*, she thought as she stood naked, nervous, and with blood running down the insides of her legs. How could she explain all that without it pointing to sex? While looking back and forth at Tony and her bedroom, she knew all hell was about to break loose.

Seeing the tears in her eyes, the shocked expression on her face and the glitter of blood on her legs, suspicion along with rage found its way into Tony's thoughts. Immediately, he passed her up, busting in her room to see Jaleel trying to crawl out the window butt naked. Without saying a word, Tony was on him with a flurry of punches.

"Tony, Stop! Please! It's not his fault!" Q'Tee shouted while jumping on her brother's back to save her true love from a beat down. It's amazing what women will do for love!

Snapping back from the past, Q'Tee wondered what Jaleel was up too. They hadn't talked since their break-up last summer. However, Ms. Gossip-to-go-with-Flo- Tiffany kept her updated with his activities whenever she called. She thought about sleeping with him again for old times sake but convinced herself it would only make things worse than it already was. Honestly, she still hadn't completely gotten over him. On the real, she did need some dick! It's been a year since her and Jaleel had sex together, or anyone else for that matter, which means she was definitely horny and way overdue.

As she started to undress, she came across the piece of paper Dontae wrote his number on. She admitted to herself that he was cute and fine. "Prison does work wonders on a nigga!" she said smiling. She debated on giving him a call but didn't want him thinking she was sweating him. Continuing to undress, she remembered him saying he had been locked up over four years. "That dick got to be good. Whoever the bitch is that got with him first probably still smiling."

With that thought, a chill went through her body and she noticed her nipples were hard. Massaging them with her fingertips sent a tingle down between her legs. Gently, she slid her fingers underneath her panties and felt the wetness saturate her fingertips.

She laid herself on the bed and began to rub and fondle her breasts as she visualized Dontae freaking her down. The heat continued to boil inside her, driving her to snatch her panties off and throw them on the floor. The desire was overtaking her body as she penetrated herself again and again with her fingers, thrusting her hips to the inward motion. Suddenly, she was overwhelmed by the tingling sensation that traveled through her body. She began to moan softly. Her body tightened up as she called Dontae's name over and over. In the process, there was a knock at the door. Q'Tee was quickly startled as she reached for something to cover up with.

"'Who is it?" she shouted angrily after being disturbed of her moment of pleasure.

"Tiffany wants you on the phone," her mother yelled from the other side of the door. "What you doing in there?"

"Nuttin', momma," Q'Tee shot back, allowing the frustration to show in her voice. "Tell her I will call her back in twenty minutes."

She sighed, "That's why I gots to get my own house with the quickness, a sistah can't even 'jack' off in peace."

Now upset that her rise to pleasure was interrupted, she grabbed some clean panties out of her dresser drawer and went to take a cold shower.

Chapter Three

The Ice Club was packed, as usual on a Friday night. Cars lined the front of the building like a car show. Custom paint jobs, chrome wheels-foreign, SUV's trucks, old schools and modern vehicles caught everyone's attention as they passed by. The line was out the door and around the corner. Niggaz waiting to get their groove and drink on, or locate a potential sex partner. For the female, the same, hoping a meal came with it. And for the hoes and skeezers, a 'trick' would suit them just fine.

Dontae was barely able to find a parking spot. The increasing number of young women, varying from all sizes and shades of color, flocked the parking lot. He couldn't believe his eyes. *I must've died and went to heaven!* he thought. He always kept an ear to the streets while in prison about the rising number of young hoes in the mix, and were willing to give the pussy up quick. Now he was seeing firsthand what all the big talk was about.

Looking at the line, he figured it was going to take forever to get in the club. Judging by the scene, he knew it was jumpin' off on the inside. *I can't wait to get up in there,* he said to himself.

As he stood contemplating on whether he should wait it out or leave, he saw Reg and Isaac walking up. He was impressed with what they were wearing--Gucci and Iceberg outfits, highlighted with their platinum jewelry. At first Dontae thought he was extra clean. After seeing them, he felt average. Even though, he had on his new baby blue Sean John warm up and a fresh pair of Air Force Ones, he still was no match for what Reg and Isaac had on.

"What it do, homie!" Isaac said, pounding fists with Dontae, "Nigga, why you still outside? All the action up in the club."

"I'm just waitin' till the line go down," Dontae said.

"Fuck that! C'mon nigga!" Isaac said, making his way with Reg to security. Dontae followed them. He stood back and watched them work their magic with security. Minutes later, they were inside the club. Just like Dontae thought, the inside of the club was off the chain. Niggaz and hoes were everywhere doing their thing. Isaac and Reg were treated like royalty. The atmosphere had changed so much. The faces he was seeing now were barely teenagers when he was partying at the club years ago. Still, he managed to see and holla at old faces, who welcomed him home with smiles and hugs.

"Here, dawg!" Reg said, handing Dontae a bottle of Cristal.

"Damn baby! You doin' it big, huh?" Dontae said appreciatively, while accepting the bottle of champagne.

"This what we do. We done already told you to join the team and get this paper," Reg said, hi-cappin' as he popped the top of his bottle of Cristal. "Just call me the number one stunna."

Dontae laughed. "I'm chillin'," he said nonchalantly.

"It's your decision. Do you!" Reg said between sips. "To each its own. But say, holla at me later so we can chop it up some more. Right now I got to mingle for a minute and see what's crackin' with these hoes."

Walking off, Reg turned around, gesturing to Dontae to look in the direction of Kayla and Ne-Ne, the same two females he and Isaac were talking to earlier in the courtyard of the projects. The girls were walking through the club.

Dontae threw up two fingers, signifying that he and Reg were on the same page. He looked at Kayla and Ne-Ne as they passed by him rolling their eyes.

Reg shouted out a few words, but the girls ignored him and kept walking.

"Girl, fuck him!" Kayla said to Ne-Ne.

Dontae overheard Kayla and sympathized with their attitude. *It's a shame to see two bad bitches go to waste, especially if they presented themselves as fair game*, he thought as he watched them gracefully walk deeper into the crowd.

Gradually, Dontae mingled deeper in the crowd himself, making his way toward the dance floor. There, he saw Lisa bouncing and dropping that ass. The light skinned brotha she was dancing with was enjoying every minute of it.

Dontae watched in amazement. *I wonder can she fuck like that?* he thought, as he grabbed his crotch off impulse.

Seeing Lisa, he expected Marquita and Briana to be floating around somewhere. He scanned the whole club, looking for them. *Maybe they in the bathroom,* he thought. Patiently, he waited for Lisa to come off the dance floor.

Finally, Lisa came off the dance floor exhausted. Dontae eased up behind her.

"Damn! You must get if from yo' momma!" he said, repeating the rap song by 'Juvenile'.

Recognizing Dontae, Lisa burst out laughing. "Boy, you crazy!"

"How long you been up in here?" Dontae asked.

"About an hour. I wanted to get here early to beat the crowd."

"I know what you mean. The line is around the corner now."

Dontae kicked it with Lisa for about twenty minutes, trying his best to persuade her to give in to getting with him after the club.

"Boy! I told you we'll see," she said smiling, knowing her mind was already made up to freak him down.

Actually, Dontae had had all he could take from sweatin' Lisa about her pussy. He figured if she was going to continue to play hard to get, he might as well use her as a pawn just to get to Marquita.

"Where yo' girls at?" he asked, mainly inquiring about Marquita.

"Briana in here somewhere," Lisa said, looking around for her. "But Marquita couldn't make it. She decided to stay at home with her man. So you know how that go."

Dontae shook his head. "Damn!" he mumbled under his breath. There went his chance to get with Marquita. *Oh well! Now Lisa will experience the "Mandingo' after all, unless she keep on trippin'. Its to many other hoes in the club I could be tryin' to talk them out of their pussy*, he thought.

The DJ had the club rocking. The dance floor was packed. Even the people who weren't on the dance floor dancing were moving to the beat wherever they stood or sat.

"Say Lisa. You want to dance?" Dontae asked.

"I don't care," Lisa said, leading the way.

On the dance floor, Dontae was no match for Lisa, and she knew it. She was working it like she was auditioning for a Beyonce "Crazy in Love" video. The more she displayed her array of booty shaking dances, the more Dontae's dick started to get hard.

Minutes later, the fast beat was replaced with the slow jam throwback of R Kelly's "Bump n' Grind".

"Ooohhh!" Lisa purred. "That's my jam!" she continued, throwing her hands in the air in a sensual way.

She reached out and pulled Dontae nearer. Wrapping her arms around his neck, she grinded seductively, rocking her hips side to side, round and round.

Dontae held on to her small waist, feeling the urgency to rest his hands at the top of her butt. The more sexual she moved, the better the sensation was feeling. He couldn't resist. Or at least his dick couldn't! His dick began to get even harder.

Lisa looked up at him, feeling his erection poking her. With no response, she pulled him into her tighter and continued to grind with a purpose.

Throughout the course of the night, Dontae mingled with a variety of women, gathering numerous phone numbers and possible hook-ups just in case Lisa played the hard to get role again. It seemed as if things were getting better by the minute.

Taking a seat at the end of the bar, he couldn't help but over hear the hyped up discussion of a group of brothas standing across from him. Quickly, Dontae focused his attention to what they were making such a big deal about.

Coming in the club were three sistahs whose presence was meant to be told.

"Them hoes is like that!" a bald head brotha said, pounding fists with his homeboy. "Look at ol' girl in the brown."

Dontae was straining his eyes to get a better view of the girls' faces. The dim lighting in the club was keeping him from seeing the total packages. From afar, everything about them stood out, mainly their shapes. All three sistahs were unique in their own way, still they were only considered as just another typical high price ghetto bitch, that managed to come up on a major do' boy. The sculptured weaves styled in the trendiest hairstyles, colored contacts, long manicured fingernails and an array of designer clothing and handbags from Channel, Baby Phat, Gucci and Louis Vuitton, all accentuated by the finest jewelry. It was obvious, they were a drug dealer's sidekick.

The three sistahs sashayed through the club, making sure they were seen. Niggaz were stopping them along the way for casual conversation or offering to buy them drinks while the jealous females turned up their noses, signifying their dislikes. Down right hatin', as others stared and whispered amongst one another, finding any type of flaw.

As they fought off the cock hounds, the threesome continued to close the gap between them and Dontae. Seconds later, the fine specimens were in full view. Dontae had to do a double take after recognizing Jasmine. "That can't be Jasmine--or is it?" he murmured, second guessing himself. Quickly, he hopped off the barstool and squeezed his way through the crowd. "Excuse me! Sorry about that! My bad!" he said as he passed up different people. Finally making his way to Jasmine, her eyes widened the moment she saw Dontae.

"Dontae!" Jasmine screamed as she rushed to him, throwing her arms around his neck, hugging him cheerfully.

Her home girls, Tina and Rhonda, looked at each other, thrown off guard by Jasmine's sudden reaction, more so curious, especially of Dontae, who they knew nothing about. To them, he was a nobody. His appearance didn't interest them enough and it definitely didn't show he had money. Their suspicion told them that he had to be someone Jasmine was creepin' with behind her man's back.

"Boy, when you get home?" she said after hugging him.'

"Yesterday!" he replied, happily.

"Man, it seem like you been gone forever."

"I feel like I been gone forever."

They both shared a laugh together.

Rudely, Jasmine's two home girls stepped in, interrupting the happy reunion.

"Ah, Jasmine, we'll be over there," Tina gestured, popping her gum. "When you get through talkin'."

"Hold up y'all" Jasmine stopped them. "I want y'all to meet someone."

Tina and Rhonda hesitated, not a least bit enthused.

"This is Dontae, an old friend of mine since high school. Dontae, this Tina and Rhonda."

Tina and Rhonda flashed fake smiles while Dontae only nodded, respecting the introduction.

Noticing the girls' conceited attitudes, Dontae's smile was replaced with a slight smirk as he stared at them as if they had shit on them. *Stuck up bitches!* he thought to himself.

Jasmine read his facial expression and so did Tina and Rhonda. Without another minute wasted, Tina and Rhonda excused themselves and hurried off, disappearing into the crowd to advertise themselves to any potential ballers that might be equipped to meet their every need.

"What up on your home girls?" Dontae asked.

"You know how money do a bitch!" Jasmine confessed truthfully. "Don't even trip behind them."

Lucky for Dontae running into Jasmine; now he could find out about Naija, being that they were best friends.

Often Jasmine's facial similarities were compared to Naija. Although Jasmine was a lighter shade of brown with a tiny black mole on her right cheek, she was very attractive and sexy. Some would agree Jada Pinkett-Smith type sexy.

Stepping back from Jasmine, analyzing her appearance, Dontae was impressed. *Damn! This bitch thicker than a mothafucka!* he thought. Her good looks, along with her two home girls, explained why the group of brothas were making such a big fuss.

The Baby Phat gear Jasmine was wearing was making a statement. The sleeveless midriff top showed off her flat stomach and belly ring. Her low rider jeans fit snugly on her firm butt, and her open toe heels exposed her neatly pedicured toes.

"From the looks of things, you must be well taken care of. Or you done hit the lottery," Dontae said admiring her.

Jasmine slightly shifted her weight to one side, placing her hand on her hip.

"You know a girl gotta do what she can to get ahead in this world, and that's by any means necessary!" she said justifying her good fortune.

"I ain't mad at ya', baby. Take care of yo' business, whatever it is you're doin'," Dontae said, thinking she was selling pussy.

Reading his mind, she said defensively, "Oh it ain't what you think it is! I ain't flat backing as an occupation. Fuck that! My shit belongs to one nigga. Lucky for me, he shows his appreciation."

As Dontae and Jasmine spent time talking, Lisa walked passed them, rolling her eyes at Dontae.

Jasmine sensed the jealousy in Lisa's reaction.

"Who is that?" Jasmine asked, basically being nosey.

Reality snapped back to Dontae instantly, remembering his chances of having sex with Lisa. "Hold up a minute," he said as he turned to go catch up with Lisa.

After a brief talk with her, assuring her that nothing was going on with he and Jasmine, he returned back to Jasmine.

"Damn nigga! That bitch got you in check like that?" Jasmine said playfully.

"Bullshit!" Dontae said smirking. "That's just some fo' sho pussy for tonight and I don't want to fuck up my chances. I can't be going home with no hard dick and shit. I spent too many of those nights in prison. I promised my dick that I wouldn't put him through that punishment ever again."

Jasmine laughed. "Boy, you is a fool," she said, still laughing.

They spent close to an hour going through different conversations. Never once did Jasmine mention Naija's name. Dontae wondered were they still friends. He figured he'd bring Naija's name up, hoping to find out her whereabouts.

"Say, where yo' girl at?" he asked.

"Who?" she replied, blankly, unaware of who he was talking about.

Dontae looked at her stupidly. "C'mon, girl. Quit playin' dumb!" he said, sarcastically. "You damn well know who I'm talkin' 'bout."

"Ooohhh! You talkin' about Naija! She...ah...ah..." Jasmine paused, totally caught off guard.

Having been caught up in conversation, she had forgotten all about the relationship Dontae and Naija had. "She chillin." As a matter of fact, we suppose to hook up later tomorrow and go shoppin," she finished.

"Oh, yeah? When you see her let her know I'm tryna holla at her. I know she fuckin' with some nigga. That's common sense. But I ain't trippin'. Just tell her to get at me."

Jasmine didn't want to be the one to break the bad news to Dontae about Naija and Tony. Besides, that was her home girl. And telling on her would be absolute betrayal. Then again, her motivation had some play in Naija's relationship with Tony. If she never would have persuaded Naija to go to the club that night, she wouldn't have never met Tony, and just maybe Naija would have stayed faithful to Dontae. *Ain't no use of me trippin' now! It's too late to mix the bitter with the sweet!* Jasmine thought. Nonetheless, she knew Naija was going to be in for a rude awakening whenever she got the news that Dontae was home, especially if they ever ran into each other after all these years.

Jasmine told Dontae bits and pieces about Naija, withholding the confidential information about her current relationship. To play it safe, she didn't bother to mention she was messing with J-Rock.

Dontae looked at her suspiciously, knowing Jasmine was hiding something about Naija. Without pressing the issue, he just played it off like he believed everything she was telling him.

Dontae figured he had talked to Jasmine long enough. Plus, Lisa kept passing by, cutting her eyes at him and making faces of jealousy. He wrote his phone number down on a napkin for Jasmine to give to Naija.

"Make sure you give this to her so that she can get in touch with me," Dontae requested, giving Jasmine the napkin.

"I will," Jasmine said, skeptical about Naija's reaction and decision to call him.

As Dontae walked off, Jasmine couldn't take her eyes off him. *Oooweee nigga! You fine as a mothafucka. Naija! Girl I love you like a sister, but you definitely have some decisions to make now,* Jasmine said to herself, wanting to get with him sexually.

The night progressed into closing time. Couples started pairing up.

The parking lot was crunk. Niggaz smoking blunts, sound systems on blast and hoes on a mission to get their man. Others headed home and some moved on to the after hour spots--Denny's, I-hop or Whataburger, for a bite to eat, while the younger crowds hung out on the strip.

Dontae stood outside in the parking lot looking around, trying to find Lisa. He was hoping her jealousy didn't lead her in the direction of another nigga. He knew he was going to be ass out if he had to mack up on some more pussy. Because usually after the club, females were already locked in on the nigga they wanted to give their pussy up too.

Continuing to look around, he spotted Reg and Isaac getting ready to leave with Kayla and Ne-Ne. *Slick mothafuckas! All that shit them hoes was talking!...Look at em'...can't wait to give up the pussy,* he thought as he smiled.

While Dontae was in the process of looking for a possible hook-up, gunshots rang out in the parking lot, scattering the crowd. *As always, a nigga gotta fuck shit up*, he thought.

People everywhere were running, screaming and ducking for cover. Vehicles were heard speeding out the parking lot, heading for safety.

In the mix of the gunfire, Dontae saw Lisa and Briana squatted down behind a truck, shielding themselves from any stray bullets.

After the brief ruckus died down, Dontae managed to persuade Lisa to let him treat her to breakfast. Then later, they went out to her apartment on the eastside. There, he ended up spending the night having hot adulterated sex. Finally, he got what he wanted after all these years. Unfortunately, the outcome wasn't what he expected.

Chapter Four

Rriinngg! Rrriinngg! Rrriinngg! The phone rang loudly, jolting Naija from her sleep. She fumbled frantically for the receiver. Finally, she retrieved it form its base, placing it to her ear.

"Hello!" she answered in a low groggy voice.

"Bitch, wake yo' ass up!" Jasmine yelled, "I don't see why you all tired and shit. It ain't like you got no job. Unless Tony put that thug lovin' on you real tough last night," Jasmine added laughing.

"No you didn't, bitch! Don't hate! The shit I do is a job, a skilled profession," Naija shot back. "And hell naw, Tony ain't put down no thug lovin'! Hell, I get a better nut playin' with myself."

Suddenly, Naija quit talking as she got up from the bed to look around to make sure Tony wasn't lurking around the corner, hearing what she was saying. After cautiously seeing he was nowhere around, she continued to talk to Jasmine.

"I'm back."

"Girl, what you doing?"

"I had to make sure Tony wasn't listening to my conversation," Naija said feeling more relaxed. "What's up?"

"Nuttin'. Just calling to see if we still goin' shopping today."

"Hell yeah! You know ain't nuttin' changed. I just got to get some ends from Tony, then it's on."

"I feel ya' home girl. I was able to get some money from J-Rock this morning when he came by to pick up lil' J.J. to take him over his grandmother's. You know I put this snapper on him just like he like it," Jasmine bragged.

"Save all your raunchy details. I ain't tryna hear nuttin' about you and J-Rock freak session. Besides, I got to put my own shit down on Tony to make sure he break bread with a bitch," Naija testified. "And right now his ass ain't nowhere to be found this morning."

"Where he at?" Jasmine asked.

"I don't know. It's no tellin' where his black ass is. He might be downstairs somewhere. Then again he might have snuck out while I was sleep to go be with one of his hoes. But if that's the case, I ain't trippin' about all that right now. There comes a time when to trip and when not to trip. And today ain't the day, 'cause a bitch need some thangs," Naija preached like the true scandalous bitch she was.

"Girl, listen to you. Spoken like a bonified playa bitch! I taught you well," Jasmine laughed, then remembered Dontae. "Giirrll, have I got something to tell you! You'll never guess in a million years who I seen in the club last night."

"Who, girl?" Naija asked, expecting the answer.

"I'ma wait until you get over here. You never know what Tony got rigged up on the phone."

"It's that confidential?"

"Yes, ma'am!

"Well, I'll be over there sometime this evening," Naija said, eager to find out what Jasmine had to tell her. "And have yo' ass ready when I get there."

"I will, bitch. Bye!"

"Bye, ho!"

When Naija hung up, she wondered what was so important that Jasmine couldn't discuss over the phone. *Probably some nigga she met in the club that she want to fuck,* Naija speculated to herself. Putting the thought in the back of her mind, she snuggled back under the covers.

It was the weekend. Time to go spoil herself on, the behalf of Tony's money. Something she enjoyed doing on a regular basis.

Looking over at the clock, she saw it was 10:42 a.m. *I might as well get up,* she said to herself. She knew she had to get prepared to work her magic when the opportunity presented itself.

She stretched, wondering where Tony was now that she thought about it. It wasn't like him to just get out of bed without trying to get a "quickie" or do something sexual unless he was already well satisfied by another female.

Naija recalled going to sleep late last night and Tony still hadn't made it home yet. She couldn't remember if he came home or not because she was faded off the Alize and vodka she drank, and the two blunts she smoked by herself.

She got up from the bed and walked clumsily to the bathroom to pee, head still pounding from last night. Afterwards, she took some aspirin, then went downstairs to look for Tony. She checked around the house. After checking the garage and seeing his Lexus was gone, she went back upstairs and prepared to take a bath.

●●●●●●

Exiting off Highway 67 onto Illinois Avenue, Tony headed into the heart of Oakcliff. Even though he had moved to the suburbs, the hood was still considered home.

Business was officially open. Time to punch in the clock to check traps and collect snaps.

Dipping through traffic in his black Lexus LS 430 with the Alpine system on blast, he fired up a blunt. Stopping at the stop light, he noticed a blue Olds Delta 88 with dark tinted windows pull up beside him. Out of reflex, he reached in his console for his chrome Beretta 9mm, quickly remembering he had left it at home out of fear of being stopped by the police in the hood, which was beginning to be a regular routine, especially, by some rookie cop trying to earn stripes. The last thing Tony wanted was a bullshit pistol case.

Based on his money and status in the dope game, the fear of jackers and the Feds was a constant reminder everyday. Jealousy and envy was all around him, playing both sides of the table. It definitely paid to be cautious or get caught slippin'. No matter the scenario, the game was a double-edged sword.

Finally, the light turned green. The Olds sped off, leaving a cloud of smoke from its tailpipe. Relieved of the unexpected, Tony returned back to relaxation mode, puffing on the blunt. As he drove, the argument he had with Q'Tee concerning Dontae came across his mind. Something about Dontae gave him the impression there was more to the story, but he just couldn't lay a finger on it right now.

Beep! Beep! Beep! The horn of a Mitsubishi Eclipse, carrying two females, caught Tony's attention as the car pulled up alongside him, redirecting his present thoughts. Always a sucka for pussy, he let down the automatic window, quickly recognizing the face of Trina, a sweet, young chocolate candy bar complexioned female that he enjoyed knocking off from time to time.

"Tony, where you going?" Trina, shouted from the passenger side of the eclipse.

"Nowhere! I'm just rollin'," Tony replied after turning down his music some.

He only told her part of the truth which is all she needed to know. His main objective was to go pick up his $100,000 from J-Rock.

"Pull over. I need to talk to you about somethin'," she requested after noticing the traffic coming behind them.

Tony whipped his Lexus out in from of them, quickly parking in a nearby church parking lot. Parking behind him, Trina got out and pranced to his side of the car. Tony watched closely through his side mirror as she approached him in some tight coochie cutter shorts. "Damn that pussy fat!" he murmured to himself. Realizing he used bad language on church grounds, he apologized to God. Even though he was a drug dealer, he respected the Word. This is something his mother instilled in him and his sister at a young age.

"What's up with the disappearing acts?" she said, swatting him on the arm. "You don't know how to return a bitch messages?

That's how it is? You get my pussy, now a bitch don't hear from you for the next two weeks. What's up with that?"

"It ain't that. You know me, I got a million and one things to do. I just been busy," he said while caressing her thigh with his fingertips, teasing her a little.

Somewhat turned on by his harmless flirting, she leaned in his window, resting her bra-less breasts on his arm. "When you gon' give me some?" she said softly while sliding her hand down in his lap to rub his dick.

Instantly, Tony became hard. Though, he had a desire to fuck her, he knew he had important business to tend too. He couldn't afford to mix business with pleasure right now. Besides, she was guaranteed pussy at any given time.

"Say, hit me up later," he told her, smiling. "Don't forget to put your code in."

"Don't play no games and have me waiting up on you," she expressed, pushing the side of his head with her finger.

"Watch yo self. Conversation ain't physical!" he said playfully.

"Whatever! I can sho' you physical," Trina said, teasingly.

As she provocatively walked back to the car with her home girl, Tony couldn't help remember how good Trina had it. She had the complete package--good head and good pussy! A nigga had the best of both worlds. Because of her skilled expertise in the sex category, Tony didn't mind breaking her off with some pocket change every now and then.

Driving off, he thought, *I got to hit that again!*

Grabbing his cell phone, he called J-Rock.

"Yeah! Wuz up wit' it!". J-Rock answered.

"What up my nigga! Where you at?"

"Down her at Shorty's, hangin out."

"You got that?"

"Already. Didn't I tell you I was gon' have it?" J-Rock said a bit agitated.

"I'm gon' swing by there in about ten minutes. I'm on Marsalis now. What they doin' down there? Any gambling jumpin' off?"

"It's a small game. It ain't enough paper in the game to raise a whole lot of noise about. I'm just waitin'. I'll be damn if I throw my money away in the crumb ass dice game," J-Rock said hi-siding.

"Okay then. I'll holla at ya' later. Maybe that shit will crank up by the time I get down there."

The sounds of Jay-Z thumped through the speakers in Tony's Lexus as he cruised the hood, bobbing his head to the beat. Reclined in the soft peanut butter leather seats, he was one paid brotha. Getting money was his trademark. He was given the game at an early age by his father's life of hustling.

After, his father's death only fueled the fire to getting his hands on some major paper. To what started out as petty weed selling in high school, to chopping down fifty packs into dime rocks and slinging them out of a dope house. Now he was flipping birds. A lot of them! Tony was known as the "Ghetto Scarface" of the hood.

His clientele was mostly local, but spread throughout surrounding cities. Living in a large city such as Dallas, Texas, the competition of major suppliers was widespread, coming from all nationalities. Nevertheless, it posed no threat to his pockets. Every now and then, large scale dealers would drop prices to broaden their exposure in order to beat the next man out. Whatever the case may be, Tony kept a set price because he kept "fire" shit that always kept his customers satisfied.

Starting out as a young buck in the dope game years ago, he was obsessed with wildin' out and spending money unnecessarily. That's usually the norm with all young hustlers. He drew a lot of unwanted attention to himself in the wrong way.

Noticed by his father's old hustling buddies, mainly Shorty, they quickly took him in, calmed him down and explained the benefits as well as the consequence behind fast money. They constantly stayed in his ear, preaching regularly. "Get in and get out! The game is sweet but it don't owe you nothing! Never let your right hand know what your left hand is doing!" From that point on, Tony began to monitor his steps. Now seven years later, he's still in the game and going strong.

Tony was definitely a ladies man who didn't mind spoiling a woman. And the women knew this. That's why so many were literally throwing themselves at him. Many wanted to take Naija's place permanently.

He was tall, standing at 6'5, weighing 255 lbs., dark and handsome. His dimples help enlighten his smile and brought added attention to his good looks. To top everything off, he had money which made up for all other shortcoming that some women said he was lacking.

His reputation was violent, if provoked. A lot of people were intimidated by his massive size, an attribute he developed during his years of playing high school football.

He was the older that his sister, Q'Tee, by six years, of whom he was very protective. Most brothers thought twice about approaching her because of the drama that came with Tony about his sister. One time he beat a brotha down that accidentally bumped into her. He thought the brotha was trying to feel on her butt on the slick tip.

Taking a right on Overton Road, he grabbed his cell phone again. This time he called Naija. The phone rang a few times before she answered.

"Hello!" Naija answered.

"What took you so long to answer the phone?" Tony questioned her with suspicion in his voice.

"I was taking a bath," she snapped, frowning.

Naija was hoping he wasn't in one of his moods because she didn't feel like putting up with his bullshit. Knowing she needed some money for the weekend, she kept a cool head and played her position.

"Yo, I'm gonna make a few stops before I come home."

"Where you at?" she asked, realizing she was in violation.

Fortunately, Tony responded with a pleasant attitude.

"I'm fix'nta go meet J-Rock and pick up some money. Then check on some other things."

"Be careful baby. I woke up this morning looking for you but you was gone. I had something for you. Just as soon as you get through doing what you're doing, I need you to hurry up and bring my dick home," she said in a sexy tone of voice with hopes of him not detecting her unconcern.

Tony smiled at her assertiveness to sex.

Hanging up, he thought, *Freaky ass!*

Throwing the cell phone in the passenger seat, he was feeling even hornier than he did when he ran in to Trina. Some kind of way, Naija knew how to turn him on completely.

●●●●●●

After hanging up with Tony, Naija laughed to herself about the fact she had him wrapped around her finger. With an appetite for fashion, jewelry and money, she knew the best way to get what she wanted was to toss some pussy his way, and he would be eating out the palm of her hand.

Naija was the prototypical good girl gone bad, once the woman, who cherished a wholesome relationship based on love, trust and honesty. Never the one to proposition her body to reap the benefits of money. Its funny how life changes! After a year or so of playing the backseat to a relationship in prison, loneliness exploited her to a new era unknown to her before, where niggaz didn't mind paying for what they wanted, mainly pussy. Whatever the cost, depending on the pockets of the hustler or the trick.

Therefore, Jasmine introduced Naija to the lifestyle. Being infatuated by the hustler's lifestyle, Naija didn't take long to adjust.

Meeting Tony three years ago only opened the doors to the playing field. And Naija entered into his game, playing to win. For months and months, they spent time together. Tony spoiled her with extravagant shopping sprees and quality time. Whatever she wanted, he bought it. Wherever she wanted to go, he took her. He showed her the time of her life. Three months into their relationship, they flew to Las Vegas for the Lennox Lewis and Mike Tyson fight. In Vegas, they spent the week shopping at the most upscale department stores, gambling at Harrah's Casino and dining at five star restaurants. Their last night in Sin City, Naija gave into the desires she had neglected since Dontae's imprisonment. Tony fell in love with her instantly, asking her to move in with him. At first, she refused. After a few months of excessive kindness, she finally accepted the offer.

Living with Tony started out like a fairy tale for the first year. Naija had developed some feelings for him until his jealousy became a problem, always suspicious of her goings and comings. Many times, she wanted to back out of the relationship. Somehow, he would always seem to win her back with his persistent pampering. As the time passed, she became accustomed to not having to work and having the finer things in life. However, her feelings were at a stand still. She never felt the love for him that she thought she would develop during their time together. Money became her main objective. Fuck a relationship! From what started out as something serious, soon became a come up to her, and Naija played the game like a specialized pro with some guidance from her home girl, Jasmine. She didn't care about him at all. All she cared about was the benefits of his money. To her Tony was a 'trick'. She only led him to believe she was madly in love with him. Hitting him off with some pussy regularly and thorough dick sucking kept everything intact. Out of the three years they have been together, she never would have guessed things would have lasted this long.

Naija sat on the side of the bed, lotioning her long legs, waiting patiently for Tony to come home so that she could put her 'thang' down. Thinking to herself, she laughed about his minute-man status. She knew it would only take seconds for him to bust a nut once she put some good loving on him. "Thank God for dildos," she said grinning.

Thirty minutes later, she sat on the couch, thumbing though the pages of a fashion magazine, wondering just how long she could play this game without Tony figuring her out. She was 26 years old. Eventually, she wanted to settle down, get married and raise a family. Just not with Tony.

Damn Dontae! Why did you have to get locked up? she asked herself.

Thoughts of Dontae began to lay heavy on her mind like so many times before. The one man she can truly say she ever loved. She still cared about him, though she figured he hated her by now, considering she fucked over him. Over the years, she thought about writing him numerous times. But after so much time had passed, she figured it would only confuse the situation. After being accused of everything under the sun, the shit got old. Soon the relationship start to go downhill, allowing her vulnerabilities to get the best of her. Deep inside, she wanted to experience that love again. As for now, her love is for some dead presidents!

● ● ● ● ● ●

Tony rode by the neighborhood spots. The scene was 'hot' as usual. Five-oh had niggaz jammed up doing shakedowns, harassing crackheads and young hustler's on the block. Seeing the drama unfold, he attempted a quick drive thru but wasn't able to get away without being recognized by the police officers in the area. In seconds, red and blue lights were flashing atop of a police cruiser. The police officer signaled him to pull over.

There were two white police officers, one older and the other. The younger one approached his car. Tony recognized Reynolds, a veteran officer who patrolled the drug infested neighborhoods. In the past, Tony and Reynolds had their fair share of run-ins, always a matter of drugs or gun possession.

Tony was glad he finished smoking the blunt that he threw out the window just in time before he was stopped. Now his fear was the lingering smell of weed left in his car. *Hopefully, they don't trip,* he thought nervously.

"Well, well, well! If it ain't Mr. Williams! How are you doing today, sir?" Officer Reynolds said amused. "You sure are in a hurry for some reason," he added speculating on the major bust he had been waiting on.

"Save all the small talk," Tony snapped aggravated. "Just tell me why you pulled me over."

"Hold on now! No need to get all hot under the collar. Honestly, Mr. Williams you sped through here like a bat out of hell. So I just wanted to find out what's your big hurry."

"Man, I ain't done nuttin' wrong. Y'all just get a big kick out of harassing me like always."

"Now settle down. I didn't say you done anything wrong. But it's my job to make sure you don't do anything wrong," Reynolds said calmly. "The thing is, by you being a highly known drug dealer, eluding a highly known drug area gives us probable cause to stop you. So let's get down to business shall we? Are there any drugs or weapons in the car?"

"Do I look stupid? All the times you've ever stopped me, where there drugs or guns in the car?" Tony shouted.

"Mr. Williams! This is a new day," Reynolds said trying to remain calm.

His younger partner, being a rookie and all, didn't know what to make out of the situation. Reacting on impulse, he kept his hand near his .38 revolver just in case Tony got violent.

"All this is a bunch of bullshit!" Tony proclaimed.

Out of nowhere, reinforcements came. Two patrol cars carrying two officers each. *They must really think I got some dope in the car,* Tony thought. He shook his head, knowing the harassment could last for hours.

During the process, a small neighborhood crowd slowly started gathering.

"Yo Tony! You a'ight?" a voice from the crowd yelled.

Not able to recognize the voice of who was checking on him, Tony threw up two fingers to the crowd, signaling he was 'straight'.

With his back-up arriving, Reynolds followed through with procedures, feeling like he had landed the big catch that just might get him a promotion. *I know this nigger got some drugs in the car,* Reynolds thought.

"I need you to step out the car with your hands where I can see them," Reynolds announced, opening the door for Tony.

The other five officers positioned themselves with their hands within easy reach of their firearms. For some reason it seem like they all had an itchy trigger finger.

Tony stepped out of the car, grinning from ear to ear.

"Put your hands on the hood and spread 'em!" Reynolds commanded.

Tony followed orders while keeping his eyes on the officers that began searching his car, making sure they didn't plant any drugs. His gut feeling always told him to never trust any law enforcement, especially after seeing the TV series "The Shield". More than likely, there was always a crooked one in the bunch, if not all of them.

Reynolds ran Tony's name into the dispatcher to check if he had any outstanding warrants. While waiting on the response to come back, Reynolds frisked Tony down, finding a small stash of cash in his pockets which was nothing to make a big fuss.

"Business must be slow," Reynolds said placing the $1,000 back in Tony's pocket.

Tony smiled at the remark, thinking to himself, *I'm glad I hadn't went to pick that money up from J-Rock.*

Returning his gaze back on the other officers searching his car, Tony saw the frustration on their faces when they came up empty-handed.

"You find anything, Ron?" Reynolds asked his partner, hoping he said yes.

"Everything's clean except for a lingering smell of marijuana," Ron answered with a southern country drawl.

Reynolds' face turned beet red, uttering, "Shit!" He signaled to his back-up that he had everything under control.

Tony wanted to laugh, but didn't. He gave a slight smirk, signifying to himself that he was untouchable.

"It seems like you are free to go, Mr. Williams. Everything else seems to be legit…this time!" Reynolds said, hating that things didn't go down the way he thought.

Tony got in his car and drove off.

Reynolds and his partner slow trailed Tony for a few blocks before finally disappearing.

Tony wiped the sweat from his brow and sighed. "That was a close call," he said as he checked his rearview mirror again to make sure Reynolds was out sight. Fully gathering his composure, he headed over to Shorty's place to see J-Rock and maybe shoot dice if there was enough money in the game.

• • • • • •

J-Rock, a slim brown skinned brotha sporting a bald fade, labeling himself as a bonafied playa, was leaning in a Chrysler Sebring, talking to two females, named Brandi and Tropic, when Tony drove up in his Lexus. Raising his head slightly, J-Rock knew exactly what Tony wanted but felt his timing was bad. J-Rock didn't feel like being bothered with Tony at the present time while he was in the process of coming up on some new pussy. Especially two freaks that were willing to 'serve' him, involving a threesome.

J-Rock acknowledged Tony as his boy and all, but at times he could act like a 'mark', and J-Rock was beginning to get sick and tried of Tony letting his money go to his head.

"Who is that?" Brandi asked, noticing Tony getting out of his car.

J-Rock didn't bother to answer her question. He was hoping Brandi and Tropic wouldn't choose up on Tony. He wanted them to keep their attention on him. On numerous occasions Tony had stolen J-Rock's shine, usually off his name alone because the image he presented.

J-Rock walked over to his Cadillac Deville, opened the trunk and removed a duffle bag with $100,000 in it and gave it to Tony.

Tony looked around nervously, making sure Reynolds hadn't double back on him. He popped his trunk, threw the bag inside and quickly shut it back, then walked back over to where J-Rock was standing.

"What up with those broads?" Tony asked, referred to the females in the Chrysler.

"Just some young freaks I met in the club last weekend," J-Rock told him.

"Oh, yeah!" Tony said, raising an eyebrow.

The mention of "freaks" was enough to arouse his curiosity. He walked over to the Chrysler to present his mack.

This is what J-Rock was afraid of. He knew Tony was going to invade his space. More so, win the young boppers.

Tony introduced himself, coming off as smooth as he could be. He conversated a brief moment with Brandi and Tropic just long enough to establish a hook-up. He was attracted to the red bone named Tropic, who happened to be the driver and also the one J-Rock took a big interest in. Tony gave her his beeper number, leaving her full of smiles. To add the icing on the cake, Tony unleashed one of his playa moves to make sure the girls would holla back at him with quickness. He pulled out the $1,000 he had in his pocket and peeled of a $100 bill and gave it to Tropic.

"Here, take this and y'all go out to eat on me," Tony said, then walked off, leaving Brandi and Tropic in total surprise.

Tony and J-Rock hung out a few minutes longer, smoking a blunt together. Tony explained his encounter with Officer Reynolds.

"Man, you better be careful. You know that fool out to get you. Reynolds ain't no joke. When he on duty I try to stay out his way," J-Rock informed Tony with a paranoid look on his face.

"I know what you mean. He been tryin' for years to catch me slippin' with some work," Tony said after puffing on the blunt, then passing it to J-Rock.

After finishing the blunt, Tony decided to go inside Shorty's Place and shoot dice.

J-Rock watched Tony go inside the building. His feelings of jealousy and envy replaced his high. "Bitch ass nigga!" J-Rock mumbled to himself, turning to go finish talking to Brandi and Tropic.

As soon as Tony stepped in the building, he spoke to the usual faces that hung around, then ordered himself a gin and orange juice.

O.C. "Shorty" Mayfield, the owner, told Tony a big dice game was going on in the back. That was exactly what Tony wanted to hear. Quickly, he walked behind the bar and pulled back the thick curtain covering the doorway heading to the back.

Shorty owned and ran the old shabby building. It was a typical hangout for the retired old school hustlers who spent their time enjoying life. Several people would stop in during the day to shoot pool, entertain themselves, and have a drink. Every so often the big time hustlers and big money gamblers would stop in and try their luck. Occasionally, crackheads would hang around in hopes of getting a handout or score a 'lick'. Every now and again, a young sexy female might swing by with a flock of her home girls just long enough to get some money from one of the old men she was messing with. Despite their married lives, the old heads always kept a young, hot, sexy thang on the side no matter the cost.

Shorty, like the rest of the old heads, had old money. Lots of it! The thing about it was he didn't flash his wealth. He kept everything plain and simple. He made his money back in the day when snitching wasn't at an all time high, selling Preludes, T's, Blues, PCV's, marijuana and syrup.

●●●●●●

A couple of hours later, after winning $7,500 in the dice game, Tony chit-chatted with Shorty about the family and business as usual. Tony had a lot of respect for Shorty, who was a good friend of his father. The rumor was out that Shorty and Gloria, Tony's mother, had a fling after his father died, which might explain all the time Shorty spent around Gloria years ago while Tony and Q'Tee were growing up as kids. But Tony paid no attention to it. In his eyes, Shorty was his mentor, along with the rest of his father's buddies that helped discipline him in the dope game and on how to be a responsible man.

After discussing some important financial propositions with Shorty, Tony headed home. He knew in his mind Naija was waiting on him to give her some money. He didn't mind spoiling her because he knew she loved him dearly. At least that's what he thought.

"Shit, them dice was hittin'," Tony said as he looked at the wad of cash he had just won. "Good thing I did have to stop by Shorty's."

During his moment of celebration, he quickly remembered the money in his trunk. He really had a reason to be nervous now. Getting stopped with $100,000 in the trunk would only be the appetizer for the Feds. He made sure he stopped at every stop sign, made all the correct turn signals and followed all driving procedures. The fact of the matter was, his Lexus was a dead give away to identifying him if the police decided to stop him.

Tony made it home at 4:30 p.m. The temperature wasn't as hot as it usually was the past several days. Yet and still it was hot enough.

Pulling in the driveway of his five bedroom house, he again escaped the unimaginable. The Good Lord is forever on his side.

Entering the house, he expected Naija to be waiting with her hand stuck out. To his surprise she was nowhere in sight which seem kind of odd.

"Naija!" he yelled as he walked through the bottom section of the house.

"Yes baby! I'm up here," Naija said, appearing at the top of the stairs in her birthday suit.

Tony stopped dead in his tracks with his mouth hung wide open, speechless!

"Are you gon' stand there all day or are you gon' bring me some dick?" she added, alluring him with a sexy pose and convincing smile.

Tony ran up the stairs taking two at a time until he reached the top where she was standing. They embraced and shared an intimate kiss. She took his hand and led him in the bedroom and helped him undress. Tony became hard instantly.

After he was completely undressed, Naija cradled his dick while pushing him down on the bed. He positioned himself as she kissed all over his body.

She placed his dick in her mouth and began to suck slowly as she massaged his testicles with her fingertips.

He moaned in pleasure. The feeling was becoming so unbearable that he wanted to scream like a bitch.

"Get on top!" he said, urgently.

Naija knew he was no match for her oral skills. Practice makes perfect. Eagerly wanting to put an end to the undesirable moment, she quickly straddled him like he asked and placed him inside of her. She went into her fake charades as if she was really enjoying herself. Tony just didn't have what it took to satisfy her sexually.

"Ooowee, baby! Right there! Give me that dick, Daddy. Tear this pussy up!" she screamed desirably like she was about to reach an orgasm.

Tony was breathing and sweating enormously, while she continued her sexual escapades rocking up and down until he finally reached his climax.

Naija tightened the insides of her pussy to make sure it was good to him. She thought to herself, *Damn I should have been an actress!* In her mind she knew Tony was pussy whooped.

Tony was in love with Naija, no question about it. He thought about asking her to marry him, but he wanted to be completely legit before he proposed. He also wanted children by her, though she stayed faithful to her birth control pills. Many times he persuaded her to stop taking them. Unfortunately, she would always say she wasn't ready for any kids right now.

As Naija got up to go the bathroom to clean herself up, Tony stopped her.

"Baby, look in my pants pockets," he said.

She picked up his pants and reached in his pocket, pulling out the wad of money he had won from the dice game. Her eyes widened at the money she grasped in her hand.

"That's yours baby. I figured you needed some cash," he announced with a big ol' smile.

"Thank you! Thank you!" she screamed as she ran back to the bed and gave him a wet kiss.

Again she turned and walked toward the bathroom, provocatively twisting her hips.

Tony stared at the roundness of her butt until she disappeared in the bathroom. As he laid in the bed, the sound of his pager snapped him out of his daze. He reached down and picked up his jeans and unclipped his pager from the side of his jeans. Checking the screen, he didn't recognize the number but he did recognize the code 69. *Trina,* he thought.

While in the bathroom, Naija counted the money $7,500. *Ch--ching!* "That was easier that I thought it would be," she whispered to herself.

Chapter Five

Weaving through traffic in her white Mercedes Benz SLK 320, a birthday gift from Tony two years ago, Naija approached North Dallas. She was hoping Jasmine was dressed and ready to go. She was already running behind schedule after having to take another bath and sucking up to Tony, making him think he was the best thing that ever happened in her life. Maybe his money but not him. Even Naija had to smile at the thought that Tony would fall for anything. If he only knew.

Turning off Northwest Hwy. onto Skillman Road, again she wondered what was so important Jasmine had to tell her. Driving into Jasmine's apartment complex, she called her mother's house. Instead of someone answering, the voice mail picked up. Naija left a message.

Naija parked next to Jasmine's Honda Accord. Before departing her car, she noticed two brothas standing by the stairwell leading up to Jasmine's apartment. When men entered her playing field, she wanted to look her best, not even a strand of hair out of place. She always anticipated the lengths men will go just to boost their egos.

She checked herself in the mirror, deciding to apply some lip gloss to her lips. Giving herself an approving look, she stepped out of the car and made her way to the stairwell leading to Jasmine's apartment.

The two brothas attentions were fixed on Naija's every step, undressing her with their eyes. Apparently, they weren't what she expected.

"Hey, lil' momma!" the dark skinned brotha said with a mouth full of gold.

Naija was offended by the way he addressed her. *Lil' momma! Nigga you must think I'm one of those hoochies you see in the club. Nigga you better check again,* she thought angrily to herself as she politely spoke and tried to step between the two men.

"Hold up baby! Let me holla at ya'," he said, slightly grabbing her elbow, stopping her.

Naija slightly jerked away, beginning to become angry by his hounding. Luckily, she was wearing her Chanel sunglasses so that he couldn't see her piercing eyes staring back at him. If not, he would have got the message a lot quicker that she wasn't interested.

"Baby, I'm married!" she said, trying to sound convincing.

"And I'm willing to share," he said, laughing at his own response along with his homeboy.

Having enough of his pestering, she shoved between them and hurried up the stairs.

"Bitch, you ain't all that!" the brotha with the gold teeth shouted.

Naija turned around with an urge to go back and check the nigga. *Fuck them broke ass niggaz,* she thought.

Making it to Jasmine's door, Naija knocked loudly.

"Come in!" Jasmine yelled.

Jasmine peeped out of the bathroom door to make sure it was Naija. After confirming Naija's presence, the stepped into the hallway with a towel wrapped around her.

"Bitch, you told me you was getting ready when I called you fifteen minutes ago!" Naija scolded Jasmine.

"I am getting ready. It ain't like you always on time. Don't front," Jasmine stated defensively.

Naija rolled her eyes while she sat her Louis Vuitton handbag down on the couch.

"You need to do something with yo' disrespectful cock hound ass neighbors."

"Who you talkin' about?" Jasmine asked, turning to walk to her bedroom.

"Some niggaz standing downstairs. One of them got a mouth full of gold."

"You must be talkin' about Quadry and Bilal."

"Whoever they is, they're not in my league."

Jasmine smirked, rolling her eyes. *Stuck up ass!* she mumbled to herself while getting dressed.

Naija sat on the floor in front of the stereo and rambled through Jasmine's CD collection until she found one she wanted to listen to. While listening to Mary J. Blige, she remembered Jasmine had something to tell her about who she saw last night in the club. Quickly, she got up off the floor and walked in Jasmine's bedroom.

"Bitch! What's so important that you have to tell me?" Naija asked, startling Jasmine.

Frowning a little, Jasmine soon remembered she wanted to tell Naija about Dontae.

"Guess who I seen in the club last night?" Jasmine asked while pulling up her jeans.

"Tramp! Just tell me. We already went through that bullshit earlier," Naija shouted, frustrated that Jasmine was prolonging the information.

"I seen Dontae last night," Jasmine said, examining the clueless look on Naija's face.

Naija recollected her thoughts. She wanted to make sure she was hearing Jasmine right.

"Who did you say?"

"Bitch, you heard me! I didn't stutter," Jasmine said with a sistah-girl attitude.

"Dontae Johnson?" Naija responded bewildered. "Girl, you lyin'."

"No I'm not. He fresh out of prison and girl he is fine! And he tryna hook up with you," Jasmine explained purposely to attract Naija's curiosity.

"What you tell'em?" Naija asked, shocked.

"C'mon home girl. You know I got your back. I didn't tell him nuttin' about you and Tony. I kept everything on the hush-hush."

"I hope you didn't give him my cell phone number," Naija said, trippin'.

"Naw, girl! You know me better than that," Jasmine proclaimed. "But he did give me his phone number to give to you. Look on top of my dresser."

Naija walked over to the dresser, picked up the napkin and looked at the phone number. Immediately, memories of Dontae resurfaced through her head. Had he served his time already? She calculated the time in her head and realized how much she had lost track of time. She wanted to call him, but what would she say? Possibly, she could call just to say hi, maybe take the initiative to apologize. She wondered what he wanted. *Probably some pussy,* she thought. *Would he cuss me out for turning my back on him?* She was in total suspense, wondering the inevitable. She placed the phone number in her pocket and decided to give the situation some more thought.

"Are you going to call him or what?" Jasmine asked, noticing the sad look on Naija's face.

"Maybe later on," Naija responded timidly.

"I'm telling you home girl, you better get you some of that fresh dick," Jasmine persuaded but at the same time feenin' for the dick herself.

"Damn, bitch! You act like you want to fuck him," Naija shouted with a sign of jealousy.

"Don't even go there with me," Jasmine said, putting her hand on her hip and rotating her neck in a circular motion.

Little did Naija know the thought did cross Jasmine's mind, based on the fact that Naija was with Tony now, and Dontae was completely out of the picture. That means Naija didn't have any room to get mad.

As good as Dontae looked last night, Jasmine was willing to keep her options open. However, she wasn't about to make her interests obvious to Naija. She knew deep down inside her heart Naija still had feelings for Dontae. Jasmine had no other choice but to respect her and Naija's friendship. In actuality, Jasmine knew the shit was about to hit the fan in a matter of time.

Jasmine took one last look in the mirror, admiring the way her apply bottom jeans fit her butt. Satisfied, she grabbed her purse.

"I'm ready," Jasmine said, heading to the door, making sure she cut off all the lights.

"It's about time," Naija said as she turned off the stereo and grabbed her purse. "I hope Heckyl and Jeckyl ain't still out there."

After spending long hours of shopping, getting manicures and pedicures and flirting with ballers, Naija and Jasmine came out the mall loaded down with shopping bags, mostly belonging to Naija. They carried everything from shoes, lingerie, clothes, perfumes, and even toys for Jasmine's three year old son.

Once they loaded everything into the car, there was barely enough room to sit down themselves. Spending a few minutes rearranging, finally they were able to squeeze into the car comfortably.

Due to hours of walking through the mall, stopping in different stores, and trying on various clothes and shoes, Naija and Jasmine had worked up quite an appetite. Unanimously, they decided on Bennigans.

At the restaurant, the maitr'd seated them at a table and handed them both menus.

"I'm starving!" Jasmine admitted.

"You're always starving, especially when someone else is paying the bill," Naija said sarcastically.

"Bitch!" Jasmine responded back with an attitude, causing a few people at the surrounding tables to turn around and look in Jasmine and Naija's direction. Jasmine paid them no mind and continued on. "Don't get brand new on me. If it's a big deal, I'll pay for my own shit."

Naija realized she unintentionally upset her friend.

"Damn Jasmine! I was just playin'. It ain't even like that with us," Naija expressed sympathetically. "You know I got your back in any circumstance."

"Yeah, right! Whatever!" Jasmine replied, still highly upset.

Naija still sensed the tension in Jasmine's voice and decided to diffuse the situation by changing the subject.

"I'm not gon' be able to go out with you tonight," Naija said.
"Why not?" Jasmine asked.

"Tony wanna take me to the casino tonight in Louisiana."

Naija and Jasmine continued their conversations while skimming through the menus until a waiter came and interrupted.

"Hello, ladies. Are you ready to order?" the waiter asked.

"Yes. Give me the chicken parmesan, baked potato with broccoli and red peppers," Naija ordered.

The waiter turned to Jasmine.

"And I will have the seafood platter with extra shrimp," Jasmine told him.

"Will that be all?" the waiter asked.

"Yeah, that's it," Naija said after looking over at Jasmine to make sure she didn't want to change her mind.

"What would you care to drink? The waiter asked as he collected the menus from the table.

"Bring us two strawberry daiquiris," Naija said.

As they waited on their food, Jasmine went to the bathroom, while Naija sat at the table thinking about Dontae again. She just couldn't stop thinking about what he wanted. *Do he want to get back together?* she thought. Right now was not possible because that meant giving up Tony and all the benefits she accomplished over the past few years. And with Dontae just getting out of prison, he didn't have anything to fill the void. But Dontae did take care of business in the sex department, remained in the back of Naija's head. However, he still wasn't equipped to meet her requirements outside the bedroom.

Naija was broken out of her trance when the waiter arrived with their drinks, followed behind Jasmine coming back from the bathroom with a smile in her face from ear to ear.

"Why you smilin' so much?" Naija asked, curious.

"See them two niggaz over there in the corner?" Jasmine pointed. Naija turned around in the direction Jasmine was pointing, locating the two dudes she was speaking of.

"Okay I see'em. What about 'em?" Naija asked, not really interested.

"They stopped me on my way to the bathroom and asked if we didn't mind us all hookin' up later. I told them I didn't mind but I had to come holla at you first to see if you was wit' it," Jasmine said, hoping Naija agreed. "Girl, they look like they gettin' money," she added, baiting Naija in.

Naija smirked. "I'm gon' pass on that one. But don't let me hold you down. Girl do yo' thang!" she encouraged.

Jasmine got up from the table again and went to talk to the two dudes.

Naija just wasn't feeling the vibe. She already had enough problems going on that she couldn't seem to solve. And she definitely didn't have the room for anymore drama.

After eating, Naija drove Jasmine back to her apartment. She helped Jasmine unload her bags along with the things for lil' J.J. and help carry the things upstairs to the apartment and sat them down on the couch.

Naija checked her gold, diamond face Bulgari wristwatch. It was 9:56 p.m. She phoned Tony's cell phone. There was no answer, only a voice mail. "I don't know why this nigga ain't got his phone on. What's the reason of having one if it's not on," Naija said, talking to Jasmine. She paged his two-way and left a message.

Naija sat around talking to Jasmine while waiting on Tony to return her message. After thirty minutes had expired, she decided to go home. On her drive back home to Los Colinas, she figured in due time, she was going to come face to face with Dontae, but right now wasn't the time.

● ● ● ● ● ●

Sunday morning the constant vibration of Tony's pager sitting on the nightstand awoke him. He squinted his eyes, blinded by the direct sunlight shining through the slightly open curtain at the Motel 6. Now fully awoke, he realized it was morning. "Damn!" He whispered under his breath while wiping the sleep from his eyes.

Grabbing his pager, he hit the display screen "Fuck!" he said angrily. Obviously, he had let a night of chasing pussy keep him from going home. On top of that, he hadn't returned any of Naija's messages. Naija had been paging him all night up until the next morning.

Tony picked up his Rolex off the nightstand and checked the time. It was 9:06 a.m. *Damn! I done fucked up,* he thought to himself.

He looked over at Trina lying beside him, still covered up. He noticed her clothes still strewn across the floor and remembered the wild time they had last night, sucking and fucking. His intentions weren't to spend the night with her. Just hit and quit it. But the freak in her took control of his thinking. After their sex marathon, sleep overtook the both of them. Now he has some major explaining to do. What was he going to tell Naija?

Tony sat on the side of the bed, thinking up a good lie to tell. Could he say he was with J-Rock? Or had she already called him? Had she been out looking for him and seen his car parked outside in the parking lot? Impossible! That's the whole reason he got a room on the other side of town so Naija wouldn't be able to find him.

Quickly, he picked up his cell phone and called J-Rock. After a few rings, a groggy voice answered.

"Hello!"

"J-Rock."

"Yeah!"

"Have Naija called you?"

"Naw man! Why in the fuck is you calling me this early in the goddamn morning?" J-Rock yelled after realizing what time it was.

"Never mind all that. Just don't answer the phone until I get there," Tony said with a bit of relief.

After hanging up with J-Rock, he challenged his brain to come up with a convincing story to tell Naija. He knew she was probably pissed, especially after promising to take her to the casino last night. *Where was my mind at? Now I done got myself caught up with this worthless bitch, Trina,* he thought, realizing he let himself get caught slippin'. *I know what I can tell her. I'll say me and J-Rock had to take care of some important business out of town. Hopefully, she will believe me without asking a whole lot of questions.* Satisfied with the story, he had to laugh.

Afterwards, he slung the covers off Trina, exposing her naked body. She mumbled sounds of discomfort, balling herself up in a knot to warm herself from the sudden rush of cool air in the motel room.

Seeing her nakedness, lust filled Tony's eyes. He decided to himself he might as well get one last nut for the road.

Naija paced around the house, waiting on Tony to call back. It had been over two hours since she last paged him. She assumed he was laying up with one of his hoes. "He must think I'm a damn fool to think he ain't out fuckin' some other bitch!" she said angrily. The thought of packing her shit and leaving crossed her mind. Many times in the past, she had let Tony get away with the same ol' shit. Always a different story but always a lie! "fuck him if he do got money! He just ain't gon' keep disrespecting me. I'm tired of this bullshit."

Then she thought, *Where would I go if I did move out?* She knew Jasmine didn't have any room and she definitely wasn't going home to her mother's. That was the last place she wanted to go. She knew her mother would continue to remind her about ever getting involved with Tony like so many time before. She wondered if she did leave, would he take back all the stuff he bought her? She definitely didn't want him to do that. *I wonder what kind of lie he got to tell this time.*

Naija contemplated on him coming home wanting some pussy to try and assure her that he wasn't out with another woman. She was already hipped to that tactic. That was the oldest trick in the books.

As she continued to pace the room, she wanted to call J-Rock but she knew he would cover for Tony like always. She decided it wasn't worth the time, figuring it was a lost cause. She knew by them being homeboys, they had each other's back in the time of need, especially now. It was the same thing with her and Jasmine. Many times before, Jasmine had covered for her during Naija's creeping sessions.

During the course of her she heard a door slam downstairs. She knew it was Tony. She stormed out the bedroom, raging, meeting him coming halfway up the stairs. Tony's eyes look like they were going to pop out of their sockets when he saw Naija. Right then, he noticed the anger written all over her face.

"Where the fuck you been all mothafuckin' night?" she yelled, getting straight to the point without any hesitation as she folded her arms across her breasts.

Tony was already prepared for the drama. Actually, he couldn't much blame her. He was definitely in the wrong. He knew he had some serious making up to do, if he talked his way out of this jam. Totally confident, he was fully prepared to give her the best lie he could tell, knowing for certain J-Rock had his back if she wanted to call him to verify everything.

"Me and J-Rock went out of town to handle some business. It was a deal I couldn't refuse," Tony told her with a straight face, hoping she believe him.

"Quit Lyin'! Naija shouted, then gathered her composure. "If that's the case, then why in the fuck you didn't call me back?"

Tony couldn't find the words to answer.

Noticing the stupid expression on his face, she punched him in the shoulder. Tony flinched to take the blow.

"You know damn well you been out fuckin' some bitch. And you expect me to fall for the okey-doke. Nigga I ain't no damn fool! Fuck around ya' dick gon' fall off while you runnin' 'round here thinkin' you being slick messing with all them nasty ass hoes. I'll be damn if I let you give me a disease. I'll leave yo' ass before I let that happen," Naija said, bluffing on the last part.

Naija knew it was no truth in what he was telling her. The same with her. She knew she wasn't going anywhere. She figured, she would accomplish more by staying than leaving.

Having taken enough of his lies, she brushed by him and hurried down the stairs. Actually, she was mad as hell. Hopefully, if she played her cards right, Tony's guilty conscience would bother him for the rest of the day and he would do his best to make it up to her by pampering her with quality time, gifts and money. She knew him far too well. Gracefully, she kicked back on the sofa, flicked on the plasma flat screen TV and waited patiently to reap the resulting benefits from the whole ordeal.

Chapter Six

Tuesday morning, Dontae slept in late. Since his release from prison five days ago, his movements have been non-stop, constantly enjoying life as a free man, partying at the club, hanging out, or riding around anywhere that was happening. In between ripping and running, he still managed to spend adequate time with Keena, mainly to have sex. Really, that's all their relationship was worth. They didn't have anything else in common, only attraction. Like a good girl, she didn't pressure him or complain about the time spent. But Dontae felt he owed her a certain amount of attention, considering she did stay down with him while doing his bid in prison. Honestly, he enjoyed her company, more so because she took his mind off Naija. Technically speaking, Keena was just a temporary replacement. Although, he told himself time and time again, she was a good girl in her own way with a big heart. Definitely an eye-catcher. Unfortunately, in his book, she didn't fit the wifey criteria to meet his standards. Besides, she was a part-time stripper, which was a definite no-no against all areas of commitments.

Finally waking up, Dontae lay comfortably for a few minutes, thinking. The past few days home had completely drained him, though time was fun. Now play time was over. He wanted to use the next couple of weeks, laying down the ground work to investigate the drug scene. He knew he couldn't rely solely on what Man-Man was telling him. A dope fiend's words have no meaning. They were the biggest con artists in the game. Dontae's knowledge of who to trust would have to rest faithfully on his own intuition. The fact of the matter is times, places and the rules of the game have changed. The first phase of his homework would be finding out who's doing what, and who to trust in moving some major dope, without the hassles of collecting his money on time.

Hopefully, he didn't have to step on any toes in the process. Then again, this is a dog-eat-dog world we live in. In order to get to the top you have to step over somebody along the way.

Seeing that it was past 11:00 a.m., he rolled out of bed, stretched and walked to the bathroom. While taking a piss, a sharp sting like needles sticking in him was felt in his dick "Ahh!" he said, wincing at the pain. After straining to finish urinating, he looked at the head of his dick and squeezed. Slowly, light yellow pus oozed out. "What the fuck is that?" he shouted, terrified at the sight of the substance. Quickly, he checked the insides of his boxer shorts, clearly seeing the dried up yellow spots that stained the fabric. Right then, he knew he was burning. But who done it? Immediately, his mind went into overdrive. "Now the only two hoes I've been with since I been home is Keena and Lisa. Every time I had sex with Keena she made me use a rubber." The process of elimination identified the guilty culprit. "It got to be that nasty ass bitch, Lisa. I knew I shouldn't fucked her without a rubber!" he said upset for not taking precautions. *Dirty bitch! Wait till I see that ho. I hope the bitch don't have AIDS,* he thought nervously.

Leaving the bathroom, he heard loud repetitious knocking at the front door. "Who the fuck is that...the police?" he said, answering his own question. The question pondered in his mind, knowing that he wasn't expecting any company.

Approaching the door, the knocking repeated again. This time harder. "Hold yo' horses, goddamnit! I'm comin'!" Dontae yelled to whoever was knocking. Checking the peephole, he saw Man-Man on the other side.

Dontae opened the door wide.

"Damn nigga! Why is you beatin' on the door like you the fuckin' police or somethin'?," Dontae scolded.

Without saying a word, Man-Man quickly darted past Dontae, persuading Dontae to shut the door.

Slowly closing the door, Dontae notice Man-Man's strange behavior. The glossy haze in his eyes told the story.

"Nigga, you on that shit, ain't ya?"

"Naw. Why you think that?" Man-Man said, turning away from Dontae.

"I can tell by yo' eyes. It don't take no rocket scientist to see you high as a mothafucka."

Man-Man didn't bother to further respond back to Dontae's accusations. He went and took a seat on the couch. True enough, Man-man was coming down off one of his three day crack binge. No sleep, no food and no shower. Despite his flaws, Man-Man still possessed a slight savvy about himself. The gift of gab still came natural, whenever drugs didn't play a vital role. During his three-day smoking spree, he was on the block helping out a youngster name Jaleel sell some rocks. Money was rolling by the minute. Jaleel decided he stacked a nice grip for the few hours he hustled. Instead of waiting to sell out, Jaleel wanted to hang out with his boys. But Man-Man's slick talking persuaded Jaleel to trust him with the remainder of the rocks, promising he will have all Jaleel's money right.

"Yeah youngsta, just leave that shit with me. Ain't no use in letting all this paper get away when I can stay out here and work the block. I guarantee you I'll have yo' paper. Just check back every so often," Man-Man said, conniving the youngsta.

The opportunity presented itself, for Man-Man a free high, and for Jaleel some extra money. So he thought! Without thinking clearly, Jaleel handed Man-Man the bag of rocks.

"You better have my money right or I'ma bust you in yo' ass!" Jaleel said, mean-mugging Man-Man while raising his shirt, showing him his .45 tucked in his waistband.

Receiving the dope from Jaleel, Man-Man took care of business like promised until things got slow. Gradually the monkey started riding his back. Every minute, the desire to take a hit was calling his name. Without a second thought, he left the block, stopping at the nearest bootlegger and bought two bottles of Thunderbird. Next, he roamed the streets, managing to find a crackhead whore. They both checked in at the Mi'Amor Motel on Scyene Ave. The rest was history, all documented in a cloud of smoke.

While Dontae and Man-Man continued to talk, a stale odor lingered in the room. Dontae turned his nose up, trying to distinguish the smell. Sniffing, he walked over to Man-Man and was stopped dead in his tracks.

"Ooowee! Goddam! You funky as a mothafucka!" Dontae said, covering his nose. "What you been doing, laying in shit?"

Man-Man raised his arm and smelled his underarms. He, himself turned up his own nose after realizing he was stinking bad. In the process of getting high, taking a bath never came to mind or anything else that was required daily.

"Say, Unc! You out there bad," Dontae told him, now feeling remorseful.

It was a hard pill to swallow, seeing his uncle strung out on drugs.

"You need to get in the tub right now," Dontae added.

●●●●●●

By today being Q'Tee's off day, she decided to spend the day looking for a job. Checking the employment office, she was lucky enough to get some referrals to possible job openings. The job market was plentiful in her associated field. She submitted applications at the different locations. Determined to take advantage of the available jobs, she also checked on other listings that she came across in the classified ads. Pleased with her potential offers, she figured she had enough searching for one day.

The temperature had shifted to the 90's. Q'Tee checked her watch. It was 1:25 p.m. Before going home, she decided to do her mother a favor and have her car washed. She knew just the spot, Sparkles' Wash and Wax Detail Shop. This was the local hangout for all the ballers in the hood of Oakcliff. The shop was owned by Jaleel's cousin, Dre'.

Pulling into Sparkles, Q'Tee's intentions of surprising her mother were soon changed the minute she saw Jaleel hanging out with his cousin and homeboys.

Recognizing Q'Tee's mother's car, Jaleel waved his hand, motioning her to stop. When she stopped, he hopped in on the passenger side. *What do this nigga want,* she thought. Jaleel opened his arms wide, expecting a hug. She leaned away, folding her arms across her breasts while giving him a look of dismay.

"Oh! A nigga can't get a hug?" Jaleel said with his arms still held wide.

Q'Tee rolled her eyes, eventually giving in to the feelings she still had for him and gave him a hug. Jaleel embraced her tightly.

"Dang boy! You gon' squeeze the air out of me," she squealed while struggling to free herself from his strong embrace.

"I'm just glad to see you, baby," he proclaimed, smiling. "I'm hoping the reason you came up here is to find me so we can hook up."

"Boy, please!" she said dryly while smirking. "I came to get my momma car washed."

Jaleel gave her a look as if saying, "Yeah right!" He scanned her body with his eyes, admiring the fact she still had a way of arousing his desires to have sex with her.

Q'Tee read his eyes and knew exactly where his intentions were heading. *Be strong! I can't give in to him,* she thought, controlling her emotions as she stared into his roaming eyes, faking a frown.

"Damn! You look good enough to eat," he expressed as he slightly licked his lips.

She inhaled softly, eyes locked in on his LL Cool J lips. Thoughts of getting her poonanny licked on crossed her mind. Immediately, she altered her thinking. This is the route she didn't want take with Jaleel, even though she was tempted.

"Don't get yourself in no trouble by your girlfriend," she said, watching the expression that came across his face.

"What girlfriend?" he lied. "Don't even trip!"

"Whatever!"

Jaleel reached over, trying to kiss her. Again, she backed away from him.

'Boy, stop!" A part of her wanted to kiss him but she took control of her hormones.

"What's up?" he asked.

"What you mean, what's up?" she responded defensively.

Brushing off the question she asked, he countered back with a look of desire in his eyes.

"Can we hook up later?"

"You have a girlfriend now."

"You know you still my girl."

Jaleel noticed the short skirt she was wearing and tried to slide his hand underneath it. She pushed his hand away. Trying once more, she stopped him again.

"Jaleel! Will you stop!" she pleaded.

He got upset and got out the car, slamming the door. She stared at him, alarmed.

"Don't be slamming my goddamn door like you done lost yo' mind!" she yelled.

"Fuck you, bitch, and move around!" he told her angrily.

"Fuck you!" she hollered back, then drove off rapidly.

"Yo' pussy ain't all that no way!" he screamed from a distant as she waited to pull into traffic.

Q'Tee was barely able to hear what he said. As she drove away from Sparkles, she glanced back in her rearview mirror, shocked at how Jaleel disrespected her. She saw him pointing his middle finger at her. She was hurt which pretty much drew the conclusion of any possibilities of them ever getting back together.

On the way home, she knew she would be giving Dontae a call now. Turning onto her street, she saw a unfamiliar new model BMW parked in the driveway. She figured her mother had company. *Probably a co-worker. Maybe momma got a man,* she thought, laughing to herself. Q'Tee pulled behind the car in her mother's Cadillac STS. She admired the new BMW M3 as she passed it walking toward the house. Again she speculated. *Probably a bill collector.*

Walking inside the house, she didn't see her mother or anybody sitting in the living room or family room. The thought of her momma getting her freak on came to her mind again and she smiled. She didn't want to be disrespectful by interrupting. Reluctantly, that wouldn't be the case after she seen her mother walking down the hallway, fully dressed and alone.

"Momma, you got company?" Q'Tee asked curiously.

"No! Why you ask that?" Gloria replied innocently.

"Then who car is that parked in the driveway?"

Gloria paused before answering the question.

"That's your car. Your brother bought it for you today," Gloria informed Q'Tee with a smile.

Q'Tee screamed at the top of her lungs as she ran out of the front door to the BMW. Opening the door to the driver's side, she sat down in the seat. Quickly, she flinched from the sun-scorched leather seats that burned her thighs. "Damn! That's hot!" she squealed, adjusting herself in the seat. She carefully analyzed every gadget, instruments and detail of her new car.

Her mother stood beside the car, admiring her daughter's joy while dangling the keys in her hand.

"Do you like it?" Gloria asked handing Q'Tee the keys.

"Like it! I love it!" Q'Tee answered starting up the car.

Scanning the stations, she programmed the radio station FM 97.9 'The beat'. 'Nelly's, Tip Drill' blasted through the speakers. Q'Tee sang along. "It must be yo' money 'cause it ain't yo' face. I need a tip drill. A tip drill…"

"Girl, if you don't turn that loud music down. I'm not gon' go through the same shit with you that I do with yo' brother about that loud ass music," Gloria preached.

Q'Tee turned the car off and grabbed the keys out of the ignition. Stepping out of the car, she walked around it, observing the outer appearance. She pictured herself rolling on 'dubs'.

Totally ecstatic about her new car, it dawned on her to call her brother after hearing her mother mention his name. She ran in the house and called him on his cell phone.

"What it do!" Tony answered after the second ring.

"Thank you, thank you, thank you!" Q'Tee shouted with joy.

"Why is you doin' all that screamin'?" Tony said, playfully.

"Boy, don't play. I'm on my way over there to take you riding."

"I guess that means you like the car."

"What kind of question is that to ask? I love it! And I love you too," she said sincerely.

"I love you too," Tony said shyly.

Tony felt touched after hanging up with his sister. They rarely expressed their love for each other even though it definitely existed between the two. To him it felt kinda good to finally say 'I love you' to her for a change.

● ● ● ● ● ●

After a long hot bath, Man-Man felt clean and refreshed. Putting on some clean clothes Dontae gave him, he looked in the mirror at himself. The person he saw staring back at him was now a stranger. The sunken face, bloodshot eyes and the bags under his eyes—he couldn't believe how he had let himself get that bad. He was once labeled a 'fresh' nigga back in the days, and now the label of dope fiend. Taking one last look at himself, he walked in the living where Dontae was.

"What you do with those funky ass clothes?" Dontae said, looking away from the TV.

"I threw them in the dirty clothes basket," Man-Man said, thinking he did the right thing.

"Ahh, hell naw! Take that funky shit and put them in a trash bag and throw them outside in the trashcan" Dontae demanded. "It's probably crabs and everything in them clothes.

"Young ass nigga, quit bitchin' all the fuckin' time like a lil' ol' ho!" Man-Man said beginning to get highly upset with Dontae's whining.

Dontae looked at Man-Man surprised at his change of voice.

"I know you ain't studding up," Dontae said, standing up to see if Man-Man's bark was as big as his bite.

Man-Man knew he had no win trying to fight with his nephew. Maybe a few years ago the shoe would have been on the other foot. He definitely would have got dead on Dontae's young ass. Now that crack redefined him, he had no strength to over-power anyone but a crack pipe. Gingerly, he went to do what Dontae had asked him to do just to clear the tension. He knew his nephew only meant well.

Man-Man disposed of his stinky clothes. Later, he and Dontae sat and rapped some more about the dope game. They covered all the in's and out's about prices, location, and major players handling weight, Finishing up their discussion, Dontae remembered he needed to go and get some penicillin.

"Say Man-Man, Doc still sell those penicillin pills at the bootlegger off Oakland?" Dontae asked.

"Yeah. Yeah. But he moved over on Metropolitan Street" Man-Man answered curiously.Thinking for a second, he added. "What's wrong with you? You burnin'?"

"Somethin like that. This ol' dirty bitch set me on fire," Dontae said, becoming angry again at Lisa.

"Boy, you gotta wrap that thang up. Everything that look good ain't always good for you," Man-Man said, knowing he was in no position to give advice. Since being strung out on drugs all his encounters with women, mainly crackhead whores, have been without a condom. Just the past three nights was the same ol' story. It's a wonder he wasn't a walking dead man.

Dontae figured as soon as his mother came home from work, he would use her car to jet over to the southside and pick up some pills.

●●●●●●

Late that evening around 4:00 p.m., Dontae and Man-Man rode to South Dallas. After heading to Doc's to purchase a bottle of Penicillin pills for $20, they rode down Dixon Street, better know as "Dixie Circle", a community within itself. Everybody between the six block radius considered themselves family, not by kin but by bond. The scene on the street was the same everyday; Oldheads hanging out under a tree, drinking, smoking weed, chasing young pussy and playing dominoes. The whole street was drug infested with Niggaz on the block or posted in the projects making that 'scilla'. The projects raised some of the rawest breeds from pimps, hustlers, killers, hoes, ride-or-die chicks, jackers, gangster, drug dealers or anything labeled criminal. Even the young thugs, a.k.a. 357 Posse, who were as young as twelve had a menacing look about themselves. They were bred to survive by any means necessary. Their signature trademarks were saggy jeans, braids, cornrows, perms with ponytails or finger waves. For the girls, everything was strictly ghetto; weaved hairstyles to hoochified outfits to a 'fly' mouth, inflamed with every curse word in the book.

Dontae creeped down the street in his mother's Honda Civic. Different stares were locked in on his unfamiliar face and the car he drove. For some strange reason, Man-Man scooted down in his seat as if he was trying not to be seen. They rode by a group of young thugs engaged in flirty conversations with a group of girls that appeared to be no more than sixteen or seventeen. Young, dumb and full of 'cum' was usually the norm growing up in the projects because of being exposed to sex, drugs, and violence at such a early age.

As Dontae passed them by, one particular thug with braids focused his attention on the car, instinctively catching eyesight with Man-Man. A light came on in his head. Suddenly, he said a few words to his homeboys, causing them to look.

Dontae made it to the end of the street, barely catching the traffic light before it turned red. Taking a left on Scyene, he decided to pull in Church's fried chicken for something to eat.

"You hungry?" Dontae asked Man-Man.

Without a moments delay, Man-Man answered. "Hell yeah!"

Man-Man was literally starving. For the past three days, his appetite for food was replaced with drugs. Now coming down off Cloud 9, his stomach was singing a song from all it's growling.

When Dontae got out of the car, he didn't notice the gray hooptie bust a U-turn in the middle of the street, then speed up into the parking lot. It's when the three young thugs jumped out the hooptie, all pointing guns at Man-Man and Dontae, that got his attention.

The tallest of the three, the one with the braids, named Jaleel, appeared to be the enforcer of the trio, slapped Man-Man upside the head with the butt of his pistol. A knot arose instantly.

Instead of bewilderment, now rage entered Dontae's sense of thinking as he stepped forward with the intention to defend his uncle.

"Don't be no hero, homie!" the medium size thug, named Tre', said raising his .380 a little bit higher, level with Dontae's head.

Dontae stopped, staring at Tre', realizing the youngster was dead serious. He looked around the area, hoping a police car cruised by or a good Samaritan dialed 911. *Where's the police when you need one? Any other time, them hoes will be everywhere!* he thought as his heart began to skip a beat. To his disadvantage, he parked in a blindspot of the building shielding himself from anyone inside that could be of some help.

"Man-Man! Where my mothafuckin' money? bitch, ass nigga! I told yo' dope fiend ass I was gon' bust a cap in yo' ass if you fucked off my shit," Jaleel said, pointing the gun directly in Man-Man's face.

Man-Man was speechless, on the brink of shedding tears. His mouth moved but the words wouldn't come out.

Dontae thought long and hard, trying to think of some way to control the situation. *I wonder what Man-Man owe this young ass nigga. It can't be much. Any nigga would be a damn fool to trust Man-man. I got about $1400 in my pocket. Maybe I can pay* *off his bill. Damn! I hate to let go of my bread like this, but fuck it! He is my uncle. No money is worth my kinfolk life,* he thought, finally coming up with an idea. It was just a matter of three thugs agreeing to the terms.

"Hey, hey homeboy! Chill for a minute. Be cool. Just put the heat up before the po-po's be all up in this bitch and then its gon' really be some drama," Dontae said, making a valid point.

The three youngsters looked at each other, checking to see if everything was cool among them. In their minds, they definitely didn't need the police riding down on them. Gradually coming to his senses, Jaleel nodded, signifying for his homies to put away their guns.

Dontae let out a long sigh of relief when they concealed their 'straps' back in their waistebands, covering them with their shirts. Now having the thugs' undivided attention, Dontae talked quick, presenting a propostion.

"What do Man-Man owe you?"

"$500!" Jaleel said, proudly.

Dontae smirked. *What! This young stupid ass nigga was ready to kill somebody over $500. Chump change! Then again, I remember back in the days $500 seem like a whole lot of money,* Dontae thought.

"Check this out. I'm 'bout to be on probably next week. What I will do is put you and your boys down with some proper work if y'all be straight up with the paper." Dontae hesitated, reading Jaleel's facial expression, making sure everything was kosher. "I'ma give you $250 on Man-Man's bill, if you squash the rest when I give y'all the packages."

Jaleel thought for a few minutes, finally agreeing to the terms with his homeboys and Dontae.

After paying the $250, Dontae talked to Jaleel, Tre' and Kwame about how much dope they were moving in the streets and the prices they were paying. Dontae wrote down their pager numbers and told them he would holla back at them in a week or so.

Everyone came out of the situation with something to gain. For Man-Man-his life; and Dontae, a possible start to getting some real paper, if he didn't get fucked in the process. The fact of the matter was Jaleel, Tre and Kwame were complete strangers. Unfortunately, Dontae had to start somewhere in order to jumpstart the paper chasin'. Hopefully, he could control the hot-headed gangsters.

During Dontae's and Man-Man's ride back home after feeding their hungry stomachs, Dontae gave Man-Man a full chastisement, explaining to him how he was throwing his life away smoking crack and living without a purpose. The shit was going in one ear and out the other. Man-Man heard the same story a million times from his sisters. Sometimes, he would take their advice and clean up his act. That only lasted a short period of time. Just as soon as he got his hands on some extra money, back to the nearest drug dealer he went.

Hopefully, Dontae could be the one to turn Man-Man's life around and bring him back to the person he use to be. It was a long road ahead of them, but Dontae was determined to beat the odds.

"Say nephew I appreciate what you done back there. That was good lookin' out," Man-Man said, rubbing the knot on his head.

"Already! You need to get yo' shit together like I told you. Who knows, the next young niggaz may not be that easy to persuade," Dontae said, looking over at Man-Man to see if the words fell on listening ears. "How's your head feelin'?" Dontae continued, noticing Man-Man massaging the knot on his head.

"It's cool. Put some ice on it and I'll be back to new again in a couple of days," Man-Man said, feeling a migraine beginning to come.

Pulling into Dontae's mother's driveway, Man-Man got out of the car to go and get some ice and take some aspirin.

Dontae sat for a few minutes, replaying everything back in his head about his talks with Sergio. He knew he needed money to get to the point in life where he wanted to be. Right now, he was at a stand still with no money, no clientele and living under the same roof with his mother. *Fuck it! I'm ready,* he thought as he rushed into the house and located his address book. He found the number to Hector, Sergio's son, in Phoenix, Arizona.

Dialing the number, Dontae's hand was shaking uncontrollably. No more than two rings, a Hispanic woman answered.

"Hola!"

"I need to speak with Hector."

"Me, no English," the woman said.

"Hector! I need to speak to Hector," Dontae spoke slowly, hoping she understood him this time.

"Si, Hector!"

A brief pause silenced the phone. Shortly after, a man's voice spoke into the receiver.

"Hola!" the man said.

"Hector? This is Dontae. What's up?"

"Poppa told me you were out. So how have you been?"

"Good. Just taking one day at a time."

"That sounds like a good thing to do. So what brings about this call? Does this mean good news?"

"That's right, there is good news. I'm ready! Just tell me what I need to do," Dontae asked nervously.

Hector let the words linger for a few seconds. "Okay then, take this number down and contact me in two weeks."

"Hold up, let me get a pen."

Dontae wrote the number down. Afterwards, he and Hector talked about other things. Hector was a discreet person. He didn't like talking about drugs over the phone.

"Tell Sergio I send my love," Dontae said.

"I will. Take care. And be sure to contact me in two weeks. No sooner or no later."

Dontae's conversation went well with Hector. Now that all the pieces were connected on the other side, he had to connect all the pieces on his side so that things will run smoothly without any screw-ups. If not, a prison cell would be waiting on him with his name and number still on it.

He needed clientele. He was skeptical about Jaleel, Tre' and Kwame, knowing they were only block hustlers. Soon he remembered Isaac and Reg. How much dope was they moving? What were they paying for kilos? Right now, they were the only ones he knew who had the clientele to move quantities of weight. The only problem is that they had their own connections.

The more Dontae thought, the more the questions popped up in his head. Where would he stash the dope? He couldn't stay at home anymore. He would never hear the end of it if his mother knew he was storing dope in her house. How could he be discreet enough to keep his mother from finding out? So many questions, but not enough answers. He figured first things first. He needed to talk to Reg and Isaac.

The next day, he went to Cellular One Mobile and purchased a two way pager and cell phone. Luckily, Keena worked there and was able to hook him up on the activation costs and a reasonable plan. Although the money Reg and Isaac gave him was slowly fading away, this was a much needed investment.

Chapter Seven

"I'm back!" Tiffany hollered on the other end of the phone. It was 1:00 p.m., a Sunday afternoon. Tiffany had just come back from being in Houston all week with Derrick. "Girl the concert was off the chain. You should've seen Usher with his fine ass. I swear all I need is ten minutes alone with him and he gonna really have something to confess about."

Q'Tee laughed at her friend, knowing if given the opportunity, Tiffany would do exactly what she said. That's just how she got down. Sex was always on her mind.

"T, you crazy," Q'Tee said, still laughing.

"You know me. Bar none...fade all!" Tiffany boasted.

"Believe me, I know!" Q'Tee said justifiably.

"We still on for the park today? Since you been back home from college we ain't been able to kick it."

"Fo' sho'! Q'Tee answered." It ain't my fault you been in Houston all week.

"Well I'm back now. Come by the house so I can give you all the juicy details about me and Derrick."

"As soon as I get dressed I'm on my way, plus I got something to show you."

Q'Tee and Tiffany cut their conversation short and hung up. They both were eager to hang out together.

Q'Tee was anxious to show off her new car to Tiffany. She knew Tiffany was going to freak out, especially since she was a stone cold car freak. Q'Tee's BMW was the icing on the cake. Q'Tee couldn't wait for them to roll up in Glendale Park this evening. Bitches were definitely gonna be hatin'.

Q'Tee had been low key about riding around or going out to the club. She mainly went to work and back home, or ran needed errands. She wanted to wait until Tiffany came back home from Houston so they could floss together. Now that her girl was back, it was on. Time to ride and be seen. And being seen was something Tiffany took pride in doing.

Friends since middle school, they became inseparable. With different personalities, they were alike in many other ways. Both were cute and fine as can get. A nigga couldn't go wrong picking either one. But for a quick fuck without any hassles, Tiffany was the chosen one. As for Q'Tee, a nigga had to be on top of his game. She wasn't coming off the pussy at all.

An hour later, Q'Tee drove up in front of Tiffany's house. Her brother, Rakim, was hanging outside with his homeboy, Rodney. Q'Tee knew Rakim always had a crush on her and she got a big kick out of teasing him.

Getting out the car, she made sure to put an extra twist in her walk. Just like she figured, Rakim's mouth dropped, eyes locked in on her every step.

"Hey, Rakim," she said in a sexy voice.

"What's up Q? You sho' lookin' good!" he said, trying to push up on her "Can a nigga get a hug?'

Q'Tee hugged him, feeling his hardness. She stepped back, smiling.

Rakim started to blush, unable to make eye contact with Q'Tee anymore.

"Where T at?" Q'Tee asked.

"She in the crib. Go on in, the door is open," Rakim told her.

Q'Tee walked through the door. As soon as she shut the door, she fell out laughing.

"Girl, what you laughing at?" Tiffany asked walking into the living room.

"Yo' brother is a trip! I gave him a hug and felt his dick get on hard," Q'Tee said in between laughs.

Suddenly, she covered her mouth with her hand, realizing she said the word 'dick' so loudly.

"Where yo' momma at?" she whispered, looking around the room, expecting Tiffany's mother to appear, fussing.

"She ain't here." Tiffany relieved Q'Tee stress. "And you gon' quit teasing my brother before he give you just what you lookin for," she added, teasing.

"Girl, please! I'm just havin' fun like I always do with yo' brother," Q'Tee replied, defensively.

"I'm just sayin' my brother old enough to fuck now. And pussy is definitely on his mind," Tiffany announced. "You know yo' shit way overdue for some dick. My brother just might be the one to take care of that need. Satisfying needs definitely runs in the family," she added, emphasizing her kinkyness.

"Tsk! Yo' brother wouldn't know what to do with this," Q'Tee said, twisting her hips around and slapping herself on the butt. "And bitch, don't be worrying about my stuff. I'm pretty sure you getting' enough dick for the both of us."

"Damn skippy! Ain't no shame in my game," Tiffany bragged.

Q'Tee shook her head, smiling. "Girl, you somethin' else. But you my nigga if you don't get no bigger!

"Already!" Tiffany confirmed. "Now let me tell you about my time in Houston."

"Hold on before you get started. I want you to come checkout my new car my brother bought me," Q'Tee said.

"What?" Tiffany screamed, running out the door. Tiffany totally geeked when she saw the new BMW M3.

"Bitch, no you didn't get no Beamer! Its about to be on now," Tiffany shouted while getting in on the driver's side. Tiffany was acting like she was the one with a new car. Q'Tee knew Tiffany was going to go wild.

"You know we gotta go riding," Tiffany said excited.

"Let's roll," Q'Tee said.

"Ah, hell naw! Look what I got on. Ain't no way in hell I'm fix'tna be caught rollin' up in a BMW looking like this. I got to get fly, cause I know niggaz is gon' be sweatin' the shit out of us," Tiffany said, heading towards her house to change clothes and fix her hair.

In the next hour, Tiffany was dressed in the sleeziest outfit she could find. She was giving Jacki-O and Lil'Kim a run for their money.

As they were leaving, Q'Tee flirted with Rakim again, by blowing him a kiss.

"Keep on playin'," Tiffany said. "Before it's said and done, my brother gon' be the one to tap that ass."

Q'Tee rolled her eyes. "Yeah, right!" Q'Tee said, sarcastically.

Riding through the neighborhoods and around town, Q'Tee and Tiffany felt like celebrities. Niggaz and bitches were breaking their necks, trying to see up in the car. Usually when a brand new beamer or expensive vehicle rode through the hood, it normally belonged to a major do' boy or his girl. Not today. Q'Tee and Tiffany stole the spotlight.

"We the shit!" Tiffany said, cheerfully. "Look at them hoes jockin'."

They continued their joyriding, talking and gossiping. Q'Tee told Tiffany about how Jaleel clowned her at the detail shop.

"What? I wouldn't take that shit! You need to have Tony kick his ass," Tiffany said.

"It ain't that serious," Q'Tee assured, still hurt by the disrespect.

On the way back to Tiffany's house, they stopped by the carwash on Hampton Road after noticing the crowd. Lo and behold, Jaleel was hanging out too.

"Speak of the devil! There go that no good ass trick right there," Tiffany blurted out angrily when she saw Jaleel.

"I see him," Q'Tee said, dryly. "Who is that girl all over him?"

"That bitch! That's Shun triflin' ass. They suppose to be messing around. She ain't shit! She fuckin' every nigga in Dallas," Tiffany said, like she had any room to talk about someone else's sex life.

"Oh! That's the bitch you was tellin' me about when I called you two months ago," Q'Tee asked.

"Yeah! That's her!

"Damn! He couldn't do no better than that?" Q'Tee said, hatin'. "She ugly as a mothafucka."

Q'Tee felt a streak of jealousy as she rode through. She watched Jaleel and Shun play around intimately. Her first instinct was to make a scene, but decided not to. However, she was going to make sure Jaleel saw her. She pulled her BMW right beside him and his new playmate, then let down the window.

"Hey, Jaleel," Q'Tee spoke in an alluring tone of voice.

Jaleel was astonished at the sight of Q'Tee. He thought for sure she was going to 'trip' out. She definitely was putting him on the spot, though he knew this was her way of getting back at him from their incident at Sparkles.

Shun gave Q'Tee a not so friendly stare.

Q'Tee paid it no mind.

"What's up Q'Tee?" Jaleel said, being social. "Who shit you rollin'?"

"Mine!" Q'Tee emphasized, proudly while looking at Shun to make sure she knew the BMW belonged to her. "My brother got it for me.

"It's tight!" Jaleel complimented.

Q'Tee gave him a bitter look that said everything she wanted to say. Jaleel recognized the look far too many times before. Out the corner of his eye, he saw Shun staring at him with suspicion. To avoid a sticky situation turning ugly, he brushed Q'Tee off.

"Say Q, it was good seeing you again. When you see yo' brother, tell him to holla at me.

Q'Tee was not pleased with him trying to get rid of her so quickly. *I know he ain't tryna act funny in front of this ugly ass bitch!* she thought. Fortunately for him, she decided to play along just to avoid a scene. She figured he wasn't worth fighting over, especially after all the shit he put her through.

"I will," she responded, rolling her eyes. Q'Tee drove off.

"Girl, did you see that nigga? He was all fucked up," Tiffany said, laughing. "You a better sport than me 'cause I'da checked him and that bitch!"

Q'Tee didn't find the scene amusing. Nevertheless, she still laughed along with Tiffany anyway. A feeling of resentment overtook her by putting Jaleel on the spot despite the way he treated her.

The two of them went back to Tiffany's house to chill until later. It was now 5:30 p.m. They wanted to hit the park around 6:45 p.m. just to give the crowd time enough to thicken up, because Q'Tee's beamer was destined to be seen.

The girls sat in Tiffany's room, gossiping like friends do, basically discussing who's doing what and who's doing who. Tiffany told Q'Tee everything that went on in Houston with her and Derrick. She also confessed about all the new niggaz she slept with in the past few months. Q'Tee knew this was nothing unusual because Tiffany was a nympho for sex. Regardless of the fact, Q'Tee still cared about her friend all the same. Q'Tee filled Tiffany in on the details about Dontae. But she left out the intimate freak session she had with herself while thinking about him.

"And you mean to tell me you ain't called him? Bitch is you crazy or are you on pussy now?" Tiffany said, feeling like she'd been let down.

Q'Tee looked at Tiffany, shocked.

"I know you didn't go there. Bitch! I'm strictly dickly!" Q'Tee said, defensively.

"I can't tell. First of all, you ain't had no dick in almost a year. And now you tellin' me you turning down penitentiary dick.

That's USDA approved--stamped by the government," Tiffany announced dramatically.

"You got to be stopped!" Q'Tee said, smiling.

"I just hate to see good dick go to waste. You might as well give me the number 'cause I definitely will put it to good use," Tiffany said, being serious as always.

Q'Tee felt like she had enough of that conversation and moved on to something else. Her and Tiffany killed time, talking until time to go to Glendale Park.

The sun was gradually going down, cooling things off a bit. Q'Tee and Tiffany didn't make it to the park until 7:15 p.m. The park was the hangout every Sunday evening during the summer if the weather permitted.

The crowd was already thick. Cars and all sorts of vehicles were bumper to bumper. The same as always. When Q'Tee and Tiffany rode through, niggaz was checking them out. The BMW brought attention to itself and added more attraction with them inside.

"There go Tony and Naija'," Q'Tee said, noticing Naija's white Benz.

"That need to be me up in that Benz, and not that tired ass ho, Naija!" Tiffany said, rolling her eyes.

Naija's Benz was backed in, profiling. Tony had got it washed earlier sparkling like it came off the showroom floor. Naija sat on the hood while Tony stood between her legs, enjoying their quality time together, smoking blunts and drinking. Tony was already buzzing from earlier, smoking weed with J-Rock and some other niggaz.

Q'Tee pulled up in front of Naija and Tony.

"I see you rollin', lil sis," Tony said, smiling as he walked to her car.

"What up big Bruh?" Q'Tee smiled back.

It's funny how they go from arguing and wanting to tear each other's head off one day, to being a loving brother and sister the next.

Tony leaned in the car, eye-balling Tiffany. Her hardening nipples were poking through the thin material of her top, drawing much attention from Tony.

'What's up, T?" Tony said desirably.

"Hey Tony," Tiffany answered softly, blushing at the same time.

"You need to holla at me."

"Nigga! You ain't gon' do right," Tiffany said, smirking. "You know that bitch got you on lockdown."

Realizing Naija was only a few feet away, Tony said, "We'll talk later."

He knew how ghetto Tiffany could be. So to avoid fucking his shit up at home any worse than it already was, he decided to catch Tiffany another time when the time was right. With a wink of an eye, he strolled back over to Naija.

Q'Tee managed to find a parking spot and backed in. Her and Tiffany got out the car with finesse. They hung out by the car, watching the activity of the crowd.

Out of nowhere appeared Dutchess, a gay friend of theirs from high school.

"Hey, tramps!" Dutchess said in his girlish voice.

Q'Tee and Tiffany couldn't control their laughter.

"Bitch what you got on?" Tiffany said, crying tears.

"Oh, don't hate!" Dutchess responded, spinning around to show off his Daisy Dukes, halter top and heels.

"I'm scared of you," Q'Tee said getting a kick out of Dutchess' girlish ways.

All three of them hung out together, laughing and talking about people. Dutchess' feminine antics kept them entertained the whole time.

Look at that bitch!" Dutchess said, pointing.

Q'Tee and Tiffany looked in the direction Dutchess was pointing, to observe a light skinned brotha hugged up with his girl.

"She just don't know I was with her man last week. He one of them down low brothas," Dutchess said, twisting his neck.

Q'Tee and Tiffany responded with "Ooouuu's and Aaahhh's".

Nightfall came. As usual, niggaz can't get together without some drama. The cause: high off weed, 'water' and alcohol, a combination that didn't mix.

Tiffany, Dutchess and Q'Tee focused their attentions to where a small crowd was gathering. Two niggaz was in a heated argument, expressing verbal slander and profanities at each other. Being nosey, Q'Tee, Tiffany, and Dutchess joined the crowd, trying to get a better view.

The .357 Posse click was at it again. They brought drama everywhere they went. They were on some gangster type shit. And it was about to be on and poppin'. A Crip, by the name of Fresh, from another hood, had stepped out of bounds. He was trying to push up on a girl named Tosha, who belonged to Kwame, a nigga from, Dixie Circle. The word shot through the park like a bullet. Minutes later, Kwame was checking Fresh about his girl. Fortunately, Fresh didn't travel alone. With his homies having his back, the nigga name Fresh wasn't trying to hear it. He and his homies squared off, ready for whatever.

BOOM! BOOM! BOOM! Gunshots rang out through the park. People ran, ducking and screaming, trying to get somewhere. Vehicles of all sorts were on the move, honking horns and maneuvering their ways through the traffic.

Q'Tee, Tiffany and Dutchess ran frantically, hoping not to catch a stray bullet. They made it to Q'Tee's car safely.

"Ooouuu child! These niggaz is crazy," Dutchess said out of breath.

"That's why we fix'nta get our asses up out of here," Q'Tee said, hurrying to get in her car. Securing herself in the car, she said, "We'll holla at you some other time, Dutchess."

Quickly, Q'Tee drove off, putting some distance between her and the showdown at the O.K. Corral.

Sirens could be heard in the distance. The only perception was somebody got shot or maybe killed. In the world we live in--a genocide era--the white man thrills himself watching Blacks kill each other. It saves White America from doing it.

The traffic of the crowd had moved to the strip on Camp Wisdom Road. IHOP, Whataburger or any available parking lot was gradually becoming packed. The gathering was only temporary. Too many niggaz in one spot, impeding the progress of white society spelled trouble. And the po-po's wasn't having it.

Q'Tee pulled up into the IHOP parking lot, looking for a place to park when she saw Naija's Benz. Her and Tiffany got out of the car and went inside the building.

"Them Dixie Circle niggaz is a trip!" Tiffany said, adjusting her short, skimpy skirt.

"One day they gon' run into the wrong group of niggaz and its gon' be some shit," Q'Tee said.

Tony waved them over to his booth. The girls walked over and sat down with him and Naija. The tension circulated instantly between Naija, Q'Tee and Tiffany.

"Y'all alright?" Tony asked, concerned for their safety.

"We straight," Q'Tee assured.

"Those young ass niggaz need to sit they ass down somewhere with all that bullshit. That kind of shit is why a mothafucka can't go nowhere and chill. I wish one of them bitch ass niggaz get out of line with me. I'ma bust'em right in the ass with somethin' hot," Tony said furiously, meaning every word.

Q'Tee sat listening to her brother run off at the mouth. She knew Jaleel was from Dixie Circle and ran with the same click of niggaz. At this point, she hadn't heard of him getting into any bullshit like what just happened several minutes ago. Now she wondered was the association with his neighborhood is what fueled the disrespectful behavior. It use to be a time when he would never disrespect her. She often told herself that she was through with him for good. But the feelings she have for him, she couldn't seem to let go, no matter how hard she tried.

While in thought, Jaleel and Shun walked into IHOP, catching Q'Tee's attention and everyone else's at the table with her. She watched them as they strolled hand in hand to their seats.

"There go yo' boy," Tony said, being funny.

"That ain't my boy!" Q'Tee said hastily. She decided to leave.

"Let's go T," Q'Tee said, getting up. "I'll see y'all tomorrow."

Q'Tee and Tiffany left out of IHOP without being seen by Jaleel.

Outside, Tiffany saw Derrick, her frequent sex partner and the one who splurged on her in Houston. He was macking on a slender chick, resembling the R&B singer, Monica, in the parking lot. He was unaware that Tiffany was walking up behind him.

Pushing him in the back, Tiffany shouted, "Nigga, what you doin'? I hope you ain't doin' what I think you doin'."

Derrick was cold-busted. He turned around to face Tiffany. "T! What you talkin' 'bout'?" Derrick asked, like he was doing nothing wrong.

"You know what the fuck I'm talkin' about! Don't play dumb," Tiffany shouted loudly, causing a scene. "You out here tryin' to get with another bitch behind my mothafuckin' back. What's wrong?" Tiffany walked up in his face, then continued. "You didn't get enough pussy in Houston?"

Angrily, the slender chick stepped up. "Derrick, who is this loud ass bitch? The Monica look alike said.

Tiffany's attention went from Derrick directly to the girl. Enraged, she swung missing her target. Derrick, quickly stepped between them and grabbed Tiffany.

"Nigga, put me down. Yeah, I ain't forgot yo' face. Bitch you got yours comin'!" Tiffany yelled as Derrick escorted her to his car. They argued among themselves until she fell weak to his sweet talking. His kiss of persuasion was all she needed, arousing her desire to be with him.

Q'Tee waited by her car for Tiffany. She thought back to Dontae. Remembering her talk with Tiffany, she felt the urge to call him, at least to occupy her mind away from Jaleel. *I don't want to sound desperate,* she thought as she weighed out her options. She definitely needed a man in her life. Masturbating was beginning to get old. She wanted the real thing, but from someone who shared her same hopes and dreams. All around her it seemed as if everybody had somebody except her.

Tony and Naija walked outside, heading to their car to leave.

"I thought you was gone," Tony said concerned.

"I'm waitin' on T. She down there arguing with Derrick."

"Don't be out here too long. It's too much shit happening."

Q'Tee nodded, respecting her brother's concern.

She watched Tony and Naija leave. Seeing them together wasn't what she wanted. Then again, it wasn't about her. The fact of the matter was that he was happy-something she wanted to experience. Happiness! She wanted to be held, pampered, loved and all the things that came in a relationship.

Clearing her head, she begin to get impatient. She looked in the direction of Tiffany and Derrick, noticing her walking toward her. From the look and the smile on Tiffany's face, it seemed as if her and Derrick kissed and made up.

Approaching Q'Tee, Tiffany said, "I'm about to roll with Derrick."

I know this bitch ain't tryna sound all sweet and innocent, when she know she a ho, Q'Tee thought to herself.

"I figured you would," Q'Tee said, sucking her teeth.

"You know how it is, that's my boo," Tiffany said smiling innocently.

Q'Tee saw the lust in her eyes. *Bitch! He just wanna fuck! You'll fall for fried ice cream,* Q'Tee thought.

The girls hugged, agreeing to hook up on a later date.

It was a lonely ride back home for Q'Tee. Yet it was a time to re-evaluate her life. More importantly, it was time to lay the groundwork to reach the full extent of her expectations and goals. Her brother had helped minimize some of her demands by purchasing her a new car. Now, her next step was a reliable job, a house and a man to share her life with. Not just any man...a special man!

Chapter Eight

Friday morning, Dontae was chillin' out at home, watching TV. Still, he was puzzled as to why Naija hadn't called yet. *I wonder did Jasmine give her my number,* he thought. It was obvious to him that Naija had a man. But, he still wanted some answers to why she fell off on him. If be, another chance at a relationship. Numerous things pertaining to her, crossed his mind. *I bet that pussy still good,* he thought, far too many times. He desired her badly next to getting his hands on some fast money.

Deep in a trance, he barely heard the phone ring. He was hesitant at first to answer, feeling it wasn't for him. Quickly, he changed that thought, realizing it could be just the call he was waiting for. When he picked up the receiver to answer, he almost choked after hearing the voice.

"May I speak to Dontae?" the woman said in a soft voice.

"This is Dontae," he responded as he tried to recognized the unfamiliar voice on the phone.

"This is Q'Tee. Your remember me?"

"Oooohhh! Hey, what's up?" Dontae replied, feeling disappointed by it not being Naija.

"Did I call at a bad time?" she asked after hearing the change in his voice.

"No! I was meaning to call you earlier but I've been tied up all day," he lied.

"That's okay. I've been busy myself."

Deeper into the conversation, Dontae became all smiles. Soon his mind shifted to the physical appearance of Q'Tee that had attracted his attention when they first met. The more they talked, the more desirable she was becoming. It had been a few days since he last had sex and he was feeling a little horny, and he was hoping she was willingly able to meet his needs.

Dontae got in a comfort zone, more so a 'playa mode' as he relaxed on the couch, evaluating the situation at hand as to how far she was willing to allow him to go.

"So, when am I gon' see you again?" Dontae asked in a smooth subtle voice.

"Whenever, now that I have a new car," she told him.

"Oh yeah! You just full of surprises."

"Not me. My brother is the one. He bought me a brand new BMW."

"That was nice of him. Now it shouldn't be any excuse for you not to come see me," he proclaimed, baiting her in.

"Mmmhh! Aren't you persistent," she said, digging him even more. "Maybe we can work something out."

"That's what I want to hear," Dontae said, then switched the phone to his other ear. "How about hooking up tomorrow, if you're not too busy."

"Sounds like you miss me already," she teased.

"If you only knew," he said, rubbing his dick, thinking about knocking the bottom out of her pussy.

"I guess I will take that as a yes. It's a possibility I can come see you around 1:00 p.m. tomorrow.

"Cool. Just call me if anything changes."

Before hanging up, Dontae gave Q'Tee directions on how to get to his house. After hanging up, he sat on the couch for a couple of minutes, thinking back to when he first met Q'Tee. *It looks like I'm gon' get in those guts after all*, he said to himself as he visualized her body once again. A tingle went through his body from the physical images that appeared in his head.

Cooling down from his heated desires, he felt bored around the house. He wanted to do something to occupy his time. He was in the mood to workout something he had neglected since he been home. Realizing he didn't have any transportation, he thought *I should've kept momma car today*. The gym was to far to walk and it was too hot to go play basketball at the park. Finally, he decided to go back to sleep.

Chapter Nine

Up early in the morning, Q'Tee felt rejuvenated. A good night's sleep had done her some justice, something she really needed. Since Tiffany kept them in the streets 24/7, last night Q'Tee decided to take a chill pill on going to the club.

Living the college life deprived her from much needed sleep as well. The all night parties, concerts and the late night club scene was a wonder how she was able to stay awake in class long enough to earn the credits she needed to graduate.

Q'Tee spent most part of the morning running errands for her mother and cleaning up around the house. Exhausted from hours of dusting, mopping and cleaning, she was in the mood for some R&R (rest and relaxation).

She flopped herself across the bed for a brief moment, reviving the lost energy she spent. "Now I see what Katy, the cleaning lady, feels like," she said, clutching her arms around the pillow. Thoughts of Dontae became vivid in her head. At 1:00 p.m. she would be meeting him. She wondered if he would try anything with her. In regards to her months of abstinence, she was hoping he did because she was definitely feeling him, and any persuasion just might be what she needed.

For a moment, she caught herself dozing off to sleep. A heavy nod woke her suddenly. "Damn! Let me get my ass up." She hopped up and went to her walk-in closet. She wanted to look good for Dontae; sexy, but not slutty! She was indecisive between a Tommy Hilfiger Khaki skirt with the matching T-shirt, or her DKNY shorts with a sleeveless top. She figured that after she took a bath she would decide.

Q'Tee took a long soothing bath, relaxing her mind at the same time. She stepped out of the tub and grabbed a towel. As she stood drying herself off, she admired her body, giving herself a full analysis as she did a 360-degree turn, primarily focusing her attention on her butt. She did a series of booty shaking dances, laughing at herself at the same time.

Overall, Q'Tee knew she was fine, an attribute she was blessed with, but tried not to let it go to her head. Completing a full body check, she placed a towel around her and went back to her bedroom to get ready.

She applied her Victoria's Secret body fragrances and lotions on her body. Glancing over at the two outfits she laid out over the bed, she was still undecided on which outfit to wear.

Searching in her dresser drawer, she selected some sexy white thong panties and a bra to match.

Looking at the clock on the nightstand, it was 11:52a.m. She remembered telling Dontae she would be over to his house at 1:00 p.m. She had a little over an hour to be dressed and make it to his house on time.

Rushing against time, she finally chose the Tommy Hilfiger outfit. After what seemed like an eternity, she was completely dressed, makeup intact, and hair whipped. She sprayed on some DKNY perfume, remembering how much Dontae liked the smell of it.

She checked the time again – 12:41 p.m. Calculating in her head, she figured that by the time she stopped and got some gas, she would make it to Pleasant Grove right on time, depending on the traffic on the freeway. She grabbed her purse and headed out the door.

Q'Tee stopped at the nearest Diamond Shamrock gas station to get some gas. Walking out of the gas station after paying for her gas, she called Dontae on her cell phone and let him know she was on her way and that she was running a little late.

Getting in her car, she noticed Jaleel pull into the gas station in his 1995 Chevy Impala. It seemed as if Q'Tee was seeing him and Shun on a regular basis. This gave her all the more reason to do her thing.

Q'Tee waved as she caught the sudden surprise on Jaleel's face when he saw her. He quickly turned away as he drove up to the next pump.

Nigga, don't act like you all that! she thought to herself as she drove off, now more excited about seeing Dontae. *Your loss is my gain.*

●●●●●●

Dontae was just getting out of the shower when Q'Tee called. He figured she was going to be late. Women! He had gotten up early this morning and worked out, then ran four miles afterwards. He flexed his muscles in the mirror. "These hoes ain't ready for me," he said as he continued to pose. His muscles were still pumped from the extended sets of flat bench presses, inclines, dumbbells and arm workouts. Despite this three week layoff, he was still able to rep his max – 455 lbs.

After brushing his teeth, applying deodorant and putting on some lotion, he got dressed. He sported a platinum FUBU Harlem Globetrotter jersey, denim short and crispy white Air Force Ones. While in prison, he made sure he kept up with the latest fashion so he wouldn't feel out of place when he got out.

Dontae checked himself in the mirror and brushed his hair, bringing his waves to life. He put on his platinum earrings, along with watch and chain that he bought at Big T Bizarre. He contemplated not wearing the jewelry, but decided what the hell. Besides, the Koreans who sold him the jewelry, nobody else knew it wasn't actually the real thing. For now, it would have to do until he was able to afford the expensive pieces.

Completely groomed, he counted his money. He had well over $300. He figured it was enough to show Q'Tee a good time. It wasn't like they were going on a cruise. Placing the money back in his pocket, he thought back to his hustling days. Even though he wasn't a baller, he did manage to keep a substantial amount of cash to do what he wanted, and when he wanted, in reference to the lifestyle he was living.

I can't wait to get my pockets right, he said to himself, lusting for the big payoff.

Later, his mother called him and told him some girl was on the phone. Again, he thought of the possibilities of it being Naija. He picked up the receiver and was pleased to hear Q'Tee's voice. *So much for it being Naija,* he thought.

"You won't believe this, but I can't find your street," Q'Tee said, shyly.

"Where you at?" Dontae asked.

"I'm right here by Skyline. Truthfully, I forgot the name of the street," she said.

"All you have to do is turn on Lomax Street and look for 4811," Dontae informed her.

She got quiet for a few seconds as she strained her eyes to look for the street signs. "I see the street and turning on it now," she said anxiously.

"I'll be outside," Dontae said, then hung up.

In seconds, she pulled up in front of Dontae's mother's house. He walked outside to meet her. They both were glad to see each other again as they hugged.

Dontae recognized the smell of her perfume from the first time they met. "Is that DKNY?" he asked.

"Yes!" she said, popping her gum, displaying her ghetto side.

"Did you have me in mind when you were spraying it on?" he asked, asserting his charm.

"Maybe... maybe not," she responded, while slightly biting her bottom lip.

"Q'Tee noticed the amount of platinum jewelry he had on. At first she wondered if it could be real. Common sense told her that a man fresh out of prison wasn't in any position to buy expensive jewelry right away. Especially when there were other things of importance to obtain, unless he had an overly generous family, or had a bunch of money put away before he went to prison. She felt like he didn't fit either category. My, my, my! Aren't you full of bling-bling," she teased as she fingered his platinum chain.

Embarrassed by the remark, Dontae knew he should've followed his first instinct by not wearing the jewelry, at least not in front of Q'Tee so soon. Quickly, he kicked into 'player mode'.

"This is just some costume jewelry I threw on until things get better," he said nonchalantly.

Q'Tee couldn't help but laugh. She was impressed by his wit and humor.

Dontae complimented her car as they rode around trying to figure out what to do.

"I bet you got all types of niggas sweatin' you now," Dontae said, making small talk.

"Naw, not really. I hardly go anywhere to be noticed," she said bashfully.

"I know one thing... it don't take much for you to be noticed," he said, playing up to her.

Q'Tee smiled fully.

"Are you hungry?" he asked.

"Starving!"

"What do you want to eat?"

"Do you know where there are any good Chinese restaurants in this area?"

"Chinese!" Dontae shouted, showing a screwed up face.

"What's the matter? You have a problem with Chinese food?"

"On the real, it's not my top ten places to eat out."

After Q'Tee's playful pouting, Dontae finally gave in to Chinese food. They had a hilarious time at the restaurant. Q'Tee was in tears laughing at Dontae trying to use chopsticks. She thought she was going to die from laughing when he dropped his chopsticks and started eating with his hands. She was starting to feel a connection with him. His down-to-earth attitude is what stood out the most. Next, it was his good looks. He didn't try to portray any fictitious images of being more than what he was. Also, his savvy personality kept her wanting to know more about him.

Leaving the restaurant, they ended up at Town East Mall. Dontae dreaded going to the mall with women. Just like he expected, she dragged him into store after store, trying on this and that. Afterwards, he ended up carrying the majority of the bags. And, the sad thing about it, not one bag had anything in it that belonged to him. What a man won't do to get some pussy!

Stopping at Braums in the mall, Dontae treated her to some ice cream, which happened to be her favorite desert--cookies-n-cream to be exact. She felt like a schoolgirl all over again.

Watching her tongue glide over the ice-cream, Dontae pictured her sucking his dick.

"Are you having a good time?" he asked while staring into her eyes.

"So far, so good," she told him, returning his stare. *I wonder what he's thinkin',* she thought to herself.

"You want to catch an early movie?"

"I'm cool with that."

They made it to the movie theater at 6:25 p.m. The movie was just starting when they walked in. They both agreed to see *I Robot*, starring Will Smith. It took a few seconds for their eyes to adjust to the darkness. Luckily, they found two empty seats in the back row.

While watching the movie, Q'Tee was thinking to herself that she had always had a fantasy about having sex in a dark movie theater. She looked around and noticed there were only a few people watching the movie. This made things all the better if she decided to carry out her fantasy. She reached over and grabbed Dontae's hand. Her insides were already wet, as wild and freaky thoughts ran through her head.

Dontae looked at her curiously, not able to clearly read the expression on her face because of the darkness.

Without any more hesitation, she leaned in and kissed him. He accepted her tongue in his mouth, kissing her passionately. He felt an erection starting to rise, and thought to himself, *It's about to be on tonight!* Q'Tee slowly pulled away and stared at his reaction, observing him carefully. She felt he passed the test. She had her own philosophy; if he kisses good, it meant that he could eat pussy good, just in case he was lacking in the dick department.

"Why you staring at me?" he asked.

"I have my reasons. Is there a problem?" she asked.

"No problem!" he answered.

Q'Tee decided to put her fantasy on hold for another time, though she was tempted to go through with it. There still was a lot to learn about Dontae to prove him a worthy prize.

After the movie, it was Dontae's idea to hang out at his mother's crib and talk. They touched on a lot of topics that brought them closer together. Also, he introduced her to his mother, and Q'Tee and Dorothy hit it off perfectly.

Q'Tee was really enjoying her time with Dontae. Each minute was getting better as it passed by. Realizing it was after 10:00 p.m., she decided she should be heading home.

"You have to leave so soon?" Dontae asked, hating that she was going.

His mother had left the house just to give Dontae the privacy he needed. He was hoping he could get 'busy' before his mother came back home.

"Yeah, I have to get up and go to church in the morning," Q'Tee said, saddened that she had to go. But it was for the best before she did something she might regret in the morning.

"I can respect that. I don't want to get in the way of a woman praising the Lord."

"Now, you're welcome to come if you want to," she said, trying to see if he was a spiritual man.

"It's not that I don't want to, but I'll have to pass this time. Please don't hold that against me," he said, smiling.

"Alright. I'ma let you make it this time," she said, growing more attached to him.

Dontae hugged her and gave her a kiss. Again, she fought back her desire to sleep with him.

"Call me when you get home," he requested after their brief kiss.

"I will," she said, catching her breath.

"When will I see you again?" he asked.

"Soon. Real soon!" she answered with a mesmerized look in her eyes.

Dontae kissed her again and this time Q'Tee backed away, keeping things from going too far.

"I think I better go now," she admitted, inhaling and exhaling.

Dontae felt he made a good impression that will broaden her curiosity to take things to the next level. So, he decided to lay off the charm and let her go.

Q'Tee went home with her panties soaked.

●●●●●●

Club G.G.'s was jumping Saturday night. It was 1:30 a.m., just an hour away from closing time. Already, niggaz and cliques of females were flocking outside to mingle, exposing themselves to a potential hook-up.

Tiffany was among the many females strutting around in short skirts, mini dresses, booty shorts, or anything revealing and sexy. She looked around the parking lot for a sexual partner with the credentials to participate in a late night creep. While eyeing several prospects, she saw Jaleel with Tre and Kwame, leaning up against his Impala, talking to some girls. The sight of him pissed her off. *Ho ass nigga!* she said to herself. She set aside her 'dick chasing' just to go and confront him about Q'Tee. She figured his ass needed a serious checkin'.

It just so happened that Jaleel had already noticed Tiffany. Seeing her walking his way, he completely stopped what he was doing and focused his eyes on her fat pussy print. Not only that, he was intrigued by the way the shorts she was wearing displayed all her curves.

"What's up, Tiff!" Jaleel said, pushing past the girl he was talking to. *Maybe this bitch will give me the pussy tonight,* he thought. He knew how Tiffany got down. She was a known freak with a reputation--a five-star freak to be exact!

"You know you wrong!" Tiffany said with a sistah-girl attitude with one hand on her hip.

"What are you talkin' about?" he asked, totally confused. He was thinking she read his mind about wanting to hook up with her.

"That shit you pulled on Q'Tee wasn't even cool. How you gon' clown her like that? Y'all been through too much shit together."

"I ain't got time to hear this bullshit about Q'Tee. Fuck Q'Tee!"

"So, that's how it is, huh? You gon' play my girl like that?" Tiffany asked, surprised at his attitude.

Jaleel just looked at Tiffany as if saying, *Bitch, what you think?* His attitude should've told her he didn't give a damn about what she was talking about concerning Q'Tee.

While Jaleel and Tiffany stood squared off in front of each other, she saw Tony pull into the club's parking lot in his new model convertible C4 Corvette, with 20 inch Giovanni wheels, and parked. Out of spite, Tiffany decided she would fill Tony in on just how Jaleel acted towards Q'Tee. She figured she would stretch the truth just a little. It didn't take much to rile Tony up about Q'Tee.

Tiffany approached Tony with one of her sexy walks. She had always been infatuated with him, so, giving him the pussy wouldn't be a problem if he wanted it. She just couldn't understand why he never got around to making a move on her, especially since she'd been friends with his sister for several years. Truthfully, she wanted to be his main girl, but it seemed as if Naija wasn't going anywhere anytime soon.

Tony peeped Tiffany coming his way when he got out of the car. His eyes went straight to the print between her legs. She saw where his eyes were staring, and put an extra twist in her hips to entice him.

"Hey, Tony," she said in a sexy voice.

"Just chillin'. What's up wit' ya?" he said, eyeing her up and down.

"You must like what you see," Tiffany said, stepping back to show herself off. "You sho' is staring."

"You holdin' like a mothafucka tonight," Tony said, admiring her voluptuous curves.

"Thank you. I try to do my best," Tiffany said, blushing. "When you gon' take me riding?" she added, moving closer to him.

"It depends on what you want to ride," Tony said, flirting.

Tiffany was caught off-guard with Tony's reply, leaving her speechless. This was her chance to get her freak on as she remembered how he came at her at the park last week.

"What you doin' later when you leave from here?" she asked, making sure she didn't let her chance of a lifetime get away.

"I'll probably go chill at Denny's," he said. "Why? You got somethin' on yo' mind?"

"I'm just seeing what's up. You the one told me we needed to talk about some things. I feel like tonight is the perfect night to do all the talking we want to do," Tiffany said, straightforward.

"I'm wit' it. Just meet me at Denny's. If I'm not there, beep me."

"I'm not gon' be chasin' you down. Either we on for tonight or not." Tiffany said, feeling like she was getting the runaround.

"Just call me 'signed, sealed and delivered'. That's what that is," Tony assured her.

This was a night he wasn't going to let Tiffany get away. She was looking too damn fine! He wrote his beeper number down and gave it to her. She placed it in her purse for safekeeping.

After establishing her hook-up, she informed him about what Jaleel did to Q'Tee. Tony took the news in calmly, even though she blew the whole ordeal out of proportion.

Tony walked over to where Jaleel was hangin' out with his homeboys and a few hoochies. His presence confused Jaleel. It wasn't common that Tony went out of his way to talk to him. Jaleel knew something was definitely wrong with this picture.

"What's up, Tony!" Jaleel said, feeling Tony out.

"Ain't nuttin', hustla'. What's crackin'?" Tony asked, all cool, calm and collected.

Jaleel wondered what Tony wanted, for him to just pop up in his face. He broke the monotony by talking about Q'Tee. Little did he know, mentioning her name made Tony even madder at him.

"Say, dawg. I seen the Beamer you bought Q'Tee."

"Yeah…" Tony paused, gathering his thoughts. "You know, I gotta take care of baby sis."

"That's good lookin' out."

Suddenly, Tony slammed Jaleel up against the car. As he stared into Jaleel's eyes, Tony could see the fear in them.

Kwame and Tre watched in amazement, contemplating on pulling their pistols. They wanted to jump in and help Jaleel. Figuratively, they knew there were consequences and repercussions in fuckin' with a nigga like Tony.

Tony wasn't planning on hurting Jaleel, only scare him. But to Jaleel, he didn't see it like that.

"If I ever hear about you disrespecting my sister again, I'm gon' get all up in yo' shit!" Tony scolded. "You hear me, nigga?" he finished, grabbing Jaleel by his collar.

Struggling to break Tony's grip, Jaleel said, "You got that."

Tony walked away, pushing himself through the gathering crowd.

Jaleel felt embarrassed, as everyone that had gathered around to watch were mumbling and smiling among themselves. Gathering his composure, Jaleel caught eye contact with Tiffany, seeing her smiling at him. He knew right then that she was the one who told Tony about what happened with him and Q'Tee at Sparkles. Never in a million years would Q'Tee dare involve Tony in her business. Jaleel looked from Tiffany to Tony's direction. *Let's see who gets the last laugh!* he said to himself.

Chapter Ten

The following week, Dontae gathered the information he needed from Reg and Isaac. They were moving 10-15 kilos of cocaine weekly, paying $16,500 for each one. Jaleel, Tre and Kwame together were good for a kilo a week. At least that's what they claimed they could move. Dontae's homework was done.

The next week, Hector agreed to ship the dope to him, no less than 20 kilos at $10,000 a piece on G.P., which was approved by Sergio. Dontae figured if he sold each kilo at $14,000, this would allow Reg and Isaac to drop their prices and pick up some more business. Also, Jaleel, Tre and Kwame could increase their clientele. At $14,000, he calculated a $4,000 profit from each kilo. With 20 kilos, this totaled out to $80,000 a week. "Damn!" he said loudly. He sat back and breathed deeply. He estimated profits that he always dreamed about having back in the day. Now in actuality, he had access to finally fulfill those dreams. With that kind of money, he couldn't splurge off the top. That would only bring unwanted attention to himself. He had to stay low key as much as possible for the sake of already having an 'X' on his back.

What if Reg and Isaac get knocked? Would they snitch me out? he thought. Based on how the system worked, there was no room for slippin'.

Dontae told himself that things were temporary. Just stack enough money to get ahead, then sit back and chill. He remembered what Sergio told him so many times before: "Get in and get out. Don't mix business with pleasure. Keep you enemies close."

Dontae figured that in six months, he would be sitting on a cool million, if first he didn't let the money go to his head and start buying everything he laid his eyes on. The good thing about this whole setup with Sergio is, Dontae had the option to quit selling drugs when he wanted to. That was the difference between Mexicans and Colombians. Colombians required a lifetime commitment, unless death or jail came into play, or a special payment was ordered.

As the weeks continued to pass, deals, transactions and purchases were made. Dontae had presented an offer Reg and Isaac couldn't refuse. Also, they simplified everything for Dontae by taking the bulk of the shipment. All Dontae did was pick up the delivery and drop everything off to his crew, then get paid. There was no need to house anything, except having to rack up a kilo for Jaleel, Tre and Kwame. With Man-Man's Chef-Boy-Ar-Dee skills, cooking the dope was no problem. Man-Man was able to bring back 18 extra ounces off each kilo because of the purity of the cocaine.

Dontae continued his regular routine by keeping an average lifestyle. No one detected anything. The only problem was that his mother and parole officer kept nagging him about getting a job. Every so often, he fronted like he was really searching for one.

By early September, money was rolling in as scheduled. In over a two month stretch, he was already over $450,000. He still managed to keep his appetite to spend at a minimum. Constantly, the desires to buy a new car and nice house had a resting place in his head. Buying anything with cash of that magnitude was absolutely out of the question. The Feds kept track of every cent spent over $10,000.

Noticing all the ballers around town flossing expensive whips with custom wheels and paint jobs, enticed Dontae to buy a fly ride. Asking his mother to buy him an expensive car was definitely not an option. On top of that, he wasn't even working. He needed someone else with a legitimate job and credit. But who? Q'Tee? Keena? Hell, naw! Suddenly he remembered conversating with Reg about where he purchased his Mercedes Benz 500CL. Reg told him about an ex-drug dealer turned preacher who owned a car lot on Loop 12 who helped people, mainly drug dealers, to purchase cars. Preacher allowed drug dealers or illegal business entrepreneurs to pay cash for any vehicle of their choice, and he would set up the paperwork as if the payments were made monthly, without any hassles from the Feds.

Dontae called Reg.

Thirty minutes later, they were pulling up to Preacher's car lot. A black, year old Jaguar SJR caught Dontae's eye. He walked over to the car, opened the door and slid into the comfortable leather seats inside the Jag. He focused his eyes on the mahogany wood grain, retractable roof, and other accessories the car had to offer.

Preacher hurried outside from his office to greet Reg and Dontae. He always had an eye for a conspirator in illegal activities. Therefore, he greeted them with open arms. They were the ones who kept the big bucks in his pockets. After a firm handshake, going through the motions, taking a test drive, and signing the papers, the deal was done. Now Dontae was the proud owner of a Jaguar.

Next, off to the rim shop.

An hour later, he was rolling on 22 inch Brabus wheels. He had just broke one of Sergio's golden rules – Don't splurge! That was a difficult task for Dontae to master, knowing he had money to spend and the supply to make more money. The next challenge that lay ahead of him was how he was going to explain a $40,000 car to his mother. Her assumption would quickly lead him to selling drugs. He knew his mother was no fool. Being a master of the streets, Dorothy wouldn't take long to find out what Dontae was doing.

Driving home, Dontae thought about what to tell his mother about the new car. *Maybe I can say it's one of my homeboy's. She know Reg and Isaac drove all kinds of expensive cars. It shouldn't be a problem for her to believe they let me keep one. Yeah, right! I must think Momma a damn fool,* he thought.

No mistaking, the damage was done. No use crying over spilled milk. He might as well go all out. He wanted to have a house built for himself and one for his mother also, he figured in due time. As of now, he needed his own place. An apartment will have to do. Staying at home with his mother wasn't playa' at all, especially now since he was pushing an expensive whip.

Wednesday morning, he was able to find a nice one-bedroom on Ferguson Road at a reasonable rate, without all those background checks. The quicker he moved in, the quicker he could get some privacy to do his thing. He was able to sidetrack his mother about the car, sticking to his original story (a lie). In due time, Dontae knew the truth was going to come out sooner or later.

By Friday, Dontae was all moved in and settled. At this point in life, he felt he was on baller status. Why not floss like ballers do!

"If Naija could see me now," he said aloud to himself. He was just barely over three months since being released from prison, and still no word from her. He chose to give up on her after not hearing from her, and concentrate on getting his money together.

Blocking the thought of Naija out of his head, he figured calling Q'Tee would put his mind at ease. Since she started working a new job, they only got a chance to spend time together on weekends. They still hadn't slept together yet, although he did dibble and dabble with Keena occasionally. He was slowly weaning himself away from her. His interest in her was only external. Despite the absence of sex between them, he enjoyed spending time with Q'Tee. She made him laugh, feel appreciated, and was easy to talk to. He felt she was the type of woman that could make a difference in his life, plus settle down with. Besides, she relieved him from all the stress over Naija.

●●●●●●

Q'Tee sat on the couch, filing her nails when Dontae called. "Hello," she answered.

"What's up, sexy?" he spoke in a smooth, deep voice.

"Nuttin'," she said, all cheesy. "Just sittin' here. What you doin'?"

"I was hoping I could see you tonight, if that's not too much to ask."

"You sound like you miss me."

"I can show you better than I can tell you," he told her, hoping she agreed.

"Listen to you! Maybe we can work something out if you promise to be gentle," she said with a feeling of eagerness.

Dontae was caught off guard with her reply. Something in her voice told him she wanted to give up the poonanny. "Come by Momma's house around 7:30p.m."

"Okay, I'll be there."

"A'ight! I'll see you later. Don't keep me waitin' too long."

"I'll try not to keep you waiting too much longer," she said with a slight hint in her voice.

Hanging up with Dontae, Q'Tee felt his interest went beyond just sex, based on the fact he never tried to force the issue on her. He was very patient and understanding. Their relationship was going into its third month. Q'Tee decided that tonight was the night to get her freak on. She had prolonged it enough. Her putty-cat was in need of a serious overhaul.

She took a shower and afterwards got dressed into something sexy. Purposely, she didn't wear any panties. She packed an overnight bag and tossed a pack of condoms in her purse just in case things got a little heated to an extent she couldn't control herself.

As she drove on the freeway to Pleasant Grove, she thought to herself that Dontae could be the man she needed in her life and to build a future with. She was impressed by his determination not to let negativity pull him back down. But here lately, she was beginning to think that he was doing something he had no business doing. It showed in his appearance, clothing and attitude. Jokingly, he always mentioned getting his hands on some quick money. She wondered if he was actually joking or telling the truth.

At 7:37 p.m., she pulled up to the curb in front of Dontae's mother's house. He was outside, shirtless and leaning on a black

Jaguar, talking on the phone. The car grabbed her attention immediately. The fresh wash and wax job had it sparkling. She wondered who it belonged to. *That shit is tight!* she thought to herself. But the sight of Dontae's chiseled body detoured her sense of thought, replacing it with the imagination of him on top of her making love to her. She felt a slight tingle between her legs. By her not having any panties on, the wetness from her pussy found its way down her inner thighs.

Noticing Q'Tee pull up, he ended his conversation with Isaac and approached her car. She hopped out and quickly rushed to give him a hug. Firmly, she pressed her body against him as she nestled herself into his muscles.

"I missed you!" she whispered, laying the side of her face on his chest.

That was music to his ears. In his mind, he knew she wanted him, but he didn't mind playing the cat and mouse game she presented, because he really liked her.

Finishing their long embrace, they stared at each other. Both of them had the same look of desire in their eyes. Q'Tee raised her hand and fanned herself.

"Is it hot out here, or is it me?" she said jokingly.

"I don't know. I was about to ask you the same thing," he played along. They both laughed.

"Are you hungry?" she asked.

"Not really. I already ate when you called."
Dontae was tired of the same old routines; movies, or going out to eat. Occasionally they would go to a play or to the comedy

club just for a change of scenery. He really wasn't into going to the club with her. That was just like bringing sand to the beach.

"So, what you want to do?" he asked.

Q'Tee thought for a minute at the question he asked. She wanted to tell him, "Let's fuck!" but decided to keep things discreet as possible and follow his lead.

"It's up to you," she said, hoping he read her mind.

"Do you want to go to my apartment?" he asked, looking away to avoid eye contact.

Q'Tee looked at him in surprise. "Apartment?" she shouted. "When you get an apartment?"

Finally, Dontae had to let the cat out of the bag, slowly but surely. There was no better time than the present.

"I'll explain it when we get there," he said. He ran into the house to grab a shirt to put on and returned in seconds. "C'mon, get in." He gestured for her to get in on the passenger side of the Jag.

Q'Tee's mind was in a frenzy while she stood with her arms crossed. "Hold up! Hold up! Wait a minute!" she said, trying to come up with the answers to questions running wild in her head.

"What's going on with you, Dontae?"

"Just get in, okay?" he said in a mild mannered voice.

"Aw, hell naw! Not until you tell me what the fuck is going on with you," she said, unleashing her true ghetto side. "Here you are, with a new fucking Jaguar sitting on dubs, and an apartment that I knew nothing about. On top of it, you have nobody's job to pay for none of this shit, which means one thing; Dontae, I'm not stupid! Common sense tells me you're selling dope again," she paused to catch her breath as she walked closer to him and got directly in his face, then continued going off on him. "How long have you been selling dope? And how long was you gon' take to tell me? As a matter of fact, how long have you had this apartment? I bet you done fucked plenty of hoes up in there, huh?"

Dontae knew the truth had to be told. If he planned on making Q'Tee his main girl, eventually he had to be straight up with her.

"Look here, Q'Tee," he said, placing her hands in his while staring directly into her eyes. "I know I should've been straight up wit' you. But I didn't' know how you was gon' react. I tried giving you hints."

She looked at him, frowning and jerked her hands away from his grasp.

Refusing to struggle with her, he released her hands.

"Trust me baby. This is all temporary. I just need to make enough money to get on my feet. You know yourself how hard it is to find a job." *Yeah, right! Like I been really looking for one,* he thought. "After I make the money I need, I'm chillin'. Then we can invest in some type of business.'

Calming down, Q'Tee felt his pain. She wasn't really upset about his hustling. It was the fact that he kept her in the blind as if he didn't trust her or feel comfortable talking to her. She knew the world strived to keep the Black man down, especially an ex-con. Hustling was usually the next alternative for a Black man to survive. All her life, she had been around hustling; her neighborhood, her father, Tony and Jaleel. So it wasn't a big deal. Because of her deep feelings for him, a big part of her wanted him to wash his hands of anything illegal. For the sake of his freedom, she hoped everything worked out for the best.

"What we have to develop is some communication. That's what makes a relationship. Without that, we have nothing. You could've came to me and explained your motives. But, you shut me out. Honestly, I hate to see you selling drugs again, but I know a man is gonna be a man. All I ask is to trust me to be there for you, respect my advice, and **please** be careful!"

Dontae knew he had a winner in Q'Tee. He hugged her gently.

Driving to his apartment, Q'Tee rested her hand on his thigh, gently massaging it. The soft touch of her hand was soothing, as his dick began to harden.

Dontae looked over at her, trying his best to restrain himself. She looked at him, noticing the desperation in his eyes. She wanted him badly just as well, to be inside her. Deliberately, she increased the anxiety by gently stroking his leg, up towards his full erection that she saw bulging through his shorts.

With the burning desire Dontae was feeling, made it hard to focus his eyes on the road. Suddenly, he felt her hand touch the swollen manhood in his shorts. The relaxing feeling made him close his eyes momentarily. As he opened them, he quickly slammed on the brakes, almost running a red light. Q'Tee snatched her hand back, then screamed.

"Are you alright?" he asked in a panicked voice.

"Yeah!" she told him, panting. "I'm okay."

Dontae leaned over and kissed her softly on the lips. She accepted his kiss willingly. As their lips parted, he looked into her eyes. "I want you!" he said desperately."

Q'Tee didn't know what to say. She was pleased with his assertiveness. Suddenly, their intense moment was interrupted by honking car horns behind them. He noticed that the light had turned green, and quickly took off.

Ten minutes later, they arrived at his apartment. Entering inside, Q'Tee looked around, admiring his taste in color coordination and style. A cozy, black sectional sofa sat against the wall leading to the door, out looking the fireplace. A black, lacquer entertainment center showcasing a 64 inch big screen TV, and a top of the line stereo, its accessories and components lined the far wall. Mixtures of plants were placed around the room, bringing the apartment to life.

"You sure ain't no woman staying here with you?" she teased. She was expecting to see clothes strewn all over the place, dirty dishes in the sink and mismatched furniture. What a surprise!

"Naw. I ain't got no woman stayin' here. If I did, do you think I would've brought you here?" he said.

She shrugged her shoulders. In reality, she knew some niggaz didn't give a damn if they did stay with a woman. They still had the nerve to bring another woman to the house. Then they had the audacity to fuck the bitch in the same bed he shares with his girl.

"Baby, I was just playin," she said pleasantly. "I'm just surprised that it's so stylish in here, like it had a woman's touch. Did your momma help you decorate?"

"Naw, she didn't help me. This is all my work. Honestly, my momma's decorating skills rubbed off on me."

"I see. How does she feel about what you're doing?"

Dropping his head, Dontae said, "I haven't really been totally honest with her yet. I have a gut feeling that she knows already. She's probably waitin' to see just how long it's gon' take me to tell her. Eventually, I'll get around to telling her everything."

Q'Tee walked up to him after seeing the hurt expression on his face and hugged him. The passion she felt for him was indescribable. She lost all recollection of other thoughts as she nestled herself in his embrace.

Dontae pressed his mouth against the side of her neck, kissing softly. She tilted her head to give him better access. Her breathing became heavy as she clutched onto his back, massaging and pulling him closer and tighter.

Gently, he made his way to her lips, brushing across them softly. She anticipated his kiss, completely turned on by his persistent teasing. Finally, he slipped his tongue between her parted lips. She responded passionately, tasting him as he explored her mouth.

His hands fondled her body, moving all over her, tracing her curves. Her body shivered at his careful touches, disturbing her most sensitive spots. He wanted her; to satisfy her; to please her; to love her; to be inside of her. He picked her up and carried her to his bedroom.

Inside his bedroom, again she was mesmerized by his style and taste. The cherry wood king size bed was accentuated with Polo by Ralph Lauren bed coverings, with matching bed skirt, pillow shams and throw pillows.

Setting her down, he went and turned on the CD player. Gerald Levert flowed through the speakers, enhancing the mood. Q'Tee felt like it couldn't get any better than this. Satisfying her need was definitely now!

They danced playfully, bumpin' and grindin' to the songs, solidifying the mood.

Q'Tee was so horny, she became the aggressor. Her hands moved meticulously over his body, removing his clothing. "I want you so bad," her voice was soft and sexy, demanding a urgency.

She slid his shorts down, squatting in the same motion. His dick was staring her directly in the face. Her slender fingers grasped his shaft, massaging it gently. Dontae moaned in pleasure from her soft touch. She took his dick in her mouth, giving him the oral pleasure she told herself she would never do until she got married. He rocked back and forth in sync with the movement of her warm mouth. She devoured every inch like a specialized pro. She got a rush she never imagined she would by giving head. Her pussy was boiling on the inside, getting wetter by the second.

Dontae felt the liquid building up in his nuts and quickly backed away from the tantalizing sensation she was giving. She looked up at him with a smile, pleased with her first time experience of giving head.

Springing to her feet, he helped her undress. Again, they kissed, adding to the excruciating stimulation. He lay her down gently on the bed. Deciding to work his way up, he slowly began to suck her toes. She wiggled and squirmed at the feeling. While in college, she remembered hearing some of the girls around the dorm talk about getting their toes sucked, and she always thought it sounded so nasty, until now. Finally, she was getting firsthand experience and enjoying every minute of it.

Without a doubt, he had her right where he wanted her. Each approach was followed through with perfection. At the sight of her glistening pussy staring at him, he fed his hunger. Other than Najia, this was the first time ever wanting to lick another woman's pussy. Something about Q'Tee was special. He caressed the tip of his tongue across her clit. She held her breath from wanting to scream. At the sight of her reaction, he furthered his journey, giving new meaning to tongue kissing by licking away at her pussy. He tasted the center of her womb, feeling her wetness cover his mouth. She began to pump her hips, accepting the slight penetration of his tongue. She tried her best to hold back that part of her that had been waiting to be released for months and months. Throbbing sensations shuddered her body, making her feel like she wanted to explode. Dontae continued his feasting journey until suddenly she screamed out in pleasure, "Oh, my GOD! What are you doin' to me? I'm commin'... I'm... cum... cummin'!" Her body went into convulsions, tightening up to release the beast inside that waited so impatiently to come forth.

Pulling him into her arms, she whispered, "Make love to me. Please!" Without hesitation, he was inside her with one thrust, filling her completely. She cried out and Dontae stopped.

"Did I hurt you?" he asked, concerned.

She shook her head 'no' and opened her legs wider, clutching onto his butt, pulling him inside her deeper, urging him to continue. The feeling was taking control of her mind. *I can't believe I'm letting this nigga run up in me raw. But it feels too good to tell him to stop,* she thought, allowing the feeling to overtake her.

They moved eagerly and wildly together, both longing for this moment. The musty aroma of sex filled the room. Dontae propped her legs over his shoulders for better leverage. She grimaced, stiffening at his every thrust. She wanted to scream, but the words wouldn't come out. With every stroke, it seemed the wetter she got. She managed to keep her eyes locked in on him to witness the look of satisfaction he was showing on his face. The feeling she was experiencing was nothing she ever experienced with the only other two sex partners in her life. Dontae quickened his movements. She could feel him swell inside her as their passion erupted into an explosive climax.

Dontae collapsed on top of her.

Q'Tee exhaled a soft sigh. She held him tightly, wholeheartedly. Their future flashed in her mind, and she realized how much she loved him.

"Does this make us official?" she asked, sincerely.

"We've been official. This was just the stamp of approval."

Right then and there, they both knew they were made for each other. They spent the rest of the night together, making love until the wee hours of the next morning.

Chapter Eleven

Saturday was the day of Tony's birthday bash/swim party at his house. It was only 2:00 p.m., still early. The party didn't officially kick off until 6:00 p.m. By it being a backyard party, Tony chose a later time to give the sun time enough to go down. Going into mid-September, summer was still in full bloom. And it was hot!

Naija and Jasmine were inside the house, preparing the last of the appetizer platters, while Tony was out back entertaining the fellas, smoking marijuana and drinking mixed drinks and Corona beer.

The smell of barbecue simmering under the barbecue pits filled the air, along with a mixture of weed that filled the blunts Tony and his homeboys were smoking.

"I can't wait to jump this party off," J-Rock said after choking on a hit of a blunt.

"Yeah, man. I'm ready for the hoes to show up. I'm tired of lookin' at all you niggaz," said a dark skinned, bald headed brother named Aaron, while accepting the blunt from J-Rock.

"You niggaz ain't gon' fuck nuttin'!" Tony said, teasing. "And J-Rock, I don't know why you frontin'. You know Jasmine ain't goin' for all that shit you talkin' 'bout."

"Jasmine ain't runnin' shit. We just got a baby together. She do her thang, and I do mine," J-Rock said. "Don't be hatin' on me 'cause you pussy whooped!"

Laughter spread throughout the group of men.

"Nigga, you got me fucked up!" Tony said defensively, not finding the remark amusing.

He wondered if there was any truth to what J-Rock said. He thought for a minute. Was he actually pussy whopped? Even though he had to admit, Naija did have some good pussy and head. Was it that obvious that he was that weak behind her? *Of course not!* he thought. *I just fucked Tiffany and Trina last week.* Honestly, since he'd been with Naija, his ratio of outside pussy had dropped. Not that it wasn't offered to him, he just didn't feel the urge to fuck with a lot of hoes like he used to. Every now and then, he could get his rocks off with a skank bitch. The real question was, was he really that much in love to hang up his playa card? The question lingered in his head until the slamming of dominoes broke his chain of thought.

"Twenty on yo' bum ass!" Aaron said, talking shit.

Quickly Tony blocked everything that he was thinking out of his head and started back kickin' it with his homies. "Give me half of that money, Mr. Marker!" Tony yelled as he slammed the domino table.

●●●●●●

Meanwhile, Naija and Jasmine had finished wrapping and putting the platters of food in the refrigerator. They sat around talking while sipping on Bartles and James wine coolers.

"I really don't care to have all them skank hoes parading around my house, being all up in Tony's face and shit," Naija said, totally against the party and the expected crowd showing up.

"For a woman who says she don't give a damn about the man, do I sense a little insecurity?" Jasmine asked, wondering if Naija had started having feelings for Tony.

"Girl, please! It ain't even like that. Besides, he ain't goin' nowhere," Naija replied, totally confident. "I just don't want them triflin' hoes to be comin' up in here disrespecting me and mine. That's all I'm talkin' about. Fuck what he do in the streets with them hoes. Up in here, it's a different story."

Jasmine sat in silence for a minute, listening and thinking. *How she gon' call somebody triflin'*, she thought to herself, thinking about Naija's scandalous ways. "How long do you plan on playin' this little game? It's been over three years, and here you are, still with Tony, but yet and still, you continue to say you don't love him," Jasmine said in a concerned tone of voice.

"I don't know," Naija signed deeply. "I ask myself the same question over and over, but can't seem to come up with an answer."

"Have you considered calling on Dontae yet?"

"I've thought about it a few times, but changed my mind. I'm pretty sure he's completely forgotten about me by now," Naija said with a puzzled look on her face.

"Maybe, maybe not. That's just a chance you gotta take. Now that I think about it, I haven't seen him in the club in a while," Jasmine said, noticing the sad look on Naija's face. "I always thought the two of you made a cute couple."

Giving thought to what Jasmine just said, Naija thought, *Bitch, please! How you gon' say we made a cute couple, and you the one urged me to holla at Tony?* Blocking that thought out of her head, Naija shifted her thinking to Dontae. She told herself a thousand times that they were made for each other. She knew he was a good man who always found a way to make her smile, something he managed to keep doing ever since high school. Naija smiled to herself, thinking back to the good ol' days. Flashbacks of their good times together and the intense lovemaking made her squirm in her seat. Startled by a burst of noise and chatter, her trip down memory lane was ended.

Tony and his crew stormed through the back patio door, talking loudly.

Najia saw the glossy haze in Tony's eyes. Right then, she knew he was on the verge of getting fucked up. He flopped down on the couch beside her. She felt irritated by his presence. It was impossible for her to keep a straight face so she frowned.

"Me and J-Rock 'n 'em fixin' to turn a few corners," Tony said with a slight slur in his voice. "Watch the meat on the grill until I get back."

Naija leaned away, avoiding the smell of liquor on his breath that was hitting her directly in the face. The real aggravation came when he leaned in to kiss her, grabbing her roughly.

"Tony, will you stop!" Naija shouted, turning away from him.

"Oh! It's like that, bitch!" Tony snapped as he stood up over her.

Everyone in the room got so quiet you could hear a rat piss on cotton. It was just that quiet. All eyes centered on Naija, waiting on her response.

She sat speechless, distraught, and mostly embarrassed. *"I know this nigga didn't call me no bitch in front of all these niggaz!"* she thought, all of a sudden with a notion to kick Tony's ass. She sprang up from the couch like a tiger in attack. She stood staring him in the face, sizing him up. Soon, she realized his big, massive body, and quickly sat back down knowing she didn't stand a chance trying to fight him.

"Tony, you really trippin' right now. J-Rock, y'all need to come get yo' boy," she said with her eyes locked on Tony's expression of guilt.

Jasmine nudged J-Rock. "Do somethin'," Jasmine told him.

"I'm not in that. That's between them two," J-Rock said, justifying his reasoning.

Jasmine slapped J-Rock on the arm.

Finally, J-Rock stepped in between Naija and Tony, resolving the situation by urging Tony to go outside. On the real, Tony didn't want things to go down like it did between him and Naija. The thought of J-Rock saying he was pussy whooped lingered in his head, touching a sensitive part of him that caused him to prove to the fellas that the category didn't fit him at all. By her reacting like she did when he tried to kiss her triggered his low self-esteem.

Watching Tony walk away, Naija was furious. Redness began to flush her cheeks, and her breathing was heavy, making her chest heave in and out.

Jasmine peeked out the window, making sure Tony, J-Rock, Darren, Chris, Aaron and Barron were leaving. After seeing all of them load up in Tony's Hummer H2, she walked back to the family room.

"Damn, he tripped out then." Jasmine said, not believing what just went on. "I ain't never seen that fool act like that."

"I know, girl. I can't stand it when he gets like that."

Shaking her head, Jasmine said, "I suggest it's time for you to start doing some serious thinking. Or packing!" she encouraged.

Getting dressed for Tony's party, Q'Tee was gradually falling in love with Dontae. Actually, she was still upset with him, though her actions didn't show it. Finding out he was selling drugs again came as a devastating blow, though she sensed it all along. She had centered so much attention on them moving in together once he secured a job that she thought he was looking for. The argument last night circulated through her head over and over. *He said it was only temporary. How long is temporary? How could you be so dumb, Dontae? The Feds are probably watching him already, especially riding around in that tight ass Jag. Be careful, Dontae. Please be careful,* she thought.

Q'Tee fought herself, trying not to give the situation much thought. But the impact of the consequences just wouldn't allow her to have peace. She wanted to call him to make sure he was still going to the party. When she asked him about going to Tony's party, he was hesitant to say 'yes'. She couldn't much blame him. It wasn't like him and Tony were best friends. On behalf of their relationship though, he agreed to go.

At this point in her life, she felt things were moving in the right direction. She had secured herself a good job with room to move up the corporate ladder. Her bank account was stable. Staying at home with her mother and having no extra bills made saving money a whole lot easier. Tony volunteered many times to help her get an apartment, but she refused. She figured he had done enough with paying for her college tuition and buying her a new car. Now it was time to do for herself.

Dontae was an important part in her life. He helped erase all the possibilities of getting back together with Jaleel. Every so often, he would call her on the phone. After he took the time out to apologize to her for his attitude toward her, she found herself holding casual conversations with him. Many times, he asked to come by and pick her up, but she turned him down, knowing all he wanted to do was have sex. Getting tired of his constant pestering about sex, she had to finally announce that she was officially seeing someone else. Jaleel acted like a good sport about things, but she knew he had larceny for whoever she was messing with. As far as she was concerned, Jaleel was a boy compared to Dontae in her book. Especially the way Dontae put his 'thing' down last night.

Even though she was upset with Dontae at first, he knew how to do all the right things to push all the right buttons. "Ooooweee! You good pussy eatin' mothafucka," she said with a big smile. Thinking back to their argument, she just couldn't resist his charm. She tried so hard to fight the feeling. Just him alone was enough. His soft touches and tender kisses sent signals straight between her legs. *Make-up sex is the bomb!* she thought. "I still can't believe I sucked his dick," she said, biting her lower lip with the feeling of doing it again.

Slipping into her Gucci sling back sandals, she glanced over at the clock. She noticed she had an hour and a half before the party started. She bought some time by calling Tiffany.

"Richardson residence."

"Bitch! Go on with all that white folks talk!" Q'Tee said, giggling.

"Pardon me!" the voice said.

"Tiffany, quit trippin'," Q'Tee said, thinking Tiffany was playing on the phone.

"I'm sorry. This is not Tiffany, this is her mother."

Q'Tee took the receiver from her head and placed her hand over the mouthpiece. "Damn!" she whispered to herself. She realized she had fucked up, especially knowing that Tiffany's mother was highly religious. Q'Tee wanted to hang up realizing she was busted. Somehow, she found the words to speak.

"I'm sorry, Mrs. Richardson. Is Tiffany home?" Q'Tee said in a low voice with a look of stupidity on her face.

"Yes, she's here," Mrs. Richardson said angrily, but managed to stay calm. "Is this Q'Tee?"

Q'Tee wanted to lie. "Yes, ma'am," she said instead.

"Listen here, young lady! The next time you call my house, watch your mouth. It's not lady-like to use all that vulgar language."

"Yes, ma'am. I'm truly sorry. It won't happen again, I promise."

Q'Tee heard Mrs. Richardson call Tiffany, and overheard Tiffany's mother confronting Tiffany about what happened. In a few seconds, Tiffany came to the phone.

"Tramp! What you doin' calling my momma a bitch?" Tiffany asked, jokingly.

"Giirrll! I thought that was you playin' on the phone. Home girl, that's my bad," Q'Tee said, still in shock.

"Don't worry about it. She'll be alright. So, what's up?"

"Guess what, girl," Q'Tee said, anxious to tell the news.

"C'mon, Q. I ain't got time to play the guessing game," Tiffany retorted.

"I did it!" Q'Tee said.

"Did what?" Tiffany asked, unaware of what Q'Tee was talking about.

"Me and Dontae," Q'Tee said shyly.

"Bitch! No you didn't!" Tiffany hollered. "Was it good, girl?"

"Let me tell ya'. Good ain't even the word for it," Q'Tee admitted, having a flashback.

Tiffany screamed joyously. "Now you know you gon' have to tell me every detail," Tiffany said, wanting a play-by-play description.

"You know I'm not the one to kiss and tell," Q'Tee said, wanting to be discreet. "I will tell you this…" she paused.

"What, girl? Tell me!" Tiffany said, anxiously.

"I sucked his dick!" Q'Tee said, embarrassed a little.

"No you didn't!" Tiffany said, almost as a whisper. She was totally shocked. "What brought all that on? He must was really puttin' his thang down for you to suck his dick."

"If you only knew," Q'Tee said, smiling from ear to ear.

"If you tell me, then I will know," Tiffany said, becoming frustrated because Q'Tee was holding back the valuable information.

"I'll tell you when we get together," Q'Tee lied. "By the way, why you didn't tell me you was fuckin' my brother?"

"Damn! How you find out with yo' nosy ass? Did he tell you?" Tiffany said. "I ain't trippin', since you all up in my business.

"Business!" Q'Tee shot back. "Yo' business is everybody business. You didn't know? But you already know my brother can't hold water. He told me the other day."

"Well, like I said, I ain't trippin'. I'm just doing me."

"That's what yo' mouth say. You know you feelin' my brother. But anyway… you coming to my brother's party? Then you can meet Dontae."

"Nah. I got a change of plans. This nigga I met the other day want to take me to the casino."

Q'Tee knew what that meant. Tiffany was probably going to give up the pussy. She knew her friend far too well.

"I guess that means you'll have to meet Dontae another time."

"I'm sorry, girl. Believe me, just as soon as I get back, I definitely got to meet the man who done turned your ass out and made you start sucking dick!" Tiffany said, laughing.

"Fuck you, T," Q'Tee said, giggling herself.

"Tell Dontae I said hi," Tiffany said.

"I will. Have fun at the casino," Q'Tee said, then hung up.

●●●●●●

Looking at his new platinum Rolex, it was 4:54 p.m. Dontae realized he needed to put some pep in his step. He had to drive all the way from Pleasant Grove to Cedar Hill to pick up Q'Tee, then back across town to Los Colinas. *Q'Tee gon' kill me if I'm late,* he said to himself. He knew he couldn't afford to get back on her bad side, knowing that she was still a little upset at him about selling drugs, even though she didn't show it.

He wasn't really feeling the party Tony was having. He had an uneasy feeling about Tony. However, this could be the time to get next to Tony and discuss business propositions. Dontae knew for a fact that Tony was pushing some major weight. He heard his name on the streets a few times. And being Tony's supplier would be the ultimate goal for Dontae. That meant big bucks at a faster pace.

Keeping the thought in mind, he took one last look at himself in the mirror. The two 2-caret diamond stud earrings glistened in his ears. "No more cheap shit now," he said as he grabbed his keys and went out the door.

Walking in the parking lot, he stopped and admired how clean his Jag was with the chrome 22's. As he sat in the leather interior, he thought back to the niggaz back in federal prison. *If they could see me now,* he thought, smiling, sliding in his Tupac CD, and "Picture Me Rollin" blasted through the speakers. He put on his Versace shades and headed for a surprise he never expected.

● ● ● ● ● ●

Q'Tee and Dontae arrived at Tony's house at 6:30 p.m. Cars, trucks, motorcycles and SUV's were parked everywhere. A few people were standing around in the front yard mixing and mingling, while the majority of the crowd was out back.

"I thought you said it was only gon' be a few people," Dontae said as he looked at the numerous amount of cars.

"Quit complaining and c'mon!" Q'Tee said, yanking his arm.

Dontae was stunned at the upscale features of Tony's house. Even the neighborhood represented money. Anyone would think Tony was a celebrity or some professional athlete based on the house and neighborhood alone. In Dontae's mind, he had plans of living large the same way as Tony in the next few months. His paper was steady stacking. Only $500,000 more and he would be done with the game.

As Dontae and Q'Tee walked up the driveway to Tony's house, he noticed several people admiring his car. A small group of girls focused their attention on him, whispering amongst themselves, trying to figure out who he was. Q'Tee wrapped her arm in Dontae's to let the curious know that he was already taken. Soft whispers of "Damn! He fine!... I need to get wit' that! ... Is that her nigga?" floated through the air, falling into Q'Tee's ears. Instantly, she flashed a devilish look as if saying, "Bitch, don't fuck wit' mine!"

Walking through the front door and into the foyer, Jasmine saw Q'Tee and Dontae arm in arm. She did a double take as her mouth hung wide open, shocked at what she was seeing. In seconds, she ended her conversation with the tall, brown skinned brotha with the diamond grill. She made her way through the crowd, bumping into people as she desperately looked for Naija. Finally, she found her outside talking to Tony and hurried and dragged her to the side away from Tony.

Tony looked at them with concern, more so, suspicion.

"What's up?" Tony asked.

"Nuttin'," Jasmine said, playing it off. "Just give me a few minutes to holla at my girl."

"It's cool," Tony assured Jasmine.

He had gotten back on good terms with Naija after realizing he was at fault for calling her a bitch and apologized. She accepted his apology with open arms, knowing it came with the royal treatment later.

Jasmine pulled Naija way from earshot of everyone.

"Girl, what's wrong with you?" Naija asked in confusion.

"Why didn't you tell me Dontae and Q'Tee are fuckin'?" Jasmine whispered, with a shocked look on her face.

"What?" Naija shouted, quickly lowering her voice while looking around to make sure she didn't bring any attention to herself from the outburst. A group of people standing nearby turned around looking in their direction being nosy, but soon went back to doing what they were doing.

"What are you talkin' about?" Naija finished.

Before Jasmine could answer the question, Dontae and Q'Tee walked out of the back door onto the patio deck.

"Bam! That's what I'm talking 'bout," Jasmine said, pointing in Dontae and Q'Tee's direction.

Seeing Dontae for the first time in all these years, Naija wanted to faint. She felt like her heart stopped beating as she stood there, staring wide-eyed. The waves in his hair, to the neatly trimmed mustache and goatee, to the muscular arms that seemed hard as a rock; he was everything Jasmine had described to her months ago. "Mmmmhh!" Naija grunted softly while shaking her head slowly from side to side.

Noticing Naija's expression, Jasmine said, "I told you that nigga was fine. Lawd have mercy!"

Naija looked at Jasmine with jealousy and rolled her eyes at her.

Dontae and Q'Tee slithered through the crowd.

Naija stepped back out of sight to keep from being seen by Dontae. She knew this wasn't the time or the place to let him see her. Then, she thought, *Could he already know about me and Tony? Do he know we live together?*

Naija and Jasmine stood back and watched Dontae and Q'Tee's every move.

Dontae was still amazed by Tony's house. The spacious backyard and swimming pool with Jacuzzi was the eye catcher. Numerous activities took place outside. People were getting their grub on, slamming dominoes, smoking blunts, hanging out by the pool, and in the pool and Jacuzzi. Just straight kickin' it. For a minute, his eyes got locked on several dime piece broads in bathing suits by the pool.

"Uuhmmm!" Q'Tee cleared her throat loudly, getting Dontae's attention. "Did you lose somethin'?" she added with a light attitude.

Dontae smiled, knowing he was cold busted.

Q'Tee spotted her brother. She and Dontae walked over to where he was standing with a group of guys, smoking blunts and drinking various drinks.

"What up, girl!" Tony said, hugging his sister and accidentally blowing smoke in her face.

"Damn, boy! Don't be blowing that shit in my face," Q'Tee yelled, frowning, trying not to inhale the smoke.

Tony noticed Dontae and quickly looked off.

I knew I should have stayed my ass home, Dontae thought, sensing his invite wasn't welcomed.

"Tight party," Dontae said.

"This bitch off the chain, ain't it?" Tony replied cheerfully.

Dontae was taken off-guard by Tony's new display of attitude toward him. Those are the most words he had gotten from Tony the whole time he and Q'Tee had been kickin' it. Dontae figured it had to be the weed and alcohol talking.

Tony noticed Dontae's shocked expression and offered him a beer.

"You want to hit this?" Tony asked, holding out the blunt to Dontae.

"I'm straight on the weed, but I'll take a beer," Dontae replied.

Tony introduced Dontae to all the fellas standing around. They all greeted Dontae with a soul-shake or a fist pound.

Q'Tee smiled at the sight of Dontae and Tony finally making some progress. *My brother never ceases to amaze me,* she thought.

Mingling together, Dontae realized that his approach on Tony wouldn't be as difficult as it first seemed. Now it was all about picking the perfect time.

Q'Tee hadn't seen Naija in the thirty minutes she had been there. She wondered where she was, not that she was concerned. It just seemed strange for Naija to be missing in action. She always made it her business to be seen.

"Tony, where's Naija?" Q'Tee asked her brother.

Suddenly, Dontae spit up the beer he was drinking when he heard the mention of Naija's name.

Tony, Q'Tee and the three other brothas standing there with them jumped back, surprised at his reaction.

"Baby, you alright?" Q'Tee asked.

"Yeah, I'm straight. Wha... wha... what name did you say?" Dontae stuttered, making sure his ears weren't playing tricks on him.

"I asked about Naija, my brother's so called girlfriend," Q'Tee emphasized as she looked at Tony while rolling her eyes.

Dontae was shocked. *It can't be the same Naija. Not my Naija,* he thought. He decided to stay calm and let everything pan out.

"I'll be back," Q'Tee said as she kissed Dontae on the lips. She left Tony and Dontae together while she went to find Naija.

Standing watching Tony and Dontae conversate together, Naija and Jasmine were in total suspense.

"I wonder what they talking' about," Naija said, bewildered.

"I don't know, but it looks like it's going to be *"Trouble, trouble!"* Jasmine said, mocking Bernie Mac in the movie,

Players' Club, while noticing Q'Tee walking through the crowd and heading in their direction.

Before Naija could duck and hide, Q'Tee spotted her and Jasmine isolated in a corner of the back yard.

Q'Tee walked briskly to them, ignoring the hisses and stares by different niggas and lesbians she passed by.

"Hey, girl! I been looking for you," Q'Tee said, like she was happy to see Naija. "You been over here this whole time?"

"Naw. Me and Jasmine just walked outside. I didn't know you was even here," Naija lied.

"I was wondering was you here. I had asked my brother about you."

"I been in the house running my mouth with Jasmine, gossiping and some mo' shit," Naija said, faking a laugh. "You remember my friend Jasmine, don't you,"

"Yeah, I remember you," Q'Tee said, talking to Jasmine. "It's been a while since I saw you. How you doin'?"

"Hey, girl," Jasmine greeted. "Ohhh, yo' hair sho' is pretty," Jasmine added, touching Q'Tee's bangs.

"Thank you," Q'Tee replied. "What y'all fixin' to do?"

"Nuttin. Just hang out over here. We don't hardly associate with a lot of people that's here," Naija said, wanting to stay undetected by Dontae.

"C'mon, walk with me over there where my brother's at. I want y'all to meet somebody," Q'Tee announced proudly.

Naija and Jasmine looked at each other simultaneously, imagining what the other was thinking.

"Meet who, girl?" Naija asked, trying to buy some time to gather her thoughts. She knew exactly who Q'Tee was referring to.

"He standing over there," Q'Tee said, looking back to see if Dontae was still standing in the same spot. "See him right there? The dark skinned guy with the white sleeveless Sean John shirt and Versace shades. Y'all c'mon."

Naija and Jasmine slowly followed behind Q'Tee as they approached Dontae and Tony. It just so happened that Dontae turned his head in their direction to locate Q'Tee, and saw Naija, Jasmine and Q'Tee coming his way. He swallowed hard at the sight of Naija with Jasmine tagging behind. Within seconds, he stood face to face, since the last time he was in the FDC Detention Center in Seagoville, Texas. He was in total amazement at how beautiful and sexy she still looked. Her pictures only lied to him. She looked better in person. By her appearance, it showed she was well taken care of.

Naija couldn't bear to look him in the face because of the regret, betrayal and unfaithfulness she felt inside. Most of all, he was looking so damn fine!

Q'Tee introduced them. "Naija and Jasmine, this is Dontae. Dontae, this is Jasmine and Naija."

Dontae and Naija greeted one another, shaking hands while he acknowledged Jasmine with a nod as he continued to hold on to Naija's hand.

Naija felt like throwing her arms around him and kissing him.

Q'Tee was a bit curious about their long introduction. "Um, excuse me! Do you two know each other?" she asked suspiciously.

Naija and Dontae were both surprised by the question, unable to come up with an answer right away. Quickly they released each other's hand and stood in silence. Expressions of guilt were written all over Dontae's and Naija's faces. Good thing Dontae had on shades because his eyes would have revealed his true feelings.

Tony stood and thought for a minute. For some strange reason, the feeling hit him again about Dontae. He just couldn't seem to lay his finger on it.

Examining Tony and Q'Tee carefully, Jasmine stepped in to save the day, breaking the silence.

"We remember Dontae from high school. It took us a few minutes to recognize him. My, my, my, Dontae. You sure have changed," Jasmine said, grazing his muscular arm with her hand. *"Ummphh!"* she thought.

Snapping out of their trances, Naija and Dontae quickly agreed with Jasmine, hoping Tony and Q'Tee bought the story without suspecting anything else.

Dontae looked over at Tony and noticed the strangest look on his face. *So this is the Tony that's been fuckin' my bitch. What a coincidence!* he thought.

During the course of the party, Naija and Dontae couldn't keep their eyes off one another. They kept their distance to avoid any suspicion or further questions.

As the party drifted into the 10:00 p.m. hour, Dontae happened to see Naija disappear into the house and figured this was a good time to make his move.

"Excuse me baby. I need to go use the bathroom," Dontae told Q'Tee.

"You need some help?" she said flirting and showing a sexy smile.

Resisting temptation, Dontae said, "Naw. But maybe later when we get back to my apartment." He winked his eye at her as he walked away.

Entering the house, he noticed the crowd was all outside and the house was completely empty. He didn't see Naija anywhere. Walking down the hall, she appeared, coming out of a back room. She was startled by his presence and let out a light, faint scream while covering her mouth.

"Boy, you scared me!" she said, holding her chest.

"My bad. I didn't mean to scare you. I was just looking for the bathroom."

"It's right there," she said, pointing to the door to the left of her.

They stood gazing in each other's eyes until the sight of one another was too much to take. Naija tried to pass by him, and Dontae blocked her path and leaned in to kiss her. She wanted to turn away, but she couldn't resist him. They kissed passionately, while embracing tightly right there in the hallway. In the heat of passion, he guided her into the bathroom, quickly shutting the door behind them, and pinned her against the door.

The longing for one another gradually increased as Naija struggled to unbutton his jeans. Finally managing to free the buttons loose, she reached inside his Ralph Lauren boxer briefs and exposed his hard dick. She closed her fist around it and gently squeezed.

Dontae let out a lingering moan, then reached underneath her denim skirt and removed her thong panties. He cupped her butt and positioned her on top of the bathroom sink. The feeling of wanting him inside her became an act of desperation as she opened her legs to receive him.

He entered her quickly but gently. The warmth of her pussy was welcoming. She hissed softly and slowly caught her breath as he reached the depths of her inner flesh. His movements started out rigid, then gradually became long, deep strokes. She was burning inside as she matched his movements in the same rhythm--wild and passionate.

They kissed again, with their tongues seeming to want to overpower the other. Suddenly, their passion became as one as they reached the point of no return. She clung onto his body, tightening her grip while wrapping her long legs around his waist. She released the burning desire that had been longing to reach its peak.

Totally out of breath, she gazed into his eyes and reality took the place of sex. Immediately, she pushed him away from her.

"What am I doing!" she said, bending down to pick up her panties.

Confused, Dontae said, "Naija, we need to talk."

"We can't! Not here," she said, stepping one leg into her panties, then the other. She ran out of the bathroom.

Dontae attempted to stop her.

"Dontae, no! You got what you wanted, now please leave!" Naija said on the verge of tears.

Naija broke free from his grasp. Luckily, no one was in the house to witness their encounter, as she hurried away, up the stairs. Dontae stood there in the hallway with his head buried in the palms of his hands, confused about what just went on.

The rest of the night was very dull to both Dontae and Naija. He played it off to Q'Tee like he was having a good time. The night didn't get any better because he ended up having to stay longer than what he expected. Tony had passed out earlier from getting too high and drunk, and had to be put to bed, leaving Q'Tee, Jasmine and Naija to chaperone the guests.

After helping to clean up, Q'Tee and Dontae finally got the chance to leave. It was after 1:00 a.m. when they said their good-byes.

"Thanks for helping us clean up," Naija said with gratitude.

"No problem," Q'Tee said.

Naija couldn't help but notice Dontae staring at her. She looked away as her mind thought back to their moment of ecstasy.

Jasmine recognized the tension between them, arousing her curiosity.

"It was good seeing you again, Dontae," Jasmine said, bringing closure to the shocking discovery between Naija and Dontae.

"The same here. And you too, Naija," Dontae said, saddened by her reverted behavior. "We should do this again sometime," he added, hinting to Naija about their sexual moment. Actually, he wanted more than just sex--he wanted her.

Naija stood in the doorway with Jasmine and watched Dontae and Q'Tee walking hand-in-hand down the driveway. She turned and looked at Jasmine, and that's when the tears began to fall.

Jasmine hugged her friend, assuring Naija that everything was going to be alright.

Chapter Twelve

Naija sat over at Jasmine's apartment, talking to her, mainly discussing the things that had transpired between her and Dontae on the night of Tony's party, three weeks ago. At this point in her life, decisions were now difficult, when before everything seemed to be so simple--just as long as Dontae wasn't in the picture. There was no doubt she wanted to see him. The few minutes they shared intimately proved that. But, at the same time, she was still stuck with a choice to make; whether to give up the finer things in life and follow her heart, or, continue to live a lie just to reap the benefits of her greed.

"Girl, I don't know what to do," Naija told Jasmine. "I still love Dontae, true enough, but it's hard to give up the life I have right now."

"I feel ya', home girl. It's definitely a fucked up situation," Jasmine said, agreeing. "Dontae been calling me damn near every day asking about you ever since he called information and got my phone number. Really, you might need to give him a call. I was in the club last weekend talking to some girls, and Dontae's name came up. And, the word on the streets is he getting' money like a mothafucka," she added.

"For real?" Naija said, giving Jasmine her undivided attention.

"Yeah. That's what I heard. That might explain why he rollin' that clean ass Jag sitting on chrome rims. If I was you, I'd see what's crackin' with him before you kick him to the curb, *again!*" Jasmine said putting emphasis on the word 'again'.

Naija smirked, wondering why Jasmine was expressing her emphasis on 'again'. She didn't need Jasmine to keep reminding her that she gave up on Dontae. Her main concern was dealing with the outcome of making the right decision that would complete her life to the fullest.

"How am I gon' call him? It ain't like I got his number," Naija said, having second thoughts.

"Girl, I almost forgot! He called me last night. At first I didn't know who was calling, interrupting my shit. You know I had company. I thought it was J-Rock at first wanting to come over. Then, after finding out it was Dontae, I was cool then. But, anyway, Dontae gave me the number to his apartment, beeper, cell phone, and the address to his apartment to give you," Jasmine said. She got up to go to the kitchen for the piece of paper with all of Dontae's information on it, that she hid in a miscellaneous drawer.

Naija took the paper and looked at the address and took a deep breath.

"Wish me luck!" Naija said, wondering the unknown.

Dontae moped around his apartment, stressed the fuck out. He still couldn't take his mind off Naija since Tony's party. It was now three weeks, going into the first week of October, and still he hadn't managed to get the answers he needed from Naija to bring some kind of closure to any possibilities of them betting back together. He managed to catch up with Jasmine and pestered her by calling frequently and inquiring about Naija. Jasmine tried her best to assure him that Naija needed some more time to think things through.

His relationship with Q'Tee was slowly falling apart when at first it was on the rise. They began to see less of each other due to his deliberate lies; always saying he had other things to do, or not returning her phone calls or messages. At this point in life, he was indecisive. He realized he was still madly in love with Naija, and his feelings for Q'Tee just didn't compare to his feelings for Naija.

He always thought that he would be able to handle whatever situation that was thrown his way about Naija. After finding out she was with Tony, he lied to himself. The fact she was in a serious relationship with Tony only complicated the situation more because of his relationship with Q'Tee.

Sitting on the couch, he replayed the night of Tony's birthday party in his mind. He closed his eyes, visualizing him being inside Naija again. How warm and good she felt. After all the years that had passed, nothing had changed. The feelings were still the same. Dontae wanted that moment back. There was so much to talk about, and a lot of questions that needed a whole lot of answering. *Was there a chance I would ever see her again?* he thought.

He walked into the kitchen and poured himself a shot of Hennessy and quickly downed it. He grimaced as the liquor scorched his throat, creating a feeling of warmth over his face. He turned on the faucet and cupped his hands, filling them with cold water, and wet his face.

He stood, leaning over the sink without any movement, continuing to let his thoughts eat away at his brain. The sound of someone knocking at the door awakened him from his reverie. He walked slowly to the door, wondering who it could be. He was in no mood for company. Without checking the peephole, he swung the door open, and couldn't believe his eyes when he saw Naija standing there looking like a Hollywood centerfold. He batted his eyes, making sure the woman standing in front of him was really Naija and not an illusion.

"Aren't you gon' invite me in?" she asked shyly.

Dontae moved to the side and motioned her inside.

Stepping inside, she looked around his apartment, pleased at the way he fixed it up.

"This is nice," she said in an effort to break the tension between them.

He nodded.

"I hope I didn't come at a bad time. I mean … I know I just popped up unexpected," she said, hoping he didn't have the notion to kick her out.

"You straight. Have a seat," he directed her to the sectional sofa.

He was still trying to get over the shock, more less, the surprise.

They both sat down silently, avoiding eye contact. Soon, Dontae got over the butterflies he felt in his stomach. This was the moment he had been asking for, and he felt it was now or never.

"Look, Naija, about that night at …"

"I know it shouldn't have happened," she said, interrupting him.

"What you mean 'it shouldn't have happened'?" he responded, with a bit of anger.

"I mean I wanted it to happen, but not like that. We both acted off impulse. I really didn't want to jump into things that quick."

Dontae didn't quite understand the direction she was going in. "So, what do you mean?" he asked.

"I just need some more time to think. A lot of time has passed between us, and a lot of things have changed," she said.

"Some more time to think, huh?" he chuckled. "You don't think four and a half years wasn't time enough for you to think?"

Naija felt appalled by the sarcastic remark. She kept cool to keep from turning the situation into an argument.

"It's just that I'm in a relationship right now," she said, trying to justify the situation she was faced with.

Dontae fell silent, allowing himself to think. "So what are you saying? You don't love me anymore?"

"What you think?" she retorted, staring at him with a straight face. "Of course I still love you. I will forever love you."

It seemed like a weight was lifted off his shoulders to finally hear her speak those words again. He sat down beside her and put his arm around her waist. The response wasn't what he expected; she pushed him away.

"No, Dontae! We can't," she said, squirming away from his embrace. "What about you and Q'Tee? Does she know about us?"

"No, she don't know about us. But I'm willing to tell her."

"How do you feel about her?" she asked, somewhat jealous.

"Hold up! This isn't about me and Q'Tee. This is about us. You don't hear me asking you about Tony," he said, raising his voice as he stood up over her.

"You don't have to get all loud," she said, becoming frustrated.

The frustration began to build up in Dontae, and the desire that he had to see Naija was gradually fading. Pacing the floor, Dontae just couldn't understand Naija.

"Explain to me; why did you come over here in the first place?"

"Cause you left messages with Jasmine that you wanted to talk to me, so I came to talk, to maybe work out our differences," she said sternly.

Dontae grinned.

"I can recall leaving messages with Jasmine over three months ago too. Did you get them?" he paused, expecting an answer. Naija looked away, feeling guilty. "That's what I thought!" he added after reading her expression. "Now all of a sudden you feel like it's time to talk."

"Like I said. I'm in a relationship and I still need time to think."

"Why does that sound so easy to say now? Did those words appear in your mind when we were in a relationship? Why couldn't you tell Tony the same thing back whenever y'all started talkin'? What was so hard about that? Huh, Naija?" he said as the anger began to build up inside.

Naija couldn't find the words to respond. She told herself time and time again in the past that she was making a big mistake.

"I'm sorry, Dontae," she managed to say.

"*Sorry! Sorry!* Is that all you can say?" he scolded. "All the shit we've been through and you let this bitch ass nigga come between us. What's so fucked up about this shit is, I asked you about that nigga Tony when I first heard you was fuckin' with him. And you denied the shit. All cryin' and shit to make a nigga think you was really being faithful. But on the real, you was fuckin' the nigga then. Truthfully, you could've been straight up with' me. I wouldn't even have tripped. I realize a woman has needs just as much as a man does. But there's a way to do anything. If you would've handled the situation like a real woman, then I would've had more respect for you. But instead, you took the easy way out by just turning yo' back on me without sayin' nuttin'. Actually, you told on yo' damn self."

"Dontae! You say all that bullshit now. But if I would've told you I was fuckin' with somebody, you would've called me everything but the child of God! And on top of that, you always called me trippin' about where I'm goin' and who I'm hanging out with. I did all I could to be supportive to you, but you didn't appreciate nuttin' I did. And now you want to throw the shit in my face like it's all my fault," Naija said defensively.

"I admit, I did trip out a few times, but I was stressed the fuck out. Put yourself in my mothafuckin' shoes! Doin' time ain't playa at all," Dontae said, feeling the pain from his prison bid all over again. "Tell me this; why is you wit' this nigga? Is it the money?"

Naija looked away from him again as if avoiding the question. Dontae could read straight through her. He shook his head.

"I can't believe that you lowered your standards to be wit' a nigga just because he got money. Whatever happened to the love? You might as well be sellin' yo' pussy, 'cause ain't no love involved."

Naija was starting to get mad. "Oh, it's like that now? So you calling me a ho?"

"You said it, I didn't. They say if you throw a rock in a pack of dogs, the first one to holla is the one the rock hit," he said, being sarcastic.

"That's the way you see me... A fuckin' ho?" she said, raising her voice. "Let me tell you somethin'! Call me what you want. But call me one paid ho. You right! I'm with the nigga 'cause he got money and I get whatever the fuck I want. Understand? That's more than I can say about yo' broke ass," she added with tears forming in her eyes.

Dontae looked at her crazy. She had definitely struck a nerve. He walked to the back and returned in a couple of minutes carrying a duffle bag and walked over to her.

Clearly she was frightened. She thought he was going to do something to hurt her. She stared up at him wondering what was on his mind.

Smiling, he unzipped the duffle bag and turned it upside down, letting the contents spill out over her head.

Out of reflex she ducked, avoiding being hit in the head.

"*Boy! What you doin'?*" she screamed, covering her head. Looking around her, she noticed bundles of money lying beside her. Her reaction showed total amazement.

"That's what that is! Do I look like I'm broke now? Yo' nigga ain't the only nigga getting' paid round this mothafucka! I may not be papered up like him right now, but my pockets sho' ain't hurtin'. As a matter of fact, since you so well taken care of, I'm gon' simplify our situation. You take yo' fake ass relationship and stick it up yo' ass and get yo' triflin', no good, scandalous ass the fuck out of my house!" he shouted, serious as ever.

Naija was shocked by his sudden change of attitude. She grabbed her Chanel purse to leave. She wanted him to change his mind and ask her to stay. They both said some harsh words to each other, but she was willing to work it out, and not leave on a bad note. The fact she still loved him was one thing. Now seeing all that money was something that drew much of her attention. She wanted to know whether it was true that he was hustling. If so, how major was he?

Telling Naija to leave was a big mistake on his part. He had let his anger make his decision. He realized this would spoil any chances of he and Naija reconciling, but a part of him said it was time to finally let to.

Standing by the door, she turned to face him with hopes of resolving their differences. He gave her an unwelcoming stare as he opened the door and let her out. Before leaving, she reached out her hand to touch the side of his face. Dontae turned away. Pulling her hand back, she stared at him sadly.

"I love you," she whispered as she walked out the door.

Slamming the door behind her, he figured he finally ended a chapter in his life, and it was time to move on. First, he had some major explaining and making up to do on behalf of Q'Tee.

Chapter Thirteen

Jaleel, Tre and Kwame had been dealing drugs for Dontae for almost four months. They were getting their hands on stacks of money far beyond what they ever dreamed of. The effects of money turned them into compulsive spenders; buying everything they laid their eyes on--cars, clothes, shoes, jewelry, and pussy! They never thought once about the value of a dollar. As long as they had the supply to make money, fuck everything else. Neither one of them desired to put back some money for a 'rainy day' or had any ideas on investing in a business. It was always splurging, getting high, throwing parties, trickin' with hoes, or whatever enjoyment they could find. And they did it big!

With their excessive spending, frequent habits overloaded their pockets. Packages were coming up short. What started out as a few hundred, routinely progressed to a few thousand. Dontae was lenient at first with the short packages, then later cut back on the amount of dope he was giving them just so they could get their heads together.

Sitting inside the dope trap on Windelken Street on the southside, Jaleel, Tre and Kwame were handling business as usual. It was 2:10 a.m. in the morning. The dope house was owned by a known crack head in the hood named Debra, a.k.a. Woodpecker. She was given the name Woodpecker because of how she gave head, bobbing her head back and forth, similar to a woodpecker continuously pecking on a tree.

Woodpecker regularly rented her house out for a swap of drugs to anyone who wanted to sell drugs there. Nonetheless, it also served as a rest haven for junkies who stopped by to smoke their dope. Unfortunately, they had to pay the piper--Ms. Woodpecker, of course.

Often, young hustlers, other crack heads or tricks would stop by late at night feeling horny and in search of a willing dope fiend whore that they could give dope or money to for a release of sexual satisfaction involving a good dick sucking and sometimes straight sex. (And we wonder why AIDS is at an all time high!)

For the past few months, Jaleel, Tre and Kwame had the spot rollin'. Word was screaming all over the hood that the dope was 'fire' – that Nutta Butta. Yellow crack cocaine that was the common drug of choice in the hood. Crack heads went crazy over the shit. They would travel miles just for a hit of 'butta'. Even if the white rock was proven to be the best, somehow crack heads were trapped in their own illusion.

●●●●●●

A gray 'hooptie' crept down Windelken Street. As the car got closer to the old dilapidated white, wood frame house, it slowed up. The two occupants inside the car paid close attention to the activities at the house and its surroundings, then slowly passed on by and parked at the end of the street.

Two jackers contemplated their next move. Evidently, both of them were waiting on the other to kick things off. This was their first jack, and their lack of experience could cost them their lives.

Ever since the altercation at the park that led to a shooting afterwards, Fresh and Gator made it their top priority to get back at Kwame and his .357 Posse. Fresh happened to catch a bullet in the shoulder. Since his recovery, he vowed to put in work. Now that Kwame, Tre and Jaleel were getting money and splurging their flamboyant lifestyles, they made easy targets.

For several months after the incident, Fresh and Gator plotted to jack Kwame, Tre and Jaleel, and whatever else came with it. By the way the clique was flossin', Gator and Fresh assumed the trio had major paper and big dope.

Every day Gator and Fresh monitored Jaleel, Kwame and Tre's comings and goings, realizing they were easy prey. Determined by the amount of traffic going in and out of the house, they speculated large quantities of dope were present. To the jackers, this was an easy come up. It was all about timing. Right now, time was of the essence. No question, they had to hit now while the getting was good. They knew Jaleel, Tre and Kwame thought they were untouchable and being robbed never crossed their minds. There were plenty of times they were caught slippin', but Gator and Fresh let them make it until now. What Jaleel, Tre and Kwame didn't know was that they were in for a rude awakening.

The jackers crept down the alleyway in the hooptie they rented from a clucker for $30 worth of crack. Standing outside the car, they observed a crack head walking down the street towards them. From his appearance, any one could see he had been up for several days smoking crack. His small afro was matted all over his head, his clothes were dirty and wrinkled, and he had an odor that was totally rank. It was obvious that this crack head was on a mission.

"Where you on yo' way to, Cuz?" Fresh asked the crack head.

The idea of using the crack head for his plan popped into his head. It was already 2:30 a.m., and he figured he and Gator had spent way too much time in the area already.

"I'm on my way to Woodpecker's," Man-Man said nervously, fiendin' to spend the $7 in his pockets. "Why, youngsta? You got somethin'?"

At the same time, Man-Man was being antsy. The desire to take a hit was driving him crazy.

"Say! Check this out. I'ma give you $100 to go over to Woodpecker's crib. While you over there taking care of yo' business, scope the crib out and come back and let me know who all is up in there," Fresh said, reaching in his pocket to peel off a $100 bill.

Man-Man's eyes lit up. Seeing the money blocked out everything else. His main focus was getting high. Now with some extra money, it was on and poppin'.

"You got that, youngsta!" Man-Man said, reaching for the money. Before he could grab it, Fresh jerked it back.

"Say ol' nigga! Don't play games," Fresh said, showing his 9mm Glock. "I got my mothafuckin' eyes on you."

"Alright, I gotcha," Man-Man said, eagerly grabbing the money. "Give me a few minutes and I'll be right back." *Suckas!* He thought.

"Hurry up and handle yo' business and meet us right here in ten minutes. And don't go in their running yo' mouth, tellin' everybody we out here," Fresh demanded.

Man-Man nodded, walking off quickly, almost running, while Gator and Fresh stepped back into the alleyway to camouflage themselves in the darkness.

"Say, cuz. You trust that dope fiend nigga like that? He might run up in there and tell them fools we out here," Gator said, bringing the situation into a better perspective.

"Hell naw! But I had to do somethin' to jumpstart this shit," Fresh explained.

Gator didn't bother to respond. *This nigga got all the sense,* Gator thought, shaking his head, trying to come up with some kind of logical reasoning.

"What, nigga?" Fresh snapped, noticing Gator shaking his head. "It ain't like you coming up wit' a game plan."

"Just chill out, Cuz. Why the fuck is you getting' all hot under the collar wit' me? Yo' problem ain't wit' me. You can miss me with all that bullshit, homie. Save all that drama for them mark ass niggaz. Remember, I'm the one down wit' ya'. It's what ever you want to do. I'm wit' it. And that's what that is," Gator said, proving his loyalty to the set.

Finally, settling their differences, the two waited patiently for the crack head to come back. Gator paced back and forth, itching to hit the lick.

●●●●●●

Inside the house, Tre, Jaleel and Kwame were getting restless, 'noid from smoking weed, popping "X" and sippin syrup practically all night. Jaleel went to the back bedroom and lay down. Feeling horny off of the "X," Tre took Woodpecker to another bedroom to get some head. Knowing him, the head wasn't going to be enough. Eventually, he would stick his dick in her. Kwame hung around up front, working the last of the dope.

A knock at the door awoke Kwame, who had dozed off. He got up from the couch and walked to the door, pistol in hand.

"Who is it?" Kwame shouted.

"Man-Man," came a response.

"Shit!" Kwame mumbled to himself. He didn't feel like dealing with Man-Man. He knew Man-Man always wanted more for his money. "I hope this nigga got some real money this time. I'm tired of fuckin' wit' crumbs."

Kwame put his Desert Eagle .45 in his waistband, then unlatched the steel bar from across the door, unlocked the door and opened it.

Man-Man walked in happily, waving the $100, ready to 'beam me up, Scotty'.

"Say, youngsta. Hook me up for $100," Man-Man said, temporarily forgetting about the jackers' instructions.

"Man-Man, where in the fuck you get $100? Who you done fucked over this time?" Kwame asked. He knew whenever Man-Man had his hands on a large sum of money, somebody had got fucked.

"See, you worried about the wrong thang. Do you wanna make this money, or what?" Man-Man said, trying to rush Kwame to give him his money's worth.

Kwame didn't bother to get into a debate with Man-Man. He knew he couldn't out talk him, and everybody in their right mind knew Man-Man was scandalous. *I see why Dontae don't fuck wit' his uncle anymore,* Kwame thought. He figured Man-Man was right. It didn't matter where the money came from. Fuck it! It was going in his pockets anyway.

"You sho' right!" Kwame said, reaching in his pocket and pulling out a bag of fifty crack packets.

Man-Man's eyes lit up.

Outside, the jackers stood around impatiently in the back alleyway. Fifteen minutes had already passed by.

"What's taking that mothafucka so long?" Gator said. "I knew you shouldn't trust that old fool. He been in there over fifteen minutes. It don't take that long to take a hit."

"I know, Cuz. That's on me," Fresh responded, becoming frustrated as well.

"Fuck this standing around! Let's ride on them bitch ass niggas, Cuz," Gator said, anxious to bust a cap in a nigga's ass.

Gator and Fresh cocked their 9mm and .380 handguns, ready for whatever. They eased down the side of Woodpecker's house, stopping to peek through each window they passed.

Stepping on the front porch, they peeked through the thin, worn curtain at the front window. Man-Man and Woodpecker were sitting on the couch getting high, while Kwame was sitting in a chair nodding, trying his best to stay awake. Jaleel and Tre were nowhere in sight.

Fresh and Gator assumed Jaleel and Tre were somewhere asleep. Still, they had to be cautious. After watching for any more activity in the house, they decided to make their move. Quickly, they kicked the door open, guns pointed.

At that very moment, Kwame thought it was a drug bust and cussed himself for forgetting to secure the steel bar back across the door. Soon, he realized it was a different scenario, after seeing the familiar faces of the intruders.

"Lay down, nigga!" Fresh shouted as he walked towards Kwame while Gator held his gun on Man-Man and Woodpecker. At the same time, they watched for any sudden movements elsewhere.

Kwame was slow about following orders. He was undecided whether he should take the jackers seriously.

It seemed as if Fresh read Kwame's mind.

"Nigga, you think this is a game?"

Obviously Fresh was dead serious, especially after coming face to face with the same nigga who shot him. The bullet from the 9mm hit Kwame square in the chest. His body shut down instantly. Fresh fired another shot, making sure God wasn't on Kwame's side.

Woodpecker screamed, while Man-Man made sure he held onto his pipe and didn't lose any dope, though he was terrified that he just might be meeting his maker, or ol' Lucifer himself.

The sounds of screaming and gunshots brought Jaleel and Tre to their feet as they both came from the back rooms, running with pistols in hand. Tre was the first to make it to the front room. His first glimpse was Kwame, dead and slumped in the chair. Tre's reaction wasn't quick enough to dodge the flurry of gunshots that rattled his body, as his own pistol fired into the air before he fell to the floor, dead.

Jaleel watched his homebody get murdered right in front of his very eyes. There was nothing he could do – it was too late. The damage was done. He was out-manned and out-gunned. The only thing left to do was save himself. He fired off several rounds, creating some distance between him and the assailants so that he could make a getaway.

Fresh and Gator ducked back into the front room. That brief delay was just enough time for Jaleel to unlock the back door and run away.

Running down the street, tears began to fall from Jaleel's eyes. Both of his homeboys were now dead. All the dope and money he had was also gone. It's sometimes odd how things go from sugar to shit!

●●●●●●

"*Ring!...Ring!...Ring*! The constant ringing of the phone awoke Dontae the next morning. He rolled over and looked at the clock. It was 7:12 a.m.

"Who the fuck is this callin' this goddam early?" Dontae said, reaching over to the nightstand to pick up the receiver.

"Hello!" he shouted. All he could hear was crying. Immediately he sat up in the bed after recognizing his mother's voice. "Momma! What's wrong with you?"

"Dontae! Hur...hurry up," Dorothy paused to find the words to say.

More concerned now, Dontae said, "Momma, you scaring me! Now tell me why you're crying."

"It's Man-Man!" Dorothy said, crying hysterically.

"What about Man-Man?" Dontae asked, thinking Man-Man done ran off with some youngster's dope again. "What he do this time?"

All Dontae could hear were slurred words in between sobs.

"Help me, Lord! Give me strength!" Dorothy cried out. "Man-Man was found dead early this morning in South Dallas in some dope house," she continued, breaking down in tears again.

"What!" Dontae yelled, dropping the phone. The tears automatically began to fall. He was breathless. "No! No! No!"

Dorothy's voice could be heard echoing through the receiver that Dontae had dropped on the bed.

"Dontae, are you still there?" his mother asked.

He picked up the receiver after getting over his initial shock.

"Yeah, Momma, I'm still here. Are you sure it was Man-Man?"

"That's what the detectives said. They want me to come down to the coroner's office to identify the body."

"I'm on my way."

After coming from seeing Man-Man's body laid out on the autopsy table at the coroner's office, Dontae took it hard. One of his main goals was to help Man-Man get off drugs and get his life together. Now Dontae blamed himself for Man-Man's death, feeling like he didn't keep a watchful eye on him and let him down by not trying harder to help him kick his habit. The fact of the matter was, Man-Man was too far gone, way beyond help. The only person that could have helped him was himself. In all actuality, he was already a walking dead man. He was diagnosed with full-blown AIDS by a nurse who happened to take his blood at the county jail when he was booked in last month on a minor drug paraphernalia case. Man-Man never bothered to tell anyone, not even his family. He faced the fact that he was going to die a slow death, so he chose to commit every chance he got to getting high.

On the way home, after dropping his mother off at her house, Dontae stopped and picked up a newspaper. On the front page of the *Metro* was an article explaining the incident with Man-Man.

DRUG DEAL GONE BAD

At 5:00 a.m., four bodies were discovered dead by an unknown person at the 1500 block of Windelken Street. The victims suffered multiple gunshot wounds, and were identified as Debra (Woodpecker) Simpson, Antoine (Man-Man) Johnson, Travan (Tre) Smith, and Kwame Woodson. The shootings occurred at a house well-known as a common drug house. Detectives are still investigating. They speculate a robbery over money and drugs that turned fatal. No suspects have been arrested.

Dontae threw the newspaper to the floor. *Tre and Kwame was there too!* he said to himself, grieving for the two youngsters.

"Where the fuck was Jaleel when all this happened?" Whatever was going on, he knew he had to cut Jaleel off completely. The investigation was going to bring some major heat, and Dontae didn't want to be implicated in anything drug/murder related. Once everything died down, he would find out personally from Jaleel what went down last night.

Chapter Fourteen

Jaleel lay low for the next two weeks. Different people he ran into who knew he was tight with Tre and Kwame kept asking all kinds of questions. All Jaleel told them was that he didn't know anything. He attended both funerals, which was a hard task, especially when he witnessed his childhood friends die before his eyes. He managed to stay strong.

Since the incident involving Kwame and Tre's murders, Jaleel had tried on numerous occasions, to contact Dontae. For some strange reason, Dontae didn't bother to call back. He even tried calling from anonymous numbers, but when Dontae called and recognized Jaleel's voice, he hung up. The little money Jaleel had was getting low, and he needed some dope, badly. With barely $5,000 in his pockets, he drove down Dolphin Road, and headed to the East Dallas projects, rollin' in his 1972 Chevy Caprice, sittin' on 20's.

Pulling into the parking lot, he saw Shun standing outside talking to J-Rock. Jaleel noticed the playful flirting exchanged between the two of them, which drew some kind of suspicion in his mind. *Is this bitch fuckin' this nigga or what?* he thought as he pulled up to the curb next to J-Rock's Yukon sitting on 24's.

At the sight of Jaleel, Shun felt a sudden fear overtake her. *Damn! How I let this nigga sneak up on me? I hope he don't embarrass me and start trippin',* she thought. Personally, she knew that Jaleel could act a fool at times.

J-Rock reached his hand slyly inside his jacket, grasping the grip on the 9mm tucked away in his shoulder holster. Although he had known Jaleel for years and probably wasn't going to start trouble, you never can tell how a nigga is going to act over a bitch. J-Rock figured he'd rather be safe than sorry.

"What it do, youngsta?" J-Rock said, eyeballing Jaleel.

"Just chillin'," Jaleel answered, with his eyes fixed on Shun.

Her guilty conscience wouldn't allow her to look him in the eyes as she tried so hard to do.

"Why you lookin' at me like that?" Shun whined, smirking and rolling her eyes. "I ain't doin' nuttin' but just talkin'," she lied.

If Jaleel had been a few minutes later, he would have missed her, because Shun and J-Rock were on the verge of leaving together.

"Did I say you was doin' somethin'?" Jaleel replied angrily. "You must be guilty." He knew she was up to no good.

Turning away from her, Jaleel focused his attention on J-Rock.

Again, J-Rock positioned himself to pull his strap if needed.

"Wuz up on some work?" Jaleel asked.

"Some work?" J-Rock repeated with a bit of surprise in his voice. "I thought you was already on."

"I was, but that shit ain't poppin' no mo'."

"So how much work you tryin' to get?"

"I need a big eight."

"What? A big eight!" J-Rock shouted. "That's all? What happened to all that paper you was gettin'?"

"My connect fell off. It ain't like I was ballin' like you and Tony," Jaleel said, admitting to his misfortune.

"Umm, excuse me?" Shun said interrupting. "It's too cold out here for me. I'll be in the house when you through talkin' to J-Rock."

Without a moment's delay, she walked off provocatively, not bothering to wait for Jaleel's response. *Cock blockin' ass nigga!* she thought, referring to Jaleel.

J-Rock caught a glimpse at her voluptuous butt as he visualized their sexual encounter last night. *Ohhhh! I dicked that hoe down last night,* he thought. Erasing the thought, he focused his attention back to Jaleel.

"So, what's up? Are you gon' hook a nigga up?" Jaleel asked.

"Say, youngsta. If you serious about gettin' some real paper, holla back at me in about an hour," J-Rock said. "And by the way, what's up on you and Q'Tee?" This was J-Rock's way of trying to find out how serious Jaleel was about Shun. As quiet as it was kept, J-Rock was sprung over the young bitch in just one night. He admitted she did have some bomb ass pussy.

"We been broke up. Ain't nuttin' happening."

"Shit! I thought y'all were still kickin' it."

"Naw, playboy. We stopped fuckin' around last summer."

"It's been that damn long?"

Jaleel nodded.

"Then why the fuck is Tony still fuckin' wit' you about Q'Tee? I heard what happened between y'all at GiGi's," J-Rock added.

"I don't know what type of time yo' boy on. But that shit wasn't cool. I know that's yo' dawg, but..." Jaleel didn't finish what he wanted to say, but the expression on his face said it all.

J-Rock heard the bitterness in Jaleel's voice and assumed he was tired of Tony bulldogging him like he was a punk or something.

"Don't let that shit get to you," J-Rock said, consoling Jaleel, but at the same time he had the same animosity toward Tony.

"I'm straight."

The whole time rapping to Jaleel, J-Rock figured Jaleel could be the missing link to his plan. All he needed was some prepping. He walked over to his Yukon, reached inside and grabbed a pen and wrote his beeper number down and passed it to Jaleel.

"Don't forget to holla at me in a hour."

"Bet," Jaleel said, taking the piece of paper.

After pounding fist with J-Rock, Jaleel walked down the sidewalk to Shun's apartment. He was about to put her ass in 'check'.

J-Rock got in his Yukon. *I love it when a plan comes together,* he said to himself. His stereo blasted 50 Cent's 'Many Men' as he drove out of the parking lot of the projects.

Chapter Fifteen

Dontae struggled to get over Man-Man's death for quite some time. It was something he had to get over and let go. Death was part of life. When it hits close to home, it's never understood. So much happened in his life over the course of a few months; some good, some bad. Dealing with the situation with Naija still lay heavy on his mind. Then there was Q'Tee, a good wholesome girl.

It was now two months later since the incident at Tony's party, and he still hadn't talked to her. She tried calling him numerous times, leaving messages on his voice mail and two-way pager. He never bothered to return the messages. After weeks and weeks of no response, she stopped calling. Now Dontae was in denial. He couldn't believe he let a good girl get away because he was being so dumb.

Honestly, it was time to move on and put the issues of Naija behind him. He figured that he had a lot of explaining to do. His work was cut out for him to win Q'Tee back. To him, she was well worth it. After coming to his senses, he admitted to himself that he acted selfish in avoiding her. In all actuality, love and happiness had been staring him in the face the whole time.

He sat on the couch, flicking channels on the TV until he caught a show on TLC showing a wedding ceremony. He thought of the possibility of marriage. This is something he always wanted to experience, ever since he was younger, but those chances were ruined by prison and Naija's unfaithfulness.

For a few minutes, he thought of any chances of he and Q'Tee being serious enough to consider marriage. He felt she was a good woman with a good head on her shoulders, and probably would make a good mother to the kids he wanted.

The cloud that was hanging over his head about Naija was now gone. He had a clear conscience to actually settle down with Q'Tee without any doubts. Naija seemed to simplify everything. He visualized Q'Tee in his mind, admiring the charming smile she presented. He couldn't help but smile himself, as he thought back to the first time they made love. The few months they were together made him feel like they'd been together an eternity.

As these thoughts lingered in his head, he soon decided on the perfect way to win her back.

● ● ● ● ● ●

Q'Tee stood in her closet going through her clothes. She couldn't make her mind up on what she wanted to wear. Being Thanksgiving, she figured a night out would do her some good, and hopefully take her mind off of Dontae for a moment, which has been going on these past couple of months.

Still undecided, she flopped herself down on the bed. She felt like crying, but fought back the tears. She tried to come up with some answers as to what was wrong between her and Dontae. Everything was going so smoothly until after the night of Tony's party.

Dontae, what are you hiding from me that you don't want to tell me? I don't know why I'm making excuses for this nigga. Hell, he just like any other nigga? Get the pussy and a bitch don't hear nuttin' else from 'em. Fuck Dontae! But how in the hell am I gon' tell him I'm pregnant? she thought. *How could I be so stupid to let him fuck me without a rubber?* Q'Tee battered herself with questions. "Maybe its best for me to be single. I hate you Dontae for doing this to me!" she said blasphemously.

Quickly she went back to the closet and selected something to wear to the club. "I'll be damned if I sit around and let a nigga stress me out. I went through enough of that shit with Jaleel," she said, psyching herself up to block Dontae out of her mind.

Suddenly, the phone rang stopping her completely. She stood frozen. Her first thought was not to answer it, thinking it may be Dontae. Truthfully, she was hoping it was him. She couldn't keep lying to herself. She missed him dearly and wanted him to remain in her life, especially for the baby.

She answered the phone slowly, hesitating before finally uttering the word, "Hello!"

"Hey girl! What's up?" shouted Tiffany.

Q'Tee closed her eyes and exhaled as her heart began to beat at its normal rhythm after hearing Tiffany's voice. Even though she would have liked it to have been Dontae, she wasn't really ready to talk to him just yet.

"What's up, T?" Q'Tee asked.

"I was callin' to see if we still hittin' the club tonight."

"Hell yeah. I'm picking me somethin' out to wear now."

Tiffany noticed the cracking in Q'Tee's voice. She knew Q'Tee was still probably stressed out over Dontae.

"Have you heard from Dontae yet?"

"Hell naw! As a matter of fact… fuck Dontae! I ain't fixin' to sit around and wait on that nigga to call. I do have a life of my own," Q'Tee said, frontin'. She wished like hell he would call right now.

"Don't even trip. It's gon' be plenty of niggaz at the club tryin' to holla at you."

"Already? I'm 'bout to get my party on!"

Q'Tee knew she was fooling herself. She doubted she would even have half of a good time without thinking about Dontae.

"Come pick me up around 10:45. I want to get their early," Tiffany said.

Q'Tee figured Tiffany would never change. She always wanted to be the life of the party and would go to any extreme to gain it. Mainly, her sole purpose was hooking up with someone. Sometimes Q'Tee wondered how Tiffany could have sex with so many niggas and not give a damn.

"I'll be there. Just have yo' ass ready when I get there," Q'Tee said before hanging up.

● ● ● ● ● ●

When Q'Tee and Tiffany arrived at Club Blue, the crowd was gradually filling in. The club scene in Dallas was nothing like the club scene in Houston that Q'Tee was exposed to during her years in college. Music celebrities, professional athletes, or any well-known persons were always a regular appearance. However, the same knuckleheads, wanna be ballers and trifling hoes, always seemed to show up on a regular basis.

Looking around at the same old atmosphere, Q'Tee thought, *What the hell! I'm gon' enjoy myself anyway.*

Q'Tee and Tiffany walked through the dimly lit club. Along the way, Tiffany received hugs from numerous niggaz. Q'Tee shook her head. *Damn! Is she fuckin' all these niggaz?* she thought. They spoke to old classmates and friends. While talking, Q'Tee noticed Jaleel and J-Rock coming through the front entrance together.

"When they start hangin' together?" Q'Tee asked, nudging Tiffany and pointing in the direction of Jaleel and J-Rock.

"You haven't heard? Jaleel is working for J-Rock now," Tiffany clarified. "That's what I heard."

If anybody wanted to know the latest gossip and news, Q'Tee knew that Tiffany knew the ins and outs of everybody's business.

Q'Tee found the news to be very surprising.

"Girl, I'm fixin' to hit the dance floor," Tiffany said after being asked to dance. On the dance floor, Tiffany was getting down and dirty.

From across the room, Q'Tee watched her friend do her thing. She laughed at the way Tiffany went beyond the call of duty, grindin', bouncin' ass, poppin' pussy. The niggaz on the dance floor spent more time watching Tiffany rather than dancing with their partners. As she watched Tiffany, different niggaz approached Q'Tee to dance, or just to carry on a friendly conversation. She wasn't feeling either one. The thought of Dontae kept running rapidly through her head.

Every so often, she would catch a glimpse of Jaleel, trying to see what he was doing or who he was with. Before she knew it, Jaleel sneaked up on her and pinched her on the butt.

"What the fuck!" Q'Tee screamed, turning around and swinging at Jaleel.

"Whoa!" Jaleel said, gathering his footing.

Recognizing who he was, she felt a bit relieved.

"Boy! Don't be doin' that shit!" she said, punching him in the chest. "I thought you was somebody else. It was about to be on in this mothafucka."

"My bad. I just couldn't help it. I seen all that ass and just had to make sure that was all you," he said, giving her a desirable look.

Q'Tee blushed, tapping him lightly on the arm. "Don't let all this ass get you in no trouble."

"Always for you, baby," he smiled while winking his eye at her.

For some odd reason, Q'Tee enjoyed Jaleel's company. It had been a while since she saw him last. She had to admit he was looking good. His appearance showed her that he was doing well for himself.

"Say, Q. You want to dance?" Jaleel asked.

"I guess."

As soon as they made it to the dance floor, Tiffany stared at them. Q'Tee noticed, but avoided eye contact with her. Avant's 'Read Your Mind' set the mood on the dance floor. *The DJ would have to play a slow song. Just my luck!* Q-Tee thought. Each couple moved in a sensual rotation. Q'Tee comforted herself in Jaleel's embrace as their hips moved in the same motion, rocking back and forth. She became captivated in the moment, completely forgetting about Dontae. She closed her eyes and let the sound of the music relax her mind.

Feeling the slight hardness of Jaleel's dick, she looked up at him. He flashed her a smile, hoping she was feeling horny.

"Tame him," she gestured downward with a nod of her head, referring to his dick.

Instead of getting mad, all she could do was smile back, knowing it was all harmless fun. Besides, she knew things wouldn't go any further than she let it. They continued to dance to the music. Then suddenly, Jaleel was spun around.

"What the fuck is this!" Shun yelled, expecting some kind of explanation. "And what you doin' all up on my man?"

"Excuse me?" Q'Tee said, feeling a bit testy.

"Bitch! You heard me," Shun shouted, drawing a crowd.

In a speed faster than light, Q'Tee was all over Shun. Shun didn't know what hit her. Hair weave and patches of clothing, mainly Shun's, were ripped and flung all over the place. Niggaz gathered around, hoping to catch a free panty shot or see some titties pop out. Tired and mad, Q'Tee went into a frantic rage as she continued to claw, scratch and swing.

Suddenly, she felt herself being hoisted up and carried out of the club. She fought to get loose, but couldn't break free from the tight grip that had her up in the air.

"Put me down!" Q'Tee shouted while trying to keep her skirt from flying up.

Once she got outside of the club, she came face to face with the person who was carrying her. Realizing that it was her brother, she felt a bit relieved, giving her a feeling of security.

"Tony, what you doin'?" Q'Tee asked.

"I need to be asking you the same question. What the fuck is you fightin' in the club for? It bet' not be over that bitch ass nigga, Jaleel!" Tony yelled.

"Hell naw! I ain't fightin' over no nigga. That bitch he fuck wit' disrespected me. She got me fucked up," Q'Tee said, looking around outside for Shun.

Q'Tee noticed Jaleel and Shun being escorted out of the club by security. Q'Tee pushed Tony out of the way with strength she never thought she had. Tony stumbled to catch his balance.

Shun saw Q'Tee running in her direction and quickly shielded herself behind Jaleel. The first beat down was enough, and she definitely didn't want another.

Trying to move out of the way, Jaleel's reaction was too slow, as he caught a punch in the face that was intended for Shun.

Tiffany grabbed Q'Tee and was able to calm her down.

"Bitch! You don't know who you fuckin' wit'! Jaleel, you better tell that bitch!" Q'Tee screamed, still trying to go after Shun.

Watching Q'Tee still trying to fight, Tony became even more furious when he saw Jaleel. By the way things were looking to him, he assumed Jaleel was the reason Q'Tee got into the fight with Shun.

Jaleel saw Tony heading his way. *Aw, shit!* Jaleel thought as he prepared to deal with the outcome. He wished he would have brought his gun with him.

"Say, man. Why is you still causing my sister problems? I thought we straightened all this shit out the last time we talked," Tony said, all up in Jaleel's face.

Jaleel turned his head away to avoid the droplets of saliva that were hitting him in the face as Tony talked.

Feeling disrespected in front of the crowd, Tony swung hard, catching Jaleel squarely on the chin. Jaleel never saw it coming. The blow dazed him for a few seconds as he staggered back to keep his footing. Everything seemed blurry. Tony followed with a two-piece, knocking Jaleel to the ground.

Quickly, Q'Tee ran to the rescue. She punched Tony fiercely.

"Tony! Stop! Leave him alone!" Q'Tee screamed.

Fending her off, Tony said," I told this bitch ass nigga to quit fuckin' wit' you, and he just don't want to listen."

"He ain't done nuttin' to me," Q'Tee said, defending Jaleel like so many times before when Tony stepped in to show his overprotective brotherly love. She helped Jaleel to his feet.

Jaleel jerked away after getting to his feet.

J-Rock watched in the distance and decided to help resolve the situation. He figured he saw all he needed to see. He walked over to Tony, and pulled him to the side to straighten the whole incident out by giving Tony the rundown on what happened to start the fight between Q'Tee and Shun.

Q'Tee looked at Jaleel and saw the embarrassment, along with anger in his eyes. For once in months, she felt sorry for him. Tony had always had a dislike for Jaleel ever since Jaleel took her virginity. Ever since then, Tony gave Jaleel a hard time. Q'Tee figured Jaleel was sick and tired of Tony's bullshit.

Jaleel returned her gaze.

Q'Tee noticed the knot that was quickly swelling on the side of Jaleel's head. He walked away quickly with Shun hurrying behind him.

Q'Tee watched him get in the car with Shun and speed off. She inhaled deeply and let out a long sigh. *How many problems can a sistah take in her lifetime? First, Dontae; then being pregnant; and now this!* Q'Tee thought as she turned and looked in Tony's direction.

Tony's eyes met Q'Tee's, realizing he had fucked up again.

Chapter Sixteen

When Naija awoke Friday morning the day after Thanksgiving, she rolled over feeling for Tony. Realizing he wasn't in bed, she wiped the sleep from her eyes and looked over at the clock to see what time it was. Seeing it was 10:07 a.m., she wondered where he was. She felt like breaking him off a lil' somethin' somethin' this morning just to put some insurance in her weekly allowance.

She got up, threw her robe on and walked into the bathroom to take a pee. While sitting on the toilet, she thought about Dontae again. Her heart was yearning to be with him. She still wondered how he got all that money. To her knowledge, his name wasn't ringing in the streets, and she would be a fool to ask Tony whether he knew Dontae was selling dope. Then again, if anybody knew, Jasmine was the one. Jasmine knew every nigga that was a baller, and all the up and coming hustlers. Naija was going to make it her business to find out the 411 on Dontae.

After washing her face and brushing her teeth, she called her hairdresser to set up an appointment for later this evening. Afterwards, she walked downstairs looking for Tony. Again, it was the weekend; time for her and Jasmine to go pamper themselves.

"Tony!" she hollered once she made it downstairs.

"In here," came Tony's reply from the game room.

Naija walked in the direction of his voice. When walked into the game room, she was stopped dead in her tracks. She was in a total trance as she saw Tony and J-Rock standing over bundles of money scattered out over the pool table.

Looking at Naija's expression, Tony said, "Damn, baby! It look like you done seen a ghost. It ain't nuttin' but money."

Naija was at a loss for words and totally forgot about asking him about some money. She was in complete amazement at the amount of money in front of her. She always knew Tony had a lot of money, but not like what she was witnessing.

J-Rock caught the look on her face and he continued to stack the bundles of money in boxes. The greed was in Naija's eyes, and now J-Rock was wondering what she was thinking.

Once Naija gathered her thoughts, she snapped out of her trance and walked to the pool table. She picked up a stack of money and examined it closely, thumbing through the huge stack to see if it was actually real, or whether her eyes were deceiving her.

"It's real," J-Rock said, after noticing the disbelief in her eyes.

After packing and taping the last box, Tony was pleased to see his accomplishments: Seven years in the game, and now a multimillionaire. He walked out of the room, down the hall to his study to make a phone call, while leaving Naija and J-Rock alone together in the game room.

Making sure Tony was out of sight, she turned to J-Rock with the same surprised look still on her face.

"How much money is that?" she asked.

J-Rock chuckled. "It's $5 million, $500,000 in each box," J-Rock said, admiring her greed.

"Are you serious?" Naija said, overwhelmed. "I will be set for life with just one box."

J-Rock looked her over, giving some thought to what she just said, and decided to test her to see where her head was at.

"With the right decisions, you can get your hands on all the money," J-Rock said, while glancing over at Naija to catch her expression.

Caught off guard, she didn't fully understand the direction J-Rock was going with the conversation.

"What are you talkin' about, J-Rock?"

Peeping out of the doorway to make sure Tony was out of earshot, J-Rock said, "I'm sayin', there comes a time in your life when you must make decisions that will benefit you."

Naija inspected his eyes carefully and figured his motives were up to no good. However, what he was saying made a lot of sense. Otherwise, she drew the conclusion that he was plotting to do something really scandalous. Looking over at the boxes, she knew it had to be something involving the money. And for a minute, greed replaced all other thoughts as she looked back at J-Rock standing there with a devious grin on his face.

Finally, Tony walked back in the room, all smiles.

"It's all set up," Tony said gladly.

"Baby, what's all set up?" Naija asked curiously.

Walking over to Naija, Tony stared her in the face, and Naija became nervous by that look.

"Baby, I'm giving up the game, and now I have to wash all this money to make it legit, so I can spend any amount of money I want to without the Feds fuckin' wit' me. In a few weeks, we can go into business for ourselves," Tony explained as he lifted her up and spun her around.

After he set her back down, Naija played like she understood, but had no idea of the procedures of washing money. All she cared about was spending it. After seeing all that money, she wanted some of it, and not the measly allowances she had been getting.

Naija started to feel lightheaded from the thought, and decided she needed to be alone to give herself some time to think.

"I'm going upstairs to lie down. For some reason I've come down with a headache," she said, feeling self-conscious.

"Go get you some rest and I'll come check on you later, after I finish down here. I got the right thing to take away that headache," Tony said, flirting.

Naija faked a smile.

"I know you do, Daddy!" she said seductively. In the back of her mind she thought, *Nigga, if you only knew! The only thing that can take away this headache, is handing over all that damn money, and it definitely ain't yo' dick! Stupid mothafucka!*

Before going back upstairs, she gave Tony a kiss. Looking over her shoulder, she looked at J-Rock and noticed the same devilish grin.

After she walked out of the room, she quickly ran up the stairs to her bedroom and threw herself on the bed with a hundred questions running through her mind.

● ● ● ● ● ●

As J-Rock was leaving Tony's house, his heart was beating faster than normal. His adrenaline was pumping non-stop. He couldn't believe he just had his hands on $5 million. Everything was laid out perfectly. He thought it would take some more planning. In all actuality, Tony simplified the whole situation for him. J-Rock's plans to rob Tony had been replaying in the back of his mind for months. He plotted so many different times, and the pieces of the puzzle were finally together. His only hang-up was Naija. He really didn't want to see her get hurt, especially if things turned ugly. He knew she was a money hungry bitch. He was hoping she took heed to what he was trying to tell her. He thought back to how her eyes lit up when she saw all that money.

Right now, time was a big factor. He decided he didn't have any more time to wait. Thinking things out more only prolonged the situation. In a few days, Tony was scheduled to drop the money off with a stockbroker that Shorty hooked him up with, to set up legit accounts. J-Rock concluded that he had to make things happen quick! Time was money, and money was time.

He checked his messages on his cell phone. He got a kick out of hearing the messages from the different women that he was involved with. Everybody wanted something; bring some diapers; bring something to eat; bring some money; bring some dick! It was bring me this and bring me that. J-Rock laughed to himself.

His moment of enjoyment was interrupted when he heard the message from Jaleel. He could tell by his voice that he was ready. J-Rock figured Jaleel had a vendetta out for Tony, but didn't know how to approach the situation. Now with the incident that happened last night at the club, J-Rock knew Jaleel was looking for some get back.

Pulling Jaleel in under his wing, J-Rock propositioned him about getting his hands on some real paper, if it meant by any means necessary. Jaleel was leery at first about anything drastic or stupid, until J-Rock mentioned it had to do with Tony. Jaleel's eyes lit up and he became all ears.

J-Rock called Jaleel back, agreeing to meet him later. After hanging up with him, J-Rock was all smiles. *Yeah, nigga! You fixin' to get yours,* he said to himself, visualizing the game plan to take Tony all the way out the game.

Chapter Seventeen

Saturday afternoon, Q'Tee still lay snuggled up in her bed with her head buried underneath her pillow. She wasn't sleep, only thinking. She thought of the events that happened at the club two nights ago. *What a disaster,* she thought. She was very upset with her brother and very sympathetic toward Jaleel. She wanted to call Jaleel and apologize for her brother's stupidity, but she figured he wasn't in the mood to talk to her.

She looked back on all the decisions she made since she graduated from college. "Maybe I should've stayed in Houston instead of coming back home," she considered. Probably her life would have been better. She only came back home to be closer to her mother, even though she was only a few miles away. Truthfully, she missed home. And, at the time she missed Jaleel. Now that she was in love with Dontae, everything changed.

It seemed like all her past experiences were repeating themselves over and over again. She thought back to Dontae and wondered if he had called while she was asleep. She rolled from underneath the covers and checked her voicemail on her cell phone and two-way pager. No messages, at least not from Dontae.

She flopped back in her bed. Again, she worried herself with thoughts. She quickly began thinking about her pregnancy and hoped the fight with Shun didn't make her lose her baby or develop complications. "It might be best if I didn't have a baby," she admitted as she buried herself under the covers.

Dontae was racing against time. He wanted everything to be right. He had spent a bit of money on food, roses, champagne, gifts, a limo and driver, and other necessities. No big deal – money wasn't a problem.

He had just dropped off 50 kilos to Reg and Isaac and collected $200,000. Business was rolling. Reg and Isaac had mad clientele. They were hitting out of town licks, taxing niggaz out the ass coming in from Oklahoma, East Texas and Louisiana. As soon as Dontae received his shipment from Hector, Reg and Isaac had over half of the work sold the same day.

Many times Hector wanted to move the shipment up to 150 kilos, now that Dontae was moving over twice as much dope than he was when he first started out. Dontae concluded that 50 kilos was enough for one week. He had millions, and was steadily stacking paper. His six months was almost up, then he would retire from the game, paid in full.

He sent all his homeboys back in prison $3,000. Sergio declined any money. He just sent his blessings.

As time was winding down, Dontae noticed it was nearing 5:00 p.m. He had called Q'Tee's mother to let her in on his plans to surprise Q'Tee. Her mother was not to let Q'Tee leave for any reason. Being that Gloria adored Dontae, she didn't mind participating in his plan. He was just hoping she could keep Q'Tee occupied until he got there. He knew things were going to be difficult. But the hard part was going to be convincing her to come with him.

●●●●●●

Q'Tee was waking up from her long, drawn out sleep. Despite all the problems she was facing, she felt she needed some rest to relax her mind. She figured she and Tiffany would hang out at the mall, and later go out to eat and maybe catch a movie that night, if Tiffany didn't have any freak session set up. *I need me a freak session,* she thought, feeling horny.

She went to her closet and grabbed her Baby Phat wool skirt and matching sweater, along with her riding boots. Afterwards she went to take a bath. As she undressed, she looked in the mirror at her stomach. She knew it was too early to detect any signs of showing, though her cravings for junk food were constant. She visualized her stomach sticking out, grimacing at the thought.

After taking a bath, she got dressed, had her hair whipped, makeup intact, and was looking like America's top model with a donk-a-donk! Taking one last look at herself, she puckered up her lips and blew a kiss at herself in the mirror. "Eat your heart out, Beyonce," she said, admiring her glamorous look.

Heading to the door, her mother stopped her.

"Don't leave right now," Gloria said, looking at her watch, trying to buy some time.

Q'Tee didn't feel like hanging around the house any longer, especially as good as she was looking. She wondered what her mother wanted.

"What is it, Momma?" she said, frowning.

"Girl, don't you get smart with me! I don't know who you think you is."

Q'Tee rolled her eyes as she shifted her weight to one hip.

Gloria struggled to think of something to tell Q'Tee to make her stick around a little while longer to give Dontae time to show up.

Q'Tee waited impatiently for her mother to say something, which happened to stall her long enough.

A big, white stretch limo pulled up in front of her mother's house. Q'Tee saw the limo and wondered what was happening.

"Who is this?" Q'Tee asked blankly. "They must got the wrong house."

Gloria fought to hold back her smile. She felt relieved to have held Q'Tee up for those few minutes. She played along like she had no idea why the limo was out front.

Q'Tee watched as the driver made his way up the walkway. She met him at the door before he had any chance to ring the doorbell.

"May I help you?" she asked politely.

"Yes, you may. I'm here to pick up a Ms. QuaTesha Williams," the driver said.

Her face was filled with bewilderment, and she became more curious as to why a limo was there to pick her up.

"I'm QuaTesha Williams, but I don't know anything about a limo coming to pick me up."

"This is compliments of a Dontae Johnson."

For a second, she fought to catch her breath after hearing Dontae's name, and the fact that he had sent a limo to pick her up.

"Where is he?" she demanded.

Without answering, the driver gently grabbed her arm. Out of reflex, she jerked away.

"Hold up now! I don't know what kind of game this is, but I ain't got time to play. So tell Mr. Dontae it was nice of him, but the game is over," Q'Tee fired off.

●●●●●●

Dontae stared out of the dark tinted windows from the back seat of the limo. It was hard to tell what she was saying, but her body language told him she was giving the driver a hard time. "I knew she was gon' be trippin'," Dontae mumbled, hoping she had a change of heart and gave him a second chance.

●●●●●●

Afraid he was pissin' Q'Tee off, the driver didn't know what to do from that point.'

Wanting so much for Q'Tee and Dontae to reconcile their differences, Gloria stepped in. She wasn't about to let Q'Tee make the biggest mistake of her life by letting a good man get away.

"Excuse me! What is your name?" Gloria asked the limo driver.

"It's Scott, ma'am," the driver said.

"Please, Scott, come on in and have a seat," Gloria said, scooting Q'Tee aside to let Scott pass. "Q'Tee will be ready to go in about five minutes."

Scott did what he was told and took a seat in the living room.

Q'Tee looked at her mother angrily

Gloria looked back at Q'Tee with an attitude. "And you!" Gloria added, talking to Q'Tee. "Follow me!"

"Momma!" Q'Tee whined. She noticed her mother's facial expression showing she meant business. In her 22 years, Q'Tee had been familiar with that look far too many times in her life. She knew that whatever her mother wanted to talk about was serious. Without putting up any more fuss, she followed her mother into the guestroom.

Looking directly in her daughter's eyes, Gloria said, "Q'Tee, there comes a time in life when you must follow your heart. Being in love is something special that doesn't just come every day. At times, it may not always be perfect, but if the situation can be resolved, try to work it out. Deep down inside your heart you love Dontae, and it's obvious he loves you. I've seen the way you've been moping around here, all stressed out over him. Whatever's going on with y'all more than likely can be worked out if the two of you just sit down and talk."

"But, Momma, I tried talkin' to him. The only thing he did was shut me out," Q'Tee stated her reasoning.

"Chile, you have a lot to learn. Men are hard to understand. Whatever's bothering them on the inside, they run from it rather than handle it. They're so egotistical they don't want women to see their soft sides. They feel like it makes them weak. I went through the same thing with your father. All I ask you to do is give him a chance to come clean. And if it sounds like a bunch of bullshit, then you have your own mind to move on," Gloria expressed, feeling admiration for Dontae.

Q'Tee let her mother's words linger for a minute. There was no doubt, she was in love with Dontae and wanted so much to have him back in her life. Realizing the truth, she hugged her mother for broadening her mind to what she really wanted.

"I love you, Momma," Q'Tee said, hugging her mother.

"I love you too, baby," Gloria said, starting to shed tears.

Breaking their hug, Gloria playfully pushed Q'Tee out of the bedroom door and up the hallway to the front foyer of the house.

"Now, go and get your man!" Gloria whispered.

Impatiently, Dontae sat in the limo in suspense. His mind was in a frenzy. His eyes stayed glued to the front door of the house. "What's taking them so damn long in there?" he said, frustrated. A couple of times he wanted to walk up to the front door and knock. His intentions were not to leave without Q'Tee hearing him out.

Finally, he saw the limo driver and Q'Tee coming out of the front door, arm in arm. Dontae's eyes bulged out of their sockets. *The moment has finally come,* he thought as he prepared to greet her.

Making it to the limo, the driver politely opened the back door for her. Instantly, Dontae and Q'Tee were staring eye to eye.

Dontae was GQ to the fullest, wearing Cartier framed glasses, a stylish Yves Saint Laurent three buttoned suit, and David Eden square toed, horn back gators, accentuated with a blue-gray mixed mink coat by Mr. Biggs' fur collection. He defined the phrase 'So fresh and so clean'!

He smiled at her presence as he slid over in the seat to give her room to sit down. At first, she wanted to make him beg for her forgiveness because of how he had been treating her these past few months. But the love and desire she had for him pushed her on inside the car. Besides, it was too cold to be standing outside.

The driver shut the door once she was inside the limo.

"Hey!" Dontae said, handing her a bouquet of roses.

She allowed herself to smile when she accepted the roses. She felt like crying, but didn't want to let him think he was getting the benefit of the doubt.

On their journey to Dontae's designated spot, he apologized to her for his actions. Also, he confessed about he and Naija's relationship before going to prison. To play it safe, he left out the details about what happened at Tony's party.

Q'Tee forgave him and agreed to start over. She was yet to tell him about her being pregnant. She decided to weigh her options to see if there was any truth in admitting that he and Naija were completely over.

They discussed their relationship until finally, they arrived at the Hyatt Regency Hotel. The driver got out of the limo and opened the door for them.

Before getting out, Q'Tee turned to Dontae and asked, "Dontae, what are you up to?" She was thinking he got a hotel room just for them to have sex. She wasn't planning on giving in that easy, even though she wanted him desperately to make love to her.

"Just c'mon, baby. Please!" he said, buttering her up.

Finally, she gave in. He led her through the double doors, into the lobby and to the elevator. They rode the glass-enclosed elevator all the way up to the Reunion Tower that overlooked the City of Dallas.

"Close your eyes," he said before the elevator doors opened.

Q'Tee smirked at his request, soon realizing he was dead serious, and closed her eyes.

Exiting the elevator into the restaurant, he surveyed the room, making sure everything was still in its proper place. With a look of approval, he allowed her to open her eyes. When she did, she was in total awe of what was in front of her. Roses and various types of flowers were scattered throughout the room; a live band was playing; the whole room was dimly lit, and a table displayed candlelight setting for two.

Dontae had outdone himself. He rented out the whole restaurant for just him and Q'Tee. It was expensive, but he figured she was worth every dime.

The maitre d' led them to their table. Dontae politely pulled out her chair, allowing her to sit down. She was amazed at the romantic setting he had prepared. She was definitely impressed, and at that moment, she erased all doubts about him playing her off the rebound.

Marinated pot roast with sides of carrots and potatoes, fresh garden salad and Crystal champagne was served.

Q'Tee was speechless. The evening was displayed with superb elegance, as the band played all the hottest slow jams. As they ate, they became more relaxed. Q'Tee was swept away, floating on cloud nine.

After dinner, they danced to several songs, intensifying the desire for one another.

Later, he led her to the hotel suite he had waiting for them. His surprises were getting better by the minute. The hotel suite looked like an upscale condo on the inside. She was fascinated at how he went overboard to prove his love. No man had ever treated her this way before. Jaleel was too gangster to have class and style, and the niggaz she dated in college were on a tight budget, limiting them from going out of their way to impress her, especially when they found out she wasn't coming off with the 'nookie'.

Attempting to sit down, Dontae stopped her.

"Hold up. Before you sit down, let me show you something," he said, grabbing her hand and escorting her to the bathroom. Inside, he presented her with a warm milk bath filled with rose petals. Once he presented the cozy setting, he left her alone.

Thank you, Momma, for not letting me give up on this nigga, she said to herself, fascinated by the royal treatment.

She undressed, then stepped in the milk-filled tub and sat down. She felt relaxed and exhilarated as the warm milk worked its wonders on her body. *This is the next best thing to being in heaven,* she thought. In more ways than one, Dontae was her knight in shining armor.

About fifteen minutes later, the sound of the bathroom door opening startled her attention as she opened her eyes. The sight of Dontae standing there butt naked hypnotized her. Her eyes focused right in on his ten inches of manhood. Q'Tee licked her lips, effortlessly imagining him in her mouth.

As he approached, her eyes never lost focus. It seemed as if the closer he got, the harder he became. Without a word being said, the chemistry between them told them what they both wanted.

Dontae stepped into the tub to join her, and they took each other to heights unknown between them, sexually, mentally and physically. Their future flashed in their minds.

After forty-five minutes of enjoyable lovemaking, they cuddled together, cherishing the moment.

Out of the blue, Q'Tee whispered, "I'm pregnant!"

Dontae's reaction was sudden, practically scaring Q'Tee. He searched for the words to say as he stared into her eyes. She returned his gaze, wondering what he was thinking. He rose quickly and sat on the edge of the tub. She rose up behind him, afraid to touch him.

"What's wrong, baby?" she asked.

Dontae turned around to look at her with tears streaming down his face. Seeing his tears, she wondered whether they were happy tears or sad tears. She grabbed him and embraced him tightly. Her tears began to fall too.

"I'll get rid of it, if that's what you want," she said tearfully.

Quickly, he pushed her back, holding her at arms length with a streak of disbelief on his face.

"No!" he said loudly.

Half confused she asked, literally crying, "Do you want me to have it?"

Dontae looked at her for a split second more and took her into his arms.

"Yes, baby! Yes! I want you to have our child!"

Chapter Eighteen

Sunday night, Naija and Tony had just made it home around 10:00 p.m. Tony figured spending quality time with Naija the entire day would make up for any lost time he deprived her from. On the real, Naija wasn't trippin' about any quality time from him as long as he kept the dollars coming. But she had to make him think he was special.

Once inside the house, he disarmed the alarm system while Naija pranced upstairs to the bedroom with her shopping bags.

Tony thought about proposing to Naija. He considered doing something special to enhance the mood, but he figured if she wanted to marry him, it didn't matter where he proposed.

In a few days, all his money would be legit. Now he could actually live a life without having to look over his shoulder. He felt as if he accomplished everything he wanted to do so far. The only things missing were a wife and kids.

Naija was undressing to get ready to take a bath. She knew Tony was going to want some pussy, especially after wining and dining her and catering to her fashion needs.

Sitting on the side of the bed in her panties and bra, she thought about Dontae again, imagining how her life may have been if she had stayed down for him. *I can't believe I let money come between my chance for happiness,* she said to herself. For fifteen minutes, she thought long and hard about ending her relationship with Tony. She felt that she had come to a dead end in her life, which now depended on making the right choices. Finally, she decided she needed to follow her heart. She admitted to herself that she really loved Dontae and wanted to spend the rest of her life with him, even if it meant giving up Tony and the benefits of his money. First, how would she explain this to Tony? How would he accept that she never loved him? All kinds of questions ran through her head.

Naija quickly grabbed her robe and put it on. "Well, here goes nuttin'!" she said, heading out of the bedroom.

As she made it to the bottom of the stairs, she heard loud voices that sounded like arguing, along with things being tossed around. At first, she told herself that Tony had the TV up too loud, something he usually did when watching a movie and utilizing his surround sound. As she got further and further down the hallway, the voices became clearer. She recognized a voice that sounded like J-Rock's.

Curiosity, more than anything, took control of her sense of thinking. Walking into the game room, she saw Tony being held at gunpoint by a younger man she soon recognized as Jaleel. Shocked, she froze in place. *I knew that wanksta ass nigga J-Rock was up to something, but I never imagined this!* she thought, paranoid.

J-Rock was opening the boxes of money and emptying the stacks in big plastic garbage bags. Simultaneously, Tony's and J-Rock's eyes met Najia coming through the doorway of the room. Being that Jaleel's back was to her, he didn't notice her, but soon caught the stares of Tony and J-Rock, and quickly turned around, feasting his eyes on Naija.

Jaleel completely lost the focus of his intentions once he saw that Naija's robe was half open, which exposed her black bikini panties and bra that covered her smooth caramel skin. After meeting Naija for the first time over at Q'Tee's mother's house years ago, he had always been infatuated with Naija. Now lust filled his eyes. *I ought to fuck her after I smoke this bitch ass nigga, Tony,* Jaleel thought.

Tony was attentive to the lingering stare Jaleel had on Naija. He quickly rushed him, tackling him similar to his days of playing linebacker in high school. The gun flew in Naija's direction as Tony and Jaleel fought and tussled on the floor. Again, Tony was the dominator, hitting Jaleel with a flurry of punches.

J-Rock realized the situation was getting out of control. He grabbed his gun and pointed it at Tony.

"Get off him!" J-Rock yelled.

Tony stood up slowly with his hands extended upward.

Jaleel lay on the floor with his eye swollen shut, and he struggled to get up. He was dazed from the beat down from Tony.

Tony watched J-Rock carefully as he approached him slowly.

"C'mon, J-Rock. Let's talk about this," Tony said, trying to convince J-Rock to have second thoughts.

J-Rock watched as Tony slowly crept. His heart was beating rapidly and sweat covered his face. He continued to hold the gun at arms' length, his hand shaking uncontrollably. In his mind, he had second thoughts, but he knew he was in too deep to turn back now. He knew it had to come down to killing Tony, and possibly Naija. Maybe Jaleel too if push came to shove.

"Just stop right there, Tony, before you make me bust a cap in yo' ass," J-Rock shouted.

Stopping, Tony begged. "We boys! It don't have to come down to this."

Tony saw he was getting across to J-Rock and continued talking. *I guess that TV shit do work,* he thought, contemplating his next move.

"We built this shit together. I love you like a brother. It ain't even 'bout the money. Your friendship is more important than this money," he added, using reverse psychology. Tony knew that if he ever got the ups on J-Rock, he was going to kill him.

After regaining his stability, Jaleel's intentions to kill Tony were desperate. No more stalling. He looked around for his gun and quickly noticed it lying a few feet from where Naija was standing, terrified. As Jaleel made a move to retrieve the gun, everyone was alarmed by his sudden movement.

Realizing what Jaleel was trying to do, Naija beat him to the gun. She picked it up and pointed it at him, stopping him dead in his tracks. He stood with his hands in the air, grimacing in pain.

J-Rock saw that Naija had the gun drawn on Jaleel. *This is not what I had expected,* J-Rock thought, as he wondered on how to bring the situation to an end. Death was the only option.

"Naija, give the gun to Jaleel!" J-Rock shouted, hoping to scare her.

Naija stood nervously, her eyes traveling from Jaleel then back to J-Rock.

"No you don't, baby! Just keep it pointed on that nigga," Tony told her with his eyes still fixed on J-Rock.

Tony analyzed J-Rock closely; his eyes; his composure. He sized J-Rock up like a boxer looking for a knockout punch. He continued to talk to J-Rock, trying to alter his thinking. *Keep him talkin',* Tony thought, moving in a little closer. He felt he was close enough to make a move. He saw the fear in J-Rock. His eyes told the story. In a million years, Tony would have never thought his own boy would try to rob him, or even try to kill him for that matter. So much for homeboys. In the game, no one is to be trusted, not even your closest friend or kin.

Tony felt it was do or die. Suddenly, he dropped below the firing range of the pistol and plowed his massive body into J-Rock's direction. On impulse, J-Rock fired a shot, clearly missing Tony as he felt his body jolted back.

There was a loud scream along with a low grunt. The bullet hit Jaleel in the chest, piercing his heart. He fell dead instantly, lying in a pool of his own blood.

Naija went into shock, panting and trying to catch her breath. The tears began to run down her face as she trembled with fear, surprise and remorse at witnessing a death.

Meanwhile, Tony and J-rock struggled to gain possession of the gun. They rolled around, fighting each other for dear life.

The gun kept sliding from their grasps. They both scurried over the floor to obtain it. Tony was able to grab it first, and he quickly stood up and pointed it at J-Rock.

"Say hello to my little friend!" Tony said, mocking Al Pacino in the movie *Scarface*, and he squeezed the trigger.

J-Rock flinched to take the impact of the bullet, but there was no shot, only clicking. He looked down at himself and noticed there was no blood. He wasn't hit! He fixed his eyes on Tony, breathing vigorously and expecting a gunshot blast to take his life.

Tony squeezed the trigger again, then again and again. Still the same results. Obviously the gun was jammed. Tony and J-Rock both stared at one another. Then they stared at Jaleel's lifeless body on the floor. Looking over at Naija, Tony noticed that she still held the gun in her hand as she stood there motionless and in tears.

"Naija, give me the gun," Tony said as he continued to watch J-Rock.

She snapped out of her trance when hearing Tony's voice. Although still frightened, the thought of the gun in her hand brought her back to reality. The conversation that she and J-Rock had Friday appeared clearly in her head. The thought of $5 million expanded her mind to what her life would be like with all that money for herself.

Her eyes surveyed the room, from Tony, to J-Rock, to Jaleel's dead body on the floor, and finally to the bags of money on the floor. She gathered her composure, now becoming the villain. She pointed the gun at Tony. He was shocked and confused by her reaction.

Stepping back, Tony said, "Baby, what you doin'? Just hand me the gun."

Naija looked at J-Rock, who still had the same gleam in his eyes that she remembered perfectly.

J-Rock noticed Naija's sudden change and wondered if she was now on his side. *Money makes a bitch do the strangest things,*

J-Rock thought. He positioned himself to move in closer to hopefully disarm her.

Naija noticed his movement and fanned the gun from side to side, from Tony and back to J-Rock, then back again.

Tony continued to sweet talk her as he inched his way toward her, extending his hand, hoping she would hand over the gun. *Just wait, bitch. I'ma beat yo' mothafuckin' ass just as soon as I get that gun from you and kill this punk ass nigga!* Tony thought.

Naija backed up with his every forward step. She shook her head back and forth.

"No, Tony. Stop!" she cried out through shedding tears.

Tony decided to charge her in the same way he did with J-Rock to dislodge the gun from her. Unfortunately, the reaction to his sudden movement caused Naija to pull the trigger. *"BOOM!"* The explosion was loud and earthshaking. Realizing she shot the gun sent Naija into a panic as the gun fell from her hand to the floor.

Watching the gun hit the floor, J-Rock ducked, avoiding getting shot from the ricochet of stray bullets.

Tony lay on the floor with a gunshot wound to his head. His body went into convulsions, shaking rapidly. The blood flowed from his head like an open faucet. He tried to speak, whispering, but no words came out. He gasped quick breaths, holding on to his last dose of life.

Naija dropped to her knees, wailing. She knelt over Tony's lifeless body. She shook him continuously, as if he had just fallen asleep. Then, reality hit her that he was actually dead.

J-Rock quickly snapped to his senses from a shocked state of mind. He stood over his long time friend, and acknowledged the fact that Tony was really dead. He looked around at the scene and immediately ran to the window and peeped out to see if any neighbors heard the gunshots. Satisfied that everything was clear, he returned and embraced Naija. He helped her to her feet, and she held on to him tightly, crying non-stop. He was thinking on how to make a clean getaway without ever being suspected. His first task was to get Naija under control.

"Naija! Quit cryin' and get yourself together!" he told her while holding her at arms' length and staring her directly in her eyes.

She kept crying and talking erratically.

J-Rock shook her hard.

"Listen!" he shouted, then calmed himself. "We have to get out of here."

Naija went from crying to whimpering, trying to regain her composure.

J-Rock saw that she had calmed down some and let out a sigh of relief.

"What we gonna do?" she asked, wanting to burst out crying again.

J-Rock looked around desperately, seeking an answer. "Finish filling those bags with the money," he told her.

Damn the money! she thought. Naija was ready to go, but she figured she might as well do as she was told. If J-Rock's motive was to rob and kill Tony, evidently it was the same for her. She started stuffing the bags with money while taking glimpses at Tony's body lying helpless in front of her. She wished he was just asleep. The tears began to fall once more.

J-Rock grabbed the guns and wiped them off with a towel. He went throughout the room, wiping areas that he may have touched. Afterwards, he helped Naija finish bagging up the money. Once all the money was deposited into the bags, they stacked the bags by the door.

"What now?" she asked, frightened.

He looked at her and noticed she was still wearing a robe, which was now completely open. He caught a sneak peek at the fullness of her breasts and the gap between her legs, but quickly focused his mind back to the situation at hand.

"First, we got to get you upstairs and put you on some clothes," he responded.

Naija looked down at herself and realized she was half naked. They hurried up the stairs to the bedroom, and Naija quickly tossed her robe onto the floor. This time, J-Rock got the full view of her standing in her thong bikini panties and bra. He shook his head at her flawless body. *Damn! I see why Tony was so sprung over this bitch,* he thought to himself while feeling a hard-on rising.

Naija grabbed her clothes she had on previously and put them back on while J-Rock paced back and forth, trying to come up with an alibi for the both of them.

"We have to get our stories together," he demanded.

"Why don't we just say it was an accident?" she suggested.

"What! Do you actually think the police is gon' believe this shit was an accident? C'mon, Naija! Use your head!" he told her.

Naija sat on the corner of the bed with her head buried in the palms of her hands. Her mind was racing a hundred miles an hour.

After several minutes had passed, J-Rock finally plotted up a story. He coached her through her whereabouts during the time Tony and Jaleel were shot and killed. She had calmed down to a minimum, but the frightening experience lay heavy on her conscience.

It was J-Rock's idea to split the money after the heat died down from the incident. Naija agreed. Relying on their alibis supposedly would erase them from ever being suspects.

After getting their stories down pat, they walked downstairs to load the money into the trunk of J-Rock's car. The gruesome scene replayed itself all over again in Naija's mind.

J-Rock walked outside, checking to see if anything seemed suspicious before getting into his car and backing into Tony's driveway. He sat for a few seconds as he went over the course of events that had just happened. "What have I gotten myself into?" he said, totally not believing what had just happened.

They loaded the bags in the trunk. Afterwards, he again went over the instructions that he wanted her to follow.

"I want you to get in your car like I told you. Go to your momma's house, get some rest and call me in the morning. And, whatever you do, don't tell Jasmine!" he explained.

She nodded in agreement as she wiped her tears.

J-Rock hugged her tightly, assuring her everything was going to be alright.

"Trust me. We're gonna get out of this," he confirmed.

They separated from their embrace. He looked at her, examining to see if she comprehended what was going on. With no other conscious purpose other than to get away paid, they departed the house, one after the other, heading in different directions.

Heavily, they both wondered if either one was to be trusted.

Chapter Nineteen

It was after Christmas, heading into New Years. Weeks had passed by after Tony and Jaleel's deaths. Their funerals were big turnouts, mainly nosy onlookers seeking something to gossip about. The scene seemed like a reenactment of Biggie and Tupac's funerals.

At Tony's funeral, Naija's guilty conscience wouldn't allow her to view the whole ceremony. At the sight of Q'Tee and her mother's grief, she fainted, more so faking as an excuse to get away. Friends and relatives led her to the family limo where she stayed until the funeral was over.

The stories that Naija and J-Rock created temporarily set well with the detectives involved in the case, after hours and hours of interrogating. The detectives were tipped that there was an ongoing beef between Tony and Jaleel, which may have escalated into retaliation on Jaleel's part and an unknown accomplice, which ended up fatal.

The investigation was still open, so that didn't put Naija and J-Rock in the clear just yet, considering that supposedly another suspect was still at large.

Naija slowly packed away her clothes in boxes. She just couldn't bear to stay in the house any longer after witnessing Jaleel's death, and being a part of Tony's murder. Besides, Q'Tee had already decided to move in, so the sooner Naija left, the better.

As she walked through the house gathering her things, she thought if she only would have gone back to Dontae when the opportunity presented itself. She wondered if there was any slim chance for them to get back together after all that had happened.

She was very self-conscious about the police finding out her involvement in the murder. She also wondered if J-Rock would mess her out of her share of the money. Her biggest worry was being able to live a normal life without going crazy or arousing any suspicion to her, once she started spending the money. She figured that once the heat died down, she would be able to buy her own house with new furniture, and move on with her life.

●●●●●●

J-Rock felt a bit relieved now that the detectives were off his back about the murders of Tony and Jaleel. It had been almost two weeks since he last talked to them. He was wondering if the case was closed. He hadn't seen anything in the newspapers or on the news about any leads or ongoing investigations.

The thought of the money was creating desires in his mind beyond his wildest imagination; luxurious houses, boats, cars, exotic trips around the world, and beautiful women of all nationalities.

Then there was the thought of Naija and the fact of having to split half of the money with her. He debated whether he should give her anything. He figured he did have the upper hand on her because she couldn't go to the police about the money. She would be implicating herself to murder. He knew she wasn't that stupid. *"Maybe I could use the money as a bribe to get the pussy,"* he thought as he visualized her in her bra and panties on that particular night.

He continued to relax on the sofa, preparing a mental agenda in his head on how he was going to spend the money. All those thoughts were immediately put on hold when Shun approached him, naked. At first, their relationship started out secretly. Now that Jaleel was dead, their involvement became more open.

He admired her smooth, dark skin spread over a brick house of a body. Despite the tender age of nineteen, her body was fully developed. Young and thick! The perfect combination.

J-Rock just couldn't get enough of Shun. Not that he loved her, but her expertise in the sex category kept him coming back. It's a shame for someone to be that young and be so freaky. Project chicks!

As Shun sat down beside him, she slid her hand inside his boxers and felt he was already hard. He let out a soft moan as she caressed his dick gently. In seconds, she devoured him into her mouth, slowly sucking, tantalizing and teasing him with her tongue.

J-Rock rocked back and forth, enjoying the magnificent dick sucking he was receiving. "You one bad mothafucka!" he moaned as he placed his hand on the top of her head, controlling her movements.

Unexpectedly, a hard knock at the door interrupted them. He jumped up quickly, hoping it wasn't one of his other female freaks deciding to pop up on their own and make themselves welcome.

Checking the peephole, he saw a group of men standing at the door wearing fatigues, jackets and bulletproof vests. Realizing they were the Feds, he griped. "Oh shit!"

Hearing him curse loudly, Shun asked sarcastically," Who is it! One of your other hoes?"

"It's the Feds!" he whispered. "Go put some clothes on."

J-Rock hurried and slid his pants on and opened the door.

"Yeah, can I help you?" J-Rock said nervously.

"Are you Jarius Miller?" the federal agent asked.

J-Rock hesitated for a second, then finally confirmed. "Yeah, that's me."

Flashing a badge the agent said, "I'm Agent Jim Jones with the FBI and we have a warrant for your arrest."

J-Rock was in disbelief as Agent Jones showed him the federal arrest warrant, which read: **"CONSPIRACY TO DISTRIBUTE COCAINE/CRACK COCAINE."**

All hopes and dreams were slowly fading away.

Agent Jones read him his Miranda Rights, and then asked him a few questions. The other officers did a thorough search of his house. After coming up empty handed, they escorted J-Rock to a waiting police car.

Shun was also taken into custody for outstanding traffic warrants.

●●●●●●

Two hours later, after his arrest, J-Rock sat in the interrogation room at the Northern District Federal Building surrounded by FBI agents and detectives. He had been indicted on a conspiracy to distribute cocaine/crack cocaine and multiple counts of drug charges.

The agents and detectives continued to drill him with questions about Tony and Jaleel's murders. The detectives informed him that he was the primary suspect in the murder investigation, basing the motives on drugs and money.

"Well, Mr. J-Rock! That is what they call you, huh, son?" the agent asked with a southern country drawl. "You Black folks shor' come up with the weirdest names."

J-Rock didn't find the agent's remarks to be amusing, but kept his cool. He was in no position to get on their bad side.

"Now that Tony is dead, that means you are liable for all the drugs listed in the indictment; the whole 500 kilos," the agent added.

"What? How you gon' charge me with all that dope? I ain't got caught with a damn thing," J-Rock shouted.

"Easy! We do what we want to. I got plenty of people willing to testify on you. Now, I advise you to start doin' some talking, boy," the agent said, as he got in J-Rock's face.

J-Rock held in his anger, although he wanted to knock the mothafucka out. He figured the agent was just bluffing to scare him into talking.

"I ain't sayin' shit until I see a lawyer."

"Ain't that some shit! You big dope boys always comin' in here requesting a lawyer, thinkin' y'all can win the case, or better yet, buy the case. Let me tell you somethin', Mr. J-Rock. That shit don't fly with us. Do you hear me, boy? This is a different ballgame now. So its best you help yourself, or its going to be some repercussions," advised the agent.

After three long hours of interrogations, J-Rock had taken all he could take. The officers gave him all kinds of scenarios that put him at the murder scene. Never once did Naija's name come up. They presented information that proved his alibis were totally bogus.

After finding out his bond was denied, labeling him a flight risk, he was booked in the county jail, a place he dreaded the most. He hated even having to sit out unpaid traffic tickets. And now he was having to stay in jail until the case was resolved, more so, found guilty. With a 99% conviction rate for the Feds, guilt would usually be the outcome unless an act of God changed the whole situation.

He called his mother, who spent the first five minutes lecturing him about 'I told you this, and I told you that!' J-Rock was in no mood for her guided words on defining his wrongdoings. He had her contact a lawyer for him.

The next day, around noon, a lawyer sat face to face with J-Rock in a conference room at the jail. The lawyer introduced himself as David Youngblood. Mr. Youngblood displayed all the information to J-Rock's case; surveillances, drug buys, recorded conversations and photos of possible drug transaction. Also, signed statements and affidavits from confidential informants.

J-Rock read through some of the paperwork. His mind became familiar with dates and places. He even noticed the time when he, Tony and Naija went to the Deluxe Inn and purchased 20 kilos. Quickly, he thought about how Naija tried to warn him about the suspicious activity of a white man, but he and Tony wouldn't listen.

"It seems they have a serious case against you, based on all the information that's in front of me," Mr. Youngblood told J-Rock.

J-Rock shook his head, agreeing with the lawyer's comments. He believed there was some truth in his words.

"Okay, Mr. Youngblood. Be straight up with me. How much time do you think I'm looking at?" J-Rock asked directly.

"Well, honestly, if it goes to trial, you could be looking at 30 to life because of the crack. But with a plea, anywhere between 15 to 20 years," Mr. Youngblood said, justifiably.

"Aw, hell naw! You got me fucked up! I can't do no time like that. I got kids and some mo' shit!" J-Rock shouted and stood up pacing.

Mr. Youngblood wasn't shocked by J-Rock's outburst. Out of his fifteen years in practice, he knew it was a routine reaction he witnessed so many times from clients that were facing lengthy prison sentences.

J-Rock sat down to settle his nerves. He wanted some closure to the situation that had just swallowed him up. He massaged his temples with his fingertips, trying to relax his mind. In actuality, it was going to take more than that.

Mr. Youngblood looked over at J-Rock and decided he had cooled off, and started back to discussing the depth of the case.

"Jarius, those are just the possibilities. I still haven't researched the case in its entirety. There's a chance I may find a loophole, and then I also may be able to pull a few strings. Just be patient. These things take time."

"Fuck pullin' some strings! See if you can pull some ropes and get me out this bullshit!" J-Rock responded sarcastically.

"I'll be back to see you in a couple of weeks," Mr. Youngblood said, gathering his things to leave. "By the way, they're moving you to the Federal Detention Center in Seagoville. It's a lot better than being here."

"A couple of weeks?" shouted J-Rock.

"Like I told you before, these things take time. It's not an overnight process," Mr. Youngblood said politely.

Mr. Youngblood excused himself from the conference room, and J-Rock was taken back upstairs to his cell.

J-Rock lay on his bunk, thinking of everything that had happened in his life over the years. Nothing could add up to what he was facing now.

Chapter Twenty

Naija was settled back in at her mother's house. She spent most of her time over at Jasmine's apartment to keep from having to hear her mother's continuous bickering.

She was lucky enough to get a job at General Motors car manufacturer. Her mother, who worked as a supervisor for 25 years, helped Naija get a job there. Having not worked in three years, it felt funny to be on the job again.

As Naija sat in Jasmine's apartment babysitting lil' J.J., she thought about how she was going to get her share of the money now that J-Rock was in jail. Jasmine informed her that the charges they had on him were serious. Naija wanted to go visit him, but knew it might bring some suspicion to her, especially from Jasmine, being that Jasmine and J-Rock were still on good terms. *I hope like hell he don't bring my name up,* Naija said to herself.

She began to feel nervous again and the thought of going away to prison for a long time, or even getting the death penalty, surfaced in her mind. She started to get fidgety. She couldn't remain still. She paced back and forth, biting her fingernails. She needed to talk to someone, quick--someone who was able to give her some insight as to what's going on and what to do.

She quickly thought about Dontae. She figured since he'd been to prison, he probably could give her some advice. The question was, could she trust him with everything that happened? Surely he wouldn't turn her in to the police.

Later on, she knocked at Dontae's door at about 8:49 p.m., unannounced. She hoped he let her in. Also, she was hoping she didn't come at a bad time, thinking he might have company, Q'Tee to be exact. She saw his car in the parking lot when she pulled up, but Q'Tee's BMW was nowhere in sight.

She adjusted lil' J.J. on her hip and knocked again, this time harder. She heard the sound of locks being opened, and within seconds, the door was swung open.

Dontae stood in the doorway with just a towel wrapped around his waist. Drops of water trickled down his body, sliding over his sculpted muscles.

It was obvious to Naija that he was in the shower. She stared at his body admiringly before he soon invited her in.

Dontae shut the door and fought back the urges that he secretly desired for her.

"What brings you by?" he asked, puzzled.

"I need to talk to you about something. Hopefully I didn't come at a bad time," she said, expecting Q'Tee to come out of the bathroom in a towel herself. Imagining him and Q'Tee making love in the shower made her somewhat jealous.

"Talk?" he asked sternly. "I thought we talked enough last time. It seemed we got a perfect understanding then."

"Please, Dontae!" she pleaded. "Just listen to what I have to say. It's very important!"

Hc just couldn't rcsist her sexy eyes.

"Let me finish taking a shower, and I'll be right back in about ten minutes. Just make yourself comfortable."

Naija occupied her time by playing with Lil' J.J. while Dontae finished showering. Images of Dontae's body flashed in her mind. She thought about going in the bathroom where he was, pretending she had to pee really bad so she could get a full view of his body. She felt a tingle run through her body. It had been weeks since she last had sex. She was definitely horny. Desperately, she wanted to experience the same feeling that he gave her the night of the party, just one more time. If so, forever!

Dontae walked back into the living room and sat down across from her. After becoming acquainted with Jasmine's son, he spent time playing with Lil' J.J. while Naija started to explain the events that happened the night of Tony and Jaleel's murders, followed by J-Rock's arrest.

After spending over an hour talking, Naija was hysterical. She was crying like she was before, as if reliving the same night all over again.

Dontae was in complete suspense as he tried to calm Naija down. He couldn't believe what he just heard.

"What am I gon' do, Dontae?" she asked, still crying.

He hesitated before speaking, trying to come up with a logical answer that didn't sound too farfetched.

She saw the worried look on his face that told her all she needed to know.

"Dontae, tell me something!"

He figured he had to be straight up with her about everything, so that she wouldn't expect anything differently if she was arrested and convicted.

"First, you need to hope that J-Rock don't give you up. The Feds have a way of twisting your arm to give them the information that they want in return for a lesser sentence," he explained.

"So you think J-Rock is gon' snitch on me?" she said, panicking.

"It's a possibility, especially if the shit is as serious as you say it is."

Dontae caught the expression on her face after what he told her. The tears began to fill up in her eyes again. He was beginning to feel sorry for her. Even though they weren't together, he still cared a great deal about her, and the last thing he wanted was to see her suffer. *But, at the same time, you can't mix the bitter with the sweet!* he thought.

"I guess I'll just have to sit around and wait to see what happens," she said, dryly.

For a minute, she thought about turning herself in and declare it was self defense. *Hopefully, the judge will be lenient on me. Please! Not in the United States,* she speculated to herself.

"I wish I could tell you somethin' you'd rather hear, but Suga, you have gotten yourself in some serious shit," he announced seriously.

Naija nodded in agreement. She enjoyed hearing him call her 'Suga'. That used to be his pet name for her back in the days. She wished like hell she had those same days back. As she briefly closed her eyes she imagined those days.

Naija figured Dontae had explained enough to fill in the blanks on what she didn't know. She decided it was time to go.

She knew Jasmine was probably wondering where she was with her child.

"Thank you, Dontae, for your help," she said, reaching to hug him.

Dontae returned her embrace as she clung to him tightly, not wanting to let go. Her body was so soft and comforting to him. This was a moment he was scared of.

As she held onto him like there was no tomorrow, she could feel the rapid beat of his heart against her chest. She knew there was still heated friction between them. She looked up at him. Not being able to resist her, he leaned in and kissed her ravishingly. She returned his kiss with sincere passion as she grind herself against his erection.

Dontae wanted this to happen, but knew it couldn't. It would only confuse the situation. And, he would be back to where he started. Right now, he had too much at stake with Q'Tee, and the fact that she was pregnant and he promised her he was through with Naija. And now, he was kissing the killer of Q'Tee's brother. He quickly backed away from her.

"We better quit," he said, gesturing in the direction of Lil J.J. as to say he didn't want to expose the child to what they were doing.

Naija pulled back and walked over to Lil J.J. and helped put on his coat and hat. Leading him to the door, she passed Dontae and whispered, "Can I come back after I drop the baby off at home?"

A part of him wanted to tell her "yes," but he had to turn her down.

"I don't think that would be a good idea, considering what just happened between us."

She was unhappy, but she knew it was for the best. She kissed the side of his cheek.

"Thanks for everything--in more ways than one!" she said sadly.

Closing the door behind her, he leaned up against it, thinking how could he keep the trust in the two women he cared so much about. He felt his future was with Q'Tee, but a part of his heart still remained with Naija.

Decisions, decisions, decisions!

Chapter Twenty-One
(One Month Later)

J-Rock sat with his lawyer again, discussing the severity of the charges against him.

"Well, Jarius," Mr. Youngblood said, exhaling deeply. "I have some good news, and some bad news."

"Lay it on me," J-Rock said, dryly.

"The bad news is the state is trying to indict you, better yet, convict you on two counts of first degree murder, in which they are seeking life in prison without parole, or maybe the death penalty depending on whether you want to play hardball," he stated while checking out the reaction on J-Rock's face.

J-Rock dropped his head in dismay. He wanted to cry, shout and kick, but he knew none of that could help him now. He needed something more powerful. A prayer and a blessing from God.

"I hope the good news is better," J-Rock said with a slight bit of hope.

"Well, the U.S. Attorney's office is offering a plea of 180 months."

"180 months! How much time is that?" J-Rock shouted.

"That's approximately 15 years."

"You mean to tell me for $50,000, the best you can get me is 15 years in the Feds and a death certificate in the state?" J-Rock shot back, highly pissed off.

Mr. Youngblood had finally gotten fed up with J-Rock's constant bitching every time he came to visit. He figured it was time to quit playing 'Mr. Nice Guy'.

"Look!" Mr. Youngblood snapped, pounding his fist on the table. "You are as guilty as O.J. Simpson, so don't give me this bullshit like you're so fucking innocent. The best thing for you to do is try and help yourself by telling me what you know about those murders!" he added, giving J-Rock the real deal on how the system worked.

J-Rock sat for a few minutes, quietly thinking. He thought all about the time he was facing, and knew he would never see freedom again unless he did some talking. He had always had a hatred toward a snitch, and now he was being forced to be one. After minutes of thinking, he finally decided to come clean with everything about the night of Tony and Jaleel's deaths, along with other information that may lead to the prosecution of the other drug dealers. He spent over two hours explaining the details leading up to the deaths.

His lawyer made written notes, as well as kept mental notes in his head. He continued to listen calmly and quietly, making sure he didn't miss anything. He figured he had to really pull some strings in the case to get J-Rock a lesser sentence. In his mind, he knew by the murders being drug related, it created such a big impact, because of the desire the courts and law enforcement agencies had on getting rid of all drug dealers, by any means necessary – whether in a jail cell or six feet deep.

"Okay, Jarius. You've given me something to work with that just might help you in the long run," Mr. Youngblood assured him. "I'll pass this information along and get back to you in a few days."

Chapter Twenty-Two

At her brother's old house, Q'Tee was lying on the couch while Dontae had his hand on her stomach, hoping to feel the baby kick again.

"You feel that?" she asked, surprisingly.

"I ain't feel nuttin'," he said, disappointed.

Q'Tee moved his hand around her stomach, trying to locate another kick. She was in her sixth month and was as big as a house. She was very excited, and also thrilled that she and Dontae were back on the right track in their relationship. She wanted a girl, but knew that Dontae was hoping for a boy. They decided not to take a sonogram. Whatever the child came to be, she knew the baby was going to be loved regardless.

She was finally comfortable staying in Tony's house. Her first few weeks were unbearable, to the point she had gone back home to stay with her mother. Too many of Tony's things kept being a constant reminder to her, and created memories.

Dontae had really been a big help by staying overnight after he would get off work, which helped ease the burden and pain. He managed to get a job working as a security guard. The pay wasn't all that, but he wasn't trippin'. He was sitting on millions. Besides, he got the job because he promised Q'Tee he would give up the dope game. More so, it got the pressure off of him from his parole officer.

She wanted him to move in permanently, but he refused. He just didn't feel comfortable knowing Naija used to lay up and fuck Tony in the same house. It was bad enough he was spending the nights. He only dealt with it on behalf of Q'Tee being pregnant. As a surprise to her, he was in the process of having a house built just for them and the baby.

As she continued to wait for another kick from her baby, she began to think about Tony not being around to see his first niece or nephew. Slowly the tears began to run down her face.

Dontae quickly noticed her sudden change and comforted her.

"Why did they have to kill him?" she cried out.

Dontae rocked her in his arms while she cried tremendously. In his mind, he wondered whether her tears were going out to Jaleel as well. Just like him, she was still holding on to distant feelings. He thought about everything Naija had told him, and mentally asked himself, *How could he not have told Q'Tee what happened?* He felt like he was stuck between a rock and a hard place, as he continued to hold her in his arms until she finally calmed down.

"I'm sorry," she said.

"It's alright. I know you still miss him," he replied sympathetically.

"We barely ever told each other we love one another, and now he's gone," she said, fighting herself not to cry again.

"He knew you loved him," he assured her.

Q'Tee gathered her composure and wiped her tears.

"When they find out who killed my brother, I hope they give them the needle," she said coldheartedly. She got up from the couch and walked out of the room.

Dontae wanted to go after her, but figured she needed to be alone. He began to think again. Ever since Naija had stopped by his apartment and confessed about the murders, she had been calling him practically every night, leaving messages. The times he caught or returned her calls, they carried on friendly conversations about old times. A few times, he invited her over. There was never a doubt in his mind that he would get busted, because he knew Q'Tee was in no shape to leave her house to drop by his apartment.

Dontae knew he couldn't allow himself to go backwards again. Soon, he was going to ask Q'Tee to marry him, but now his guilty conscience was starting to get the best of him. He knew she would never forgive him if she found out he knew all along that Naija was the one who killed her brother. One day, everything was going to surface. What's done in the dark will come to the light! Believe that.

●●●●●●

Waiting to see his lawyer again, J-Rock was nervous when he walked in the conference room at the detention unit, and noticed his lawyer accompanied by two unknown men dressed casually in business suits. He sat down and studied the faces of the other two men.

"Jarius," Mr. Youngblood said as he introduced the two men, "This is Ken Powell of the U.S. Attorney's Office, and this is Detective Nick Anderson."

J-Rock greeted them both with a slight nod as they stared at him as if with a vengeance.

"Mr. Miller, I hear you have some valuable information to tell us," Detective Anderson said, pulling out a small notepad and pen.

J-Rock nodded as he straightened his posture in his chair.

The detective positioned his tape recorder so that it would pick up J-Rock's statements clearly. Then, he motioned for J-Rock to proceed. J-Rock nervously explained the incident once again, this time crying as he went on.

All three men wrote their share of notes as they continued to listen to J-Rock's detailed story through sniffles and pauses.

After going through a series of questions, the detective and U.S. Attorney felt satisfied with J-Rock's cooperation. They excused him from the room for several minutes as they discussed standard procedures concerning J-Rock.

As J-Rock waited in another room, he wondered if he had done the right thing. He hated to have to snitch on Naija, but he felt she was the ticket to lesser time, along with the names of other drug dealers he dealt with in other cities.

Finally, his lawyer called him back into the room.

"Here's the deal; If what you're telling us turns out to be true, then we can drop the first degree murders down to involuntary manslaughter, which by chance just might get you ten years in state prison," the lawyer said.

J-Rock let out a sigh of relief and relaxed more freely in his chair.

"Now, with this federal case," J-Rock sat at attention. "We might be able to get that 180 months down to 120 months, which is ten years and likely to run concurrent, so you'll be out in eight years," the lawyer confirmed.

J-Rock wanted to jump and scream, but instead he said a silent prayer, then shook everyone's hands.

"Don't get happy now. Those are just the recommendations based on whether you're being straight up with us," U.S. Attorney Powell said.

"Everything's straight up. You can count on that," J-Rock responded assuredly.

Chapter Twenty-three
(Three Months Later)

The courtroom was packed with family members, friends, nosy outsiders and reporters. Naija was on trial for first degree murder. Today was her final day in court. The verdict could change the rest of her life, for the good or the bad.

J-Rock managed to get a deal for nine years on his federal case due to his cooperation. Now, his testimony in Naija's trial will be missing the piece he needed to seal his fate. Not only did he win the system, but he won for the money he and Naija had stolen from Tony. He successfully convinced the authorities that he and Naija only took a small portion of Tony's money; $100,000, which he told was divided evenly between the two of them. In all actuality, J-Rock had the $5,000,000 stashed away for safekeeping until he got out of prison. Only one person could put their hands on the money when needed to – his mother.

Naija looked around the crowded courtroom, identifying faces. She saw her mother and sister, along with her friend, Jasmine. They all waved, showing their support. As she continued to look around the courtroom, her eyes fell upon the cold stares of Q'Tee and her mother, Gloria. Naija quickly turned away, embarrassed to dare look at them. If only she could turn back the hands of time. She never intended any of this to happen. *Apologizing to them will never justify or take the place of a life,* she thought remorsefully.

Blocking what they thought of her out of her mind momentarily, she soon realized she didn't see Dontae. She drifted her eyes around the courtroom again, hopefully to see him sitting somewhere she may have overlooked. Apparently, he was nowhere to be found. *That's funny. He's been here for all my other hearings, and today, the day of sentencing, he's not here,* she thought, confused. She wondered where he could be. *Maybe he's still having it hard dealing with Q'Tee concerning the fact that he withheld vital information from her about Tony's death,* she thought. Naija massaged her temples, not able to cope with the turmoil.

Quickly, Naija's attention was brought back to reality by the judge entering the courtroom from his chambers after waiting for the jury to deliberate. The judge ordered silence in the courtroom as he pounded his gavel loudly. Silence flooded the courtroom immediately.

"Jurors, have you reached a verdict?" the judge asked.

"Yes, your honor. We the jury find the defendant guilty of first degree murder!" the jury representative said.

Naija couldn't believe her ears. She was in complete shock.

The chatter in the courtroom erupted, along with crying.

Q'Tee caught a glimpse of Naija's response to the verdict. In a way she felt sorry for her, but feeling sorry for stupidity just didn't mix.

"Order in the court!" the judge shouted as he pounded his gavel repeatedly. After the noise was brought down to a silence, he began with the sentencing phase. "Ms. Naija Taylor, will you please stand."

Naija stood up slowly. Her knees felt weak because of the heavy burden she was now carrying. She focused her eyes forward, staring directly at the judge, noticing his hard features. She wondered what he thought of her.

The judge examined her closely. *My child, how did you ever get yourself into something as serious as this. The price to pay behind living life in the fast lane,* he thought sympathetically. He has seen on many occasions young men and women alike waste their lives away behind stupid mistakes.

"Ms. Taylor, would you like to say anything on your behalf before sentencing?" he asked.

Sniffling, she wiped away the tears from her eyes and the snot from her nose. "Yes, your honor, I would." She paused, gathering her thoughts. She took a deep breath and continued.

"I would like to apologize to the family of Tony Williams. I truly understand that there's nothing I can possibly say to justify what I did or bring Tony back, for that matter. I promise you that everything that has been presented to you is not all true. I am guilty for my actions, but I am not the heartless animal the court portrays me to be. I just pray and hope that one day you will forgive me. I am truly sorry!" As Naija finished up her final words to the court and Tony's family, the tears began to fall again. She cried hysterically. The bailiff had to come calm her down.

Q'Tee also cried, mostly for her brother. She felt the sincerity in Naija's words. She figured Naija was regretful, although the whole incident was over money. It just so happened her brother's life was taken as well. Q'Tee sensed it all along that Naija's greed for money would soon catch up to her, but it wasn't expected to end up like this.

After Naija gained her composure, the judge continued. "Well, Ms. Taylor, my heart goes out to you. I really hope you can learn from all that's happened. Frankly, I'm here to uphold the law and see that justice is served for the victim and for the defendant."

"Ms. Taylor, you have done a senseless thing with little thought for the lives you were going to effect. Why? Over money, I assume. Obviously, you had every motive to benefit from the financial gain of Mr. Williams' money if you had successfully gotten away with this heinous crime."

"Therefore, I sentence you to a term of fifty years in the Texas women's penitentiary, to be served immediately. Court is adjourned!" The judge pounded his gavel, left the bench and headed back to his chambers.

Naija dropped to her knees. She screamed over and over. Streams of tears ran down her face. "NO! NO! NO! NO! Lord, don't do this to me!" she shouted. Her mother, sister and Jasmine ran over to comfort her. The bailiff let them have a few minutes alone.

"It's gon' be alright, baby," her mother said, teary eyed as she hugged her oldest daughter tightly. "Just be strong. The Lord will make a way."

Naija nodded her head, assuring her mother that she would be fine. Sadly, their time had to come to an end when the bailiff stepped in and announced it was time for Naija to go. She quickly hugged her baby sister and Jasmine. Finally, she was handcuffed and escorted out of the courtroom.

● ● ● ● ● ●

Dontae waited out front on the steps of the courthouse. He kept pacing, often taking glimpses at the engagement ring he had in his pocket. For once in his life, he was finally making the right decision.

He saw Q'Tee wobbling out of the doorway of the courthouse with her mother. Even in her ninth month, she still looked good. Dontae assumed the trial was over. He couldn't bear to watch it any more, especially after keeping Q'Tee in the dark about everything. A part of him kept asking whether he was there for Q'Tee, or was he there for Naija. Undecided, he chose not to show up in the courtroom any more.

Dontae knew for sure Q'Tee was still angry with him, but he couldn't blame her for being mad. He really had to prove that he was deeply in love with her. This time, a fancy dinner, a live band and elegant hotel suite, filled with a night of sensual lovemaking wasn't going to win her back. His only chance of hope was the fact that she was carrying a part of him in her body.

As he approached Q'Tee, she threw her hand up, stopping him.

"I ain't got time, Dontae!" She pushed past him.

"Q'Tee, please hear what I got to say," he begged. "Baby, I love you!"

Q'Tee stopped, turned around and frowned at him angrily. She walked over to him and stood directly in his face, staring him in his eyes. Then she slapped him across the face viciously.

Her mother, Gloria, was shocked at her daughter's reaction and afraid of Dontae's response.

Dontae turned his head from the impact as he raised his hand to rub the side of his face to soothe the stinging. He flexed his jaw to alleviate the slight pain. Slowly, he turned to face her, trying to read her mind and her intentions.

Feeling like she had conquered her frustrations, Q'Tee said, "How dare you say you love me! You don't even know the meaning. How could I be so stupid as to ever involve myself with you." Her words ripped Dontae's heart apart. "And, by the way the bitch you really love just got fifty years! I figure she needs your love and support more than I do," she emphasized sarcastically.

Dontae swallowed hard, imagining how Naija must be feeling right now. He continued to plead with Q'Tee for her forgiveness. Clearly, she stood her ground.

Suddenly, Q'Tee felt the pain shudder through her body. She started to feel lightheaded and grabbed on to Dontae.

"Dontae! I think the baby is coming!"

Dontae panicked while looking around at her mother for some assistance or advice. Quickly, they hurried Q'Tee to the car and off to the hospital.

●●●●●●

After returning to her cell, Naija finally faced the reality that she was going to prison for a very long time. She called her family and Jasmine. They all assured her that they would stay supportive by writing and coming to visit. That helped ease the pain some. Her biggest worry was Dontae and why he didn't show up today in court. He had promised her he would be supportive despite the problems she caused in his relationship with Q'Tee. Naija couldn't seem to understand his disappearance, especially since they had gotten closer as friends these past few months. She admitted that she needed him more so in her life, to help endure the setback that had devastated her life. She wondered if he knew what her sentence was. She decided to call him.

The phone rang a few times, and she wondered why he hadn't answered or the voicemail hadn't picked up. After the forth ring, Naija was shocked at the response.

"You have reached a number that has been changed. If you feel that this is an error, please hang up and dial again," the recording said.

Naija hung up and tried calling again, and got the same response. She then called his cell phone number, and the number was no longer in service. Violently, she slammed the phone down and began to cry. She soon realized that Dontae had finally erased her from his life for good. Now she understood what it meant to need someone you truly loved to be there for you throughout the struggles of the lowest points in life. A lesson taught, a lesson learned.

●●●●●●

At the hospital, Q'Tee gave birth to a baby boy, weighing seven pounds and three ounces, after being in labor for six hours. Despite the heartaches, she dealt with the death of Tony, and the drama with Dontae and Naija; it now was replaced with happiness. As she held her baby in her arms, she smiled at Dontae.

Dontae enjoyed the birth of his first child. He realized he had a family to call his own. He gave Q'Tee and his baby boy a kiss.

"I love you," Q'Tee expressed.

"I love you too," Dontae replied.

Being so caught up in the moment, he had forgotten all about his proposal. Quickly, he remembered the ring in his pocket and fumbled inside to reach it. Getting down on one knee, he presented the ring to her.

"Will you marry me?" he asked.

Q'Tee was shocked as tears began to flow from joy. She took a slight glance at her mother. Gloria gave her a nod of approval.

Turning back to face Dontae, Q'Tee shouted, "Yes! Yes! Yes!"

Dontae placed the ring on her finger, then kissed her hand.

Gloria was overjoyed. She finally got a grandchild, and now she was getting a son-in-law, of whom she was definitely proud.

During all the excitement of planning the wedding, the nurse walked in, interrupting the happy moment.

"My, my, my, this is a happy room," the nurse said.

"It is! We're getting married!" Dontae said proudly.

"Congratulations! First a new baby, and now a wedding. How lucky can a girl get in one day," the nurse said, smiling and winking at Q'Tee. "I must say, your day has been filled with nothing but joy."

Q'Tee smiled and looked at Dontae.

"It surely has," Q'Tee said, admiring her soon-to-be husband.

Holding the clipboard, the nurse asked, "Have you named the little fella yet so I can put it on his birth certificate?"

Q'Tee, Dontae and Gloria looked at each other, realizing they hadn't named the baby because of being caught up in the wedding plans.

"Oh my God! We haven't decided on a name for the baby!" Q'Tee said, totally ecstatic. "What should we name him?"

Dontae thought for a few minutes, and decided on the perfect name.

"How about Anthony? In remembrance of Man-Man and Tony."

Epilogue
(One Year Later)

Living happily married was the life Dontae had always dreamed of. Now he was finally experiencing everything he sought out to do. At times, he replaced Q'Tee with the thought of Naija, and wondered what life would have been like if they had gotten back together. Unfortunately, Naija was a thing in the past. He was very much in love with Q'Tee. She was everything in a woman that he could ever ask for. Most of all, she made him happy and completed him in every aspect of living.

Dontae took the money he made in the dope game and invested it wisely. He started his own real estate company and built the dream house he always wanted for his family. Also, he set up trust funds for his two children: his son, Anthony, and his newborn daughter, Daisha.

Q'Tee, herself, finally got the position she wanted in the company she worked for. She was the top sales accountant for a prestigious mortgage company. She enjoyed married life as well. Dontae catered to her and the kids' every need. What more could she ask for in a man?

Dontae sat in his study, going through the mail. As he isolated the bills from the miscellaneous mail, he came across an envelope that caught his attention. The handwriting was very familiar, but no return address was written. Out of curiosity, he opened the envelope. He was in for the shock of his life when he saw what was inside.

Dear Dontae:

     I'm probably the last person you want to hear from. I was just sitting here in my cell thinking. As always, you popped in my thoughts. If you're wondering how I got your address, I got it from ol' trustworthy Jasmine (smile). I hope you're not mad. The last thing I want to do is come between your happiness. I had my chance and blew it. You showed me the meaning of true love, and instead, I took it for granted. Sure, we had our share of ups and downs. But who doesn't? Instead of working out our differences, I chose the coward's way out and surrendered myself to a world beneath my character God! I wish this all was a dream. That I can wake up and everything will be back to normal. Unfortunately, it's not that easy. In all my life, I never wanted to be anyone else until now. This may sound funny, but I wish I was Q'Tee. I'm the one who's supposed to be your wife, the mother of your children, and live happily ever after. Right now, I envy Q'Tee. I know I'm wrong to say it, but I'm supposed to be wearing the title of Mrs. Dontae Johnson. Not her! It's too late to bitch now, huh? I had my chance and fucked up. All I can say is thank you for the good times, and for showing me what love was all about. If I never hear from you, or never cross paths again, always know you will forever hold a place in my heart.

Love,
Naija

     Dontae threw the letter down on the desk. Again, thoughts of Naija ran through his head. A part of him was glad to hear from her. However, he had to continue to block her out of his life. He grabbed the letter and tore it into small pieces, and dropped them in the trashcan. Clearing his mind, a knock at the door halted his thoughts.

Hurrying to the door, he opened it. The sight that appeared on the front porch was a scene that will replay in the back of his mind over and over.

The Feds arrested Dontae on conspiracy charges. Reg and Isaac cooperated with the government and gave up Dontae as their supplier in return for a lesser sentence.

Six months later, Dontae went to trial and was found guilty. He received a sentence of 360 months in federal prison.

J-Rock resided in FCI-Beaumont medium correctional facility. He was asleep in his room on the top bunk. He was feeling tired from working p.m. kitchen, and decided to hit the rack early. Being so sound asleep, he didn't hear the door to his room open and shut.

Suddenly, his mattress was snatched from the top bunk, with him falling to the floor. The three unidentified inmates stabbed him repeatedly. Screams for help could be heard throughout the run, but no one made it their business to come to his aid. That's what it was... only business!

After the assailants were through putting in work, they left the scene the same way they came in, cool, calm and collected.

When J-Rock's body was found, he was dead from multiple stab wounds to his torso, face and hands. Also, there was a note found on his body that read, "SNITCHES GET DEALT WITH".

Dealing with a lengthy sentence and a lost love was too much for Naija to handle. She started to break down mentally. Psychiatrists evaluated her, labeling her mentally disabled – crazy to be exact! She now resides in the psychiatric ward in the women's prison in Gatesville, Texas. Presently, she is still undergoing tests and evaluations. As of now, no improvement has been gained. She is watched around the clock until further review. Her records state she is borderline suicidal.

Q'Tee is still being the typical good girl ... For now!

Street Knowledge!
"So Real You Think You've Lived It!"

Upcoming Novels From Street Knowledge Publishing

Coming Fall of 2006

No Love-No Pain
By: Sicily

The Hunger
By: Norman R. Colson

Coming 2007

Bitch Reloaded
By: DeJa King

Dopesick 2
By: Sicily

Playin' For Keeps
By: Gregory Garrett

Stackin' Paper
By: JoeJoe and DeJa King

Shakers
By: Gregory D. Dixon

Sin 4 Life
By: Parish M. Sherman

Dipped Up
By: Visa Rollack

No Other Love
By: "Divine G"

M.U.C.C.
By: Ronald Jackson

Lust, Love, & Lies
By: Eric Fleming

Dirty Livin'
By: Fernando Seirra

The Fold
By: Tehuti Atum-Ra

Street Knowledge Publishing Order Form

Street Knowledge Publishing, P.O. Box 345, Wilmington, DE 19801
Email: jj@streetknowledgepublishing.com
Website: www.streetknowledgepublishing.com

For Inmates Orders and Manuscript Submissions
P.O. Box 310367, Jamaica, NY 11431

Bloody Money
ISBN # 0-9746199-0-6   **$15.00**
Shipping/ Handling Via
U.S. Priority Mail   **$4.05**
Total   **$19.05**

Me & My Girls
ISBN # 0-9746199-1-4   **$15.00**
Shipping/ Handling Via
U.S. Priority Mail   **$4.05**
Total   **$19.05**

Bloody Money 2
ISBN # 0-9746199-2-2   **$15.00**
Shipping/ Handling Via
U.S. Priority Mail   **$4.05**
Total   **$19.05**

Dopesick
ISBN # 0-9746199-4-9   **$15.00**
Shipping/ Handling Via
U.S. Priority Mail   **$4.05**
Total   **$19.05**

Money-Grip
ISBN # 0-9746199-3-0   **$15.00**
Shipping/ Handling Via
U.S. Priority Mail   **$4.05**
Total   **$19.05**

The Queen of New York
ISBN # 0-9746199-7-3   **$15.00**
Shipping/ Handling Via
U.S. Priority Mail   **$4.05**
Total   **$19.05**

Don't Mix The Bitter With The Sweet
ISBN # 0-9746199-6-5   **$15.00**
Shipping/ Handling Via
U.S. Priority Mail   **$4.05**
Total   **$19.05**

Purchaser Information

Name: _____

Address: _____

City: _____ State: ___ Zip Code: _____

Bloody Money ___

Me & My Girls ___

Bloody Money 2 ___

Dopesick ___

Money Grip ___

The Queen of New York ___

Don't Mix The Bitter With The Sweet ___

Quantity Of Books? _____

Make checks/money orders payable to:
Street Knowledge Publishing